Author: Dennis D. Gagnon, age 17, 1970.

Illustrator: Mina Schwind, age 17, 2018.

The Party Line

Dennis D. Gagnon

ARCHWAY PUBLISHING

Archway Publishing books may be ordered through booksellers or by contacting:

Archway Publishing
1663 Liberty Drive
Bloomington, IN 47403
www.archwaypublishing.com
1 (888) 242-5904

ISBN: 978-1-4808-5829-9 (sc)
ISBN: 978-1-4808-5831-2 (hc)
ISBN: 978-1-4808-5830-5 (e)

Library of Congress Control Number: 2018901314

Print information available on the last page.

Archway Publishing rev. date: 07/22/2019

Contents

To H. G. Wells and Jules Verne, those intrepid explorers of untrodden territories, who themselves were beneficiaries of the great and unsurpassed Edgar Allan Poe; let this present work be my modest memorial to these three great beings.

Primum non nocere. (First, do no harm.)
—Hippocratic Oath

The finest emotion of which we are capable is the mystic emotion. Herein lies the germ of all art and all true science. Anyone to whom this feeling is alien, who is no longer capable of wonderment and lives in a state of fear is a dead man. To know that what is impenetrable for us really exists and manifests itself as the highest wisdom and the most radiant beauty, whose gross forms alone are intelligible to our poor faculties—this knowledge, this feeling ... that is the core of the true religious sentiment. In this sense, and in this sense alone, I rank myself among profoundly religious men.
—Albert Einstein

All is therefore clear and lucid in consciousness: the object with its characteristic opacity is before consciousness, but consciousness is purely and simply consciousness of being consciousness of that object. This is the law of its existence.
—Jean-Paul Sartre, *Transcendence of the Ego*

Cogito ergo sum. (I think, therefore I am.)
—René Descartes, *Meditations on First Philosophy*

Preface

The larger story here is a false retrospective, a fictional account of musings that really did shape my early life and mind. Paradox, contradiction, and relativity play a big role in my tale. Rather than being aberrations, these qualities seem to define reality. Yet there is constancy, invariance, running through our lives. In my later years, I can see that the thoughts and concerns that occupy the attention of the young characters in my story are not so unique; there are universals that run through the fabric of our human existence.

Who am I? How do I live life as a good person? What is the nature of evil, and how can I lessen that evil in the world? What is life? What is death? Should I use reason, faith, or emotion to guide my actions? What is suffering? Do we have free will? Is there something out there in the world beyond myself? How should I treat others? These are some of the existential questions asked by a responsible human. In retirement and enjoying the duties of a part-time philosophy professor, I find that these questions arise naturally in my course discussions. I sometimes feel these are stale and worn questions.

My young charges invariably disintegrate that cynical attitude. For them life is a fire hose, and they joyfully face their whole beings into the onrushing stream. I cannot escape their excitement in vicarious rapport. My young students keep me alive, and I wish to return the favor for that valuable service. What more respectful and intimate gift can I offer then a fictional rendering of my own early trials and experiences, when—as the natural cycle now bestows upon my young students—the multiplying synapses of my being were awash with the creative juices of existence?

Acknowledgment

Thank you, Luella Englehart, Ph.D., my beautiful wife, for your careful edits of this work. I give utmost thanks to my older brother, Rick E. Gagnon, for the early inspiration and encouragement that allowed me to continue work on this book. Also, many thanks to Mark McIntire, a colleague in the philosophy department at Santa Barbara City College, for his careful review and critique of the major themes in this work. I would like to thank all the friends and family I burdened with early drafts of my story—drafts that were literally rough but were smoothed out as best I could, given their wonderful comments. Finally, my book has benefitted tremendously from the careful and expert editors at Archway Publishing. Thanks, everyone.

Introduction

This work is an autobiographical science fiction, with an emphasis upon the word "fiction." My story includes a ghost, a phoenix, a monster, dragons, battles between good and evil in an aethereal realm, and spiritual teachers. All of these are fictional.

This is the tale of an extremely thoughtful young adventurer in his junior year of high school in 1971 coming of philosophical age. The young man grapples with the nature of reality and his place in it. He ponders the distinction between appearance and reality and the explanatory power of scientific methodology—especially as applied to the special theory of relativity and early thoughts on quantum mechanics—from which he concludes that there is nothing but consciousness. He is led to reason that no material realm exists. In this hidden realm of pure consciousness, he deals with the nature of good and evil and our relationship to others. He is confronted with life-and-death issues that require mindful and responsible resolution.

Some of what this young man undergoes is based upon my own experiences at the same age, although the vast majority of the events depicted here are pure fiction. At that age I really did stumble upon the notion I called the "party-line theory of consciousness," from which the book receives its title. I will leave a description of that theory to the interior pages of this book. This theory strongly shaped my developing worldview for many years, and I have never entirely abandoned it. The dream sequence in a later chapter of this book did happen much as it is depicted, with the recent addition of an oblique reference to string theory. I did have a childhood friend whose first name began with the letter *D* and who is the inspiration for the pivotal character in this philosophical science fiction. This story reasonably captures the essence of my relationship with D—— in our childhood years. The way the character D. is portrayed in the rest of the book is widely divergent from my actual childhood friend. This work is a belated attempt to come to terms with D——'s early death at sea.

While a young woman by the name of Percy plays an important role in my tale, I have never met a young woman by that name. This is not to say that I have never met strong, self-determined women with personality traits similar to those I have ventured to depict in my character Percy. Thank goodness for strong women.

I have written this tale with the general reader in mind who does not have a grounding in philosophy. I hope the reader will find that the philosophical issues discussed arise in a natural manner, such as a young searcher may have confronted them and wrestled to a reasonable resolution. With very few exceptions, I refer to no philosophers or philosophical systems by name. However, the reader who is knowledgeable in philosophy may see in these pages hints of Homer, some pre-Socratic philosophers (especially Heraclitus and Empedocles), Sophocles, Plato, Aristotle, René Descartes, Sir Isaac Newton, Gottfried Wilhelm Leibnitz, John Locke, David Hume, Immanuel Kant, J. S. Mill, Friedrich Nietzsche, Charles Sanders Peirce, Sigmund Freud, Carl Jung, Albert Einstein, Karl Popper, Jean-Paul Sartre, Ludwig Wittgenstein, W. V. O. Quine, Daniel

Dennett, Bas van Fraassen, Tim Maudlin, Lao-Tzu, K'ung-fu-tzu (Confucius), Mencius, Wang Yangming, the Buddhist philosopher Nāgārjuna, the Hindu classic *The Bhagavad Gita,* M. K. Gandhi, the book of Job, and the Sermon on the Mount. I fully realize that it is presumptuous to claim that I have captured the thoughts of these folks and works in my book. But I claim nothing of the sort. What I do claim is that in the process of uncovering my tale, I have discovered *hints* of these folks and ideas—insofar as *I* view what my narrative has uncovered. The reader may find altogether different influences. If nothing else, I should think that this book would be of interest simply as an illustration of how these different folks and ideas may be brought together in one work of science fiction. *I* certainly had fun in this archeological exercise.

Prologue

Impetuously, I dived back into the aethereal realm and sought out D. Immediately the visualizations of my surroundings became very dark and I was filled with a severely cold chill. I felt the body of the birdlike monster wrap itself around me like the coils of a giant serpent while its wings enclosed me in a shroud. Its beaked face was close to my ear, and it hissed, "There you are. I've been calling you. You have certainly taken your precious time to come to your friend's aid. Being the courageous person you are, I can only take that delay as an indication of your respect for my immense power!"

Frightened, but being careful not to fall into my highly polished and insulting street repertoire, I said, "Look, I don't have any quarrel with the United Lodge of Divine Wisdom. Just leave D. and me alone!" I felt I was suffocating.

The dark monster replied, "The United Lodge of Divine Wisdom! It is a baby compared to my power. I could will them away in less than an instant. However, some of its participants are important components in my base. And I heartily thank them for that. Really, though, I have participants from everywhere." And then it roared, "I am the very manifestation of will to power!" At this perhaps overzealous estimate of its own exalted significance, it again roared, but this thunderous noise was a roar, hiss, squawk, squeal, cry, and laugh all at once combined into a deafening and horrifying cacophony of evil. That noise lasted far too long.

Once I was no longer cringing from the awful noise and the ringing in my ears ceased, I asked, "What do you want with D. and me? If you are so powerful, then why do you care about us?" I asked this last question with a bit of sarcasm, and I received a severe tightening of its coils about my body in return.

"You should be more careful not to exhibit a lack of respect for your superior, little man." There was a slight pause, and it continued. "I don't give a damn about D. I've only been using him to get to you. Once you and I have reached our agreement, I will no longer have a use for him; he is entirely disposable."

I did not like his use of the word "disposable," but I tried to keep my mind clear of fear and upwelling thoughts—I did not want to give too much away to this monster. It was the hardest exercise I had encountered in the aethereal realm up to that point.

"Okay," I said, "so what do you want of me, then?"

After I asked the question of what the monster wanted from me, out of fear and a sense of self-preservation, I began to construct my protective bubble. The monster popped that protective sphere like a soap bubble being attacked by an adventurous toddler. The monster squealed in delight in bursting my protective bubble. I tried again, and the monster happily played with the bubble, blowing on it and waving at it to make it quiver; the beast then poked it with a sharpened claw, causing it to disappear in a dispersing mist. I saw it was no use in trying to construct my transparent protective envelope, and I asked again, "What do you want of me!?"

At this point, it gave what could have been interpreted as a slight, albeit evil, smile. It loosened its coils around me slightly and said, "Good, now we are negotiating."

I tried hard not to think to myself, *We are doing nothing of the kind!*

"Are you sure?" it asked. "You haven't heard my offer. I have a lot to offer. I think you'll come around; they all do ... eventually." It gave another evil laugh. It continued, and its words felt like a drill boring through my skull and into the soft matter within. "You are a strong-willed kid, to say the least—more so than I've seen in a very long time. I need you to join with me; become one of my privileged participants. With your will added to mine, we could only grow stronger! We would increase our power a hundredfold!" With that it inserted a salivating proboscis into the hole in my skull and started probing my brain; no, it began probing my very mind!

"No!" I yelled, and I pushed out the proboscis and began filling the hole in my skull. With the enormity of the effort required to repair my skull, I was starting to lose my concentration—and with that, my will.

"But just look what you would have to gain," it said. "You will become immortal by becoming a part of me. We will go on indefinitely, harvesting evil and suffering to sustain myself. Oh, there will never be a dearth of that pestilence upon Earth; I will make sure of that!"

It was getting darker and colder. I was hardly able to muster the energy to shout "Forget it, you pig! I don't want anything to do with you!" With that D. was revealed about five feet away from us, cringing on the ground, in a faint and narrow beam of light that barely showed the immense pain on his face.

There was a flash of lightning with a smell of rotten eggs in the air. D. convulsed in pain and shouted, "No! No more!"

"Maybe I can compel you to join my conversation?" the monster softly asked me. "Do you really see no reason to merge with my being?" It smiled. "Or, maybe some pain on both of your parts would be more persuasive?"

D. barely whispered, addressing the monster, "Be careful of tickling this dragon's tail, fella; I've seen his bite." I was stunned to hear D. refer to me as the dragon in this situation.

"Silence!" roared the monster, and D. went into a prolonged session of violent convulsions, crying out and splattering spittle in every direction.

But I am getting ahead of myself in conveying this tragedy, as it took place in 1971, when D. and I were seventeen years old. The real story begins earlier, in 1962. I will begin my story there.

1

Bullying Bullies

As young boys in elementary school, D. and I were quite the team. If someone saw one of us, the other was soon spotted. When viewed side by side, however, one would be impressed by how different we appeared. I was short for my age and skinny; D. was tall, with long, powerful legs. But we had a certain affinity, recognizing in each other an interest in social and moral phenomena—as far as that interest would go for young schoolboys, that is. We loved exploring the psychological boundaries of the society in which we both felt unfairly imprisoned. However, we usually endeavored to be fair in our dealings with others. That recognition of the intrinsic worth of others allowed us to reap the benefit of constant amusement as privileged viewers of the absurd comedy in which we all played parts. And we loved playing our parts. As much as we loved to recite the script of life, with full knowledge it was only a script, we also loved occasionally and randomly changing those roles. We enjoyed the effect those rewrites had on the other actors in our play, forcing spontaneous improvisations to the altered script. As stated, we were usually careful to be fair to others. At least we liked to think that we tried.

Then again, D. and I could be quite ruthless in our dealings with some of the more unsavory characters in our societal morality play. We lived to bully bullies. In that regard, we often played the risky game of tickling the dragon's tail.

There was a family in our neighborhood that was, to put it bluntly, a family of bullies—everyone but the mother, that is, who paradoxically was one of the nicest people I ever met. One of the bullies in that family stood out from the others as a giant in the bloody vocation. He was everything the bully script called for. He was big, on the heavy side (actually, downright fat), mentally about as sharp as a flat tire, and as mean as, well, as mean as the one he labeled his "old man," which was saying a lot.

A short tale provides insight into the moral movement of his machinelike and soulless integrity. One afternoon, D. and I were aimlessly roaming about the neighborhood and exerted the sustained effort necessary to climb a chain-link fence in order to enter the empty high school football stadium. The stadium was built on a steep, sloping hill. The parking lot at the top of the hill was level with the ticket gate and the top of the bleachers. Climbing over the fence from the top parking lot gave us a perfect view of the field below. At about the fifty-yard line, maybe ten yards into the field, stood our favorite bully with his back to us. His complicit girlfriend, whose role I think was being played at the time by a young girl by the name of Mary Lou, stood beside him, laughing. Her back was to us as well. A foot or so in front of the bully, facing us, knelt Bud, his face looking up pleadingly at the bully.

Now, Bud was a special person. He was a student at our school, but we saw very little of him. He was in our class but not in our classroom. They instructed him, with a couple of other special students, in a small building that was somehow associated with our school grounds but separated from it by a chain-link fence with barbed wire along the top. Bud joined us for class photos, forever being the subject of confusion when families, years hence, tried to identify that stranger with ill-fitting clothes and a goofy smile off to the side in the front row. When we had a school festival or holiday performance, Bud was brought in to play a bit part. One year our festival had a maritime theme, and Bud was given the role of a foghorn; he proudly and loudly proclaimed, "Ugh, ah!" whenever the performance conductor pointed at him.

Once, Bud was still on the playground when we all went out for recess. Unlike the other students in our grade, and being forever curious, D. and I approached him and said, "Hi."

Bud was delighted to say "Hi" back to us. He showed us a slender stick he had found and immediately began a story. "My dad," he said, "says that a single stick can be broken but a bunch together can never be broken. That's why we should all stick together!" He frantically looked on the ground for sticks. He found none besides what he already had. We left him there forlornly gazing at the fragile little twig he held in his nearly empty hand.

Sometime later, when I was alone and somewhat bored, I decided to test Bud's bundle-of-sticks claim. I took a small bundle of about ten to fifteen small sticks and held them in my hands. Try as I might, I could not even begin to break the sticks in half as I held them in a bundle. However, I was not deterred. I laid the bundle before me and took each stick up in turn and broke it in half. I carefully laid the left-hand piece to my left and the right-hand piece to my right. When I had completed this process of breaking each stick in half, I had two bundles of sticks, one to my left and one to my right. I took up the left-hand bundle in my left hand and the right-hand bundle in my right hand and held the two bundles together so it appeared as if I held one unbroken bundle. I then went through the motion as if I were breaking the original single bundle in half. "There," I said aloud to myself, "I've broken a bundle of sticks!" I did not feel that I had cheated in any way. From my point of view, I had legitimately broken the original bundle in half.

As I was saying earlier, from our position at the top of the stadium seats, we could see the backs of the neighborhood bully and his attending girlfriend, with Bud on his knees closely before them. We shouted to the bully, "Hey, pig, what's ya doin'?"

The bully, startled, turned around, zipping up his fly. He shouted, "Hey, you runts, get out of here or I'll pound ya!"

One of us shouted back the requisite reply "You and what army?"

This academic intercourse provided poor Bud with just enough time to wipe his face, stand up and run toward the fence. The bully said, "Oh, man," and started trotting after Bud. Bud made it to the fence, scaled it faster than a cat, and disappeared among the school buildings. Mary Lou stood there like a marble statue. D. and I decided it was time to make ourselves scarce. We turned and ran to the fence behind us and quickly climbed over it, yelling insults to the bully as we disappeared into the adjoining residential area.

D. and I loved bullying that particular bully—and others too. For a time, I kept a slingshot in my back pocket, but I did not use it to hurl stones. My shot of choice was the fruit from a Natal plum. A Natal plum is a thorny, dark-green shrub with a fragrant flower that looks like an oversize jasmine blossom. It also has a red, fleshy fruit about the size of a small Roma tomato. This being Southern California, there was always a handy supply of my preferred projectile. The Natal plum is a rather solid fruit and can pack a reasonable impact when hurled with sufficient force. But it also splatters with a satisfying spread of deep-red pulp. I must confess that it probably hurts a bit to be shot with one of these fruits hurled from a powerful slingshot.

When we spied one of our bully targets, D. and I sneaked up behind and pelted him with our precisely targeted Natal plums. Before the bully could finish cursing and accidentally cover his hand with the fruity pulp by massaging his wounded back, D. and I would be off and running. The bully did not have a chance of catching us with this head start. That was the first of our three techniques for getting out of trouble even faster than we had gotten into it—running.

As I said, I was short for my age and no competition for D. in the quick sprint. But what I lacked in initially getting out of the starting blocks I made up for in endurance. Given a little time to catch up, I would run alongside D. We could literally run for hours, and I'm literally using the term "literally" here. D. and I loved to run. We routinely ran circuits around the extensive territory we considered ours at least once a week just to make sure all was well within our self-determined domain.

On these runs, we conversed about all things important to young boys. One topic that arose quite often was the Catholic Church. D. belonged to a devoutly religious family, and in his childhood and young adulthood he progressed through the whole route of maturity waypoints devised by the ecclesiastical authorities. His experiences with these significant milestones along his spiritual path provided us with endless conversational opportunities, with me usually playing the role of the devout atheist. D. was very concerned for my soul, not being able to wrap his head around the idea that one could lead a moral life and yet not have even the beginnings of a belief in God or adherence to any religion. I forgave him for his chauvinistic ignorance, as I knew he forgave me for my lack of faith.

Another weapon in our arsenal used to extricate ourselves from uncomfortable situations was that we were proficient in getting people to see what was not there. This takes a little explaining. We were very young, maybe in our first or second grade in elementary school, when D. and I discovered the power of suggestion. Our use of that power was innocent at first. I think it was D.'s idea, but one day at school, during recess, he said, "Let's play a trick. We can look down this drain and pretend to see something. Let's see what other kids do."

I said, "Okay," and I went over to the to drain, which was covered by a two-foot-by-two-foot rectangular iron grating and started staring at the wet greenish sludge about one foot below. We did not call out to the other kids; we did not call attention to ourselves in any obvious way. Eventually, after staring for quite some time, I said to D., "Do you see it? There it is!"

"No, I don't see it," D. said, though he soon added, "Oh yeah, there it is. Cool! Do you think *it* sees *us*?" We went on in this manner for a couple of minutes, and soon we had a large group of kids jostling around us trying to see "it." Many proclaimed that they saw it and tried to give a description of it to the other kids gathered around. D. and I got up off our hands and knees and sauntered away to watch from a short distance. The kids continued to catch glimpses of it, and some started telling stories about how it had gotten itself down that drain in the first place. This went on until the end of the recess, when even a couple of the teachers had to pull themselves away from looking down the drain and go back to providing adult guidance to their young charges.

D. and I were amazed and excited with the result of our experiment. We were just kids, of course, so we did not have a prolonged discussion about the psychological mechanisms in play here; we just knew that we were now in possession of a new tool with which to pull the strings of others. And what do the young do with a newly discovered tool? We played it out for all it was worth, of course. We got very good at using it. Eventually we started using it to get out of sticky situations.

One rather failed example of attempting to use this power to make others see what was not there concerns a bottle of Coca-Cola. D. liked to take a bottle of Coke and, placing his thumb over the mouth of the open bottle, shake it vigorously. He would then point the bottle away from himself, remove his thumb from the mouth of the bottle, and exult in the height of the ensuing spray. I think part of his enjoyment in this maneuver was getting covered by a thin mist of Coke. He only did this out of doors, of course. But one slow afternoon, when we had nothing much else to do than watch an old black-and-white Basil Rathbone movie about Sherlock Holmes, D.

decided to perform his trick in the TV room of his parents' house. The idea was to sufficiently agitate the carbonated sugar solution but then see how long it would take to ever so slightly relax his thumb and slowly release the pressure, not allowing a single drop of the tasty liquid to escape from the bottle. We were playing the risky game of tickling the dragon's tail again, and we were completely absorbed by it.

I do not know how long it would have taken D. to slowly release the pressure from that bottle with no resultant explosion; we did not have the opportunity to record that particular datum. D.'s older brother came into the room, observed the experiment we were performing, and promptly retreated to go and inform his father. Now, D.'s father was one of those people who very infrequently gets ruffled by anything; he was an easygoing sort, devoted to loving his wife and three sons. But I had been visiting D. for most of the weekend by now; we had been getting into one thing after another, and D.'s father was pushed just a fraction over the line. He marched into the TV room and demanded the Coke bottle from D. D. looked more serious than at any time I had ever seen him and said, "Dad, I can't give it to you."

D.'s dad sternly demanded, "D., you give me that Coke right now!" I was watching this skit secure in my anticipation of the final scene—someone was going to end up being covered in a heavy spray of Coca-Cola.

I looked past D.'s father, over the shoulder of D.'s onlooking brother, through the short hallway, and out the front window with a view to the driveway, and I said, "Is that a cop?"

D.'s father yanked his attention from D. and looked intently at me, trying to ascertain my game. "Yeah," I said, ignoring D.'s father's gaze and still looking out the window on the other side of the house, "I saw a cop out on the driveway. D., did you see him too?"

D. said, "Yeah, I saw him. What's a cop doing out there on our drive?" At this point, D.'s brother yelled out to his mother, who was in another part of the house, that *he* had seen a cop in the driveway. D.'s brother, mother, and father all went out the front door to determine whether they could be of any assistance to the nonexistent officer. D. sighed in relief, looked at me, turned around and tripped over the coffee table, releasing the contents of the Coke bottle onto the ceiling above, creating a representation not unlike a monochromatic Sistine Chapel viewed by a myopic patron of the arts. I was sent to spend the rest of the weekend at my parents' home. Debriefing with one another, D. and I later decided that the ruse would have worked if the coffee table had not been in the way.

Appropriately, the third weapon in our arsenal was humor. It worked quite well. D. was a natural at it. Those times when our quickness and agility failed us, or when we could not distract our antagonists by conjuring shiny nonexistent objects, we relied upon humor to release us from uncomfortable situations. If we were cornered by a group of bullies we had roused, we would revert to something akin to an Abbott and Costello routine. Our antagonists would end up scratching their heads, trying to figure out what we were talking about, and this would give us just enough time to run for it.

One time a nasty brute had us penned up in a dead-end alleyway, and he said, "I told you guys a hundred times not to come here. Now you're going to get it."

D. immediately shot back, "I've told you a million times, don't exaggerate!" Now, that seems silly of course, but it worked. The jerk was temporarily distracted, and we instantly took advantage of that beguilement to run away.

Another time, we were stuck in a similar manner, and one of our assailants said, "Okay, you guys are in trouble now. We're going to beat you to a pulp!"

D. responded, "If we had our football uniforms on, we'd show you!" Again, it does not sound like much in the telling of the tale, but it does not take much to distract the weak willed. Besides, I thought it was really funny.

Of course, engaging in the risky game of tickling the dragon's tail meant that occasionally we would end up being bitten by that dragon. D. was not there with me once when our favorite neighborhood bully, the one that had molested Bud, trapped me between himself, his older brother, and his cousin—all monsters. He and his brother decided they would initiate their younger cousin into the joys of beating someone into oblivion. Their cousin was not quite as big as they were, but he was substantially bigger than I, and he had the family proclivity toward viciousness. The bully's brother pushed his cousin at me, while the bully pushed me at his cousin. The cousin was coming at me with something resembling a smile on his ugly face owing to his anticipation that he would soon be causing me great pain and suffering. I saw only one way out of this situation. I decided to let myself go and see what may come. A feeling of freedom and power washed across my body. That scintillating experience of completely uninhibited will washed down from the top of my head to the soles of my feet, loosening every fiber of my being and readying me for any spontaneous action of my choosing. I was not thinking about what I was going to do; I was totally immersed in its execution.

Without warning and without any of the other verbal niceties required by the social rules of childhood combat, I quickly approached my assailant and kicked him hard in the testicles. When he doubled over in pain, I immediately punched him in the side of the head with all the force I could muster. He fell over on the ground to my left, moaning and holding his crotch. I kicked him as hard as I could in his unprotected face. His head snapped back from the impact with an audible crack. My two ambulatory assailants just stood there stunned, and I ran away as fast as I could. One, two, three, and I was out of there on four.

D. had a similar experience once, though unlike my solitary experience I was with him at the time. Again, three thugs had caught us, and two of them held me while the biggest one challenged D. to a final face-off. D. was more than ready, having been egged on and taunted by this thug for weeks now. They started sparring, and D.

quickly dived in at his opponent's torso, avoiding his antagonist's fists by going under them. This knocked the both of them down, and they started wrestling.

My two captors, holding me fast on either side, began chuckling in derision; but I did not see anything funny for them to be laughing at. From my knowledge of D., I was aware that I was watching him methodically execute a perfect plan of engagement. Eventually D. was on top of the thug's back, holding one of his opponent's arms up behind his shoulder and holding the back of his opponent's head with his other hand, grinding his surprised face into the scree of gravel and broken bits of glass covering the asphalt. D.'s face and neck muscles were straining at the effort, but he looked more than determined. It was relentless. Eventually the thug to my right let go of me and went to his colleague's defense. As I was released on my right side I immediately swung to the left and planted an upward-slanting punch to my other captor's solar plexus, nearly exhausting the entire contents of his lungs. He let go of me and doubled over trying to inhale, momentarily frustrated in his attempt to reexpand his chest. Meanwhile, D. had seen his competitor's accomplice approaching and kicked his feet out from under him and sprang to his own feet. As we would have preferred in the first place, D. and I took off running.

When we were about thirteen or fourteen years of age, D. took to sailing his boat out of our local marina and into the Santa Barbara Channel. He was devoted to his boat, and I became devoted to hobbies on more solid ground—camping in and hiking the mountains of our neighboring national forest. However, I did accompany D. on many boating adventures. On these yachting excursions, more than once we violated standard sailing etiquette and even maritime law by sailing close to fast-moving container ships and tankers. On those occasions, we would routinely hear alarm bells going off on the behemoth vessels and their crews warning us away with bullhorns. Once, sailing near a tanker, we were becalmed by the wind shadow caused by the tanker's hulk, and we were nearly capsized by the enormous wake it left behind as its massive iron hull narrowly missed our miniscule wooden boat. D. and I considered that day's adventure a particularly exciting outing. We told no one.

Such are the frolics of teenage boys given responsibility beyond their maturity. Looking back on those days, I would have to say that both D. and I suffered from an overassessment of our abilities in the water. Not only was D. a very good sailor, but he was also a certified Junior Lifeguard and very much at home in the water. I did not know the first thing about sailing, but I could follow directions. Neither was I a certified Junior Lifeguard, but I was just one level in swimming ability below the level of Junior Lifeguard and had spent years swimming with the local AAU swim team. I think that we calculated (or, more likely, assumed) that no matter what happened, we could both swim and float on the currents that would eventually bring us onto shore. We did not even consider the wearing of life vests; such was the extent of our deluded confidence—our hubris. For any emergency we were to encounter in the Santa Barbara Channel, though we did not actively entertain any such event, we unconsciously agreed to rely solely upon our skills in the water. Fortunately, we had survived those days and had not been engaged in such risky behavior for many years by the time the events being primarily recounted here occurred.

All of this has been told to help place into perspective what comes later in my story, and to allow an understanding of my devastation as I helplessly watched D. die in my arms. I have recounted these early tales also to illustrate that, contrary to the instructions of Resident Teacher—a character you will meet later in my tragic tale—there are times when quickness is a virtue. Or, if quickness is not exactly a virtue, it is at least sometimes necessary for one's survival. Concerning that dark birdlike monster, I wish I had acted more quickly.

11

The Party Line

As we began high school, D. and I grew apart. We were still the best of friends, but we began to see less and less of each other. He was devoted to his boat, and I became involved in sports and playing the oboe in the school orchestra. We were both good students, but for some reason we had no classes together in the whole of our high school tenures—as if the public school system had some notes deep in their files to the effect that D. and I should never be placed together in the same class. However, we were both prone to leading solitary, introspective, and peaceful teen lives, despite what some of our family members, priests, and teachers predicted of us based upon our earlier childhood behavior.

I became interested in science and philosophy, while D. became interested in mathematics and psychology. On the rare occasions we bumped into one another, we would excitedly share what we had recently been reading in our respective areas of interest. Even though we saw less of each other in our latter teens, when we did get together it was like old times. We loved to laugh in retelling stories of our earlier childhood. However, we spent much of our time away from one another, to mature along separate lines. It was during one of those many times absent from D. when I first contemplated the notion of the party line. That notion, the party-line theory of consciousness, impelled me to leap to the view that the world is filled with gods.

Many people are not acquainted with the concept of a party line. Although a legitimate use of the phrase, I do not refer here to a dogmatic adherence to a set of beliefs or attitudes insofar as one belongs to a particular group, as in "One must stay true to the goals and objectives of the party line." Rather, I use this phrase in an entirely different way.

Telephonic service in its early days, and in difficult-to-reach locales and difficult times, was often a shared service. This service connected a number of customers to a single line, or telephone number, across households or businesses. Customers needed to work out among themselves who would use the service when and how to share that service. This was a party line. A caller could literally pick up the phone and listen to and participate in a previously initiated conversation. I became acquainted with party lines because a family down the street subscribed to that type of service in the 1960s.

The party line as a telephonic service is an antiquated mechanism, but there are modern analogues to it, one of which may be the online forum. There are differences between an online forum and a party line, of course, but they both share the property that many different people could be using the service to conduct a group conversation. This "party-line effect" is the psychological foundation of modern social media and is what paradoxically led me as a youth to see the world as filled with gods. It even helped me to explain to myself why some people have come to believe in a supreme God.

Unfortunately, a consequence of the party-line effect is also the existence of pure, unmitigated evil in the world. I do not mean just to say that there are evil people or people who commit evil acts, but that Evil, in itself, exists just as gods, and maybe even God, exists.

In 1971, when I was about seventeen years old, I decided to conduct a series of experiments in what I at the time assumed to be a form of extrasensory perception. I was a complete novice in this phenomenon, if it even is a legitimate phenomenon to be investigated. It was a long string of events and thoughts that led me to conduct these experiments at that time. An important part of those antecedent events included the fact that I had been reading Erich von Däniken's *Chariots of the Gods*. Based upon what I read in that book, I considered it at least a merely logical possibility that aliens from distant planets had had some contact with the planet Earth in the remote past. I was open to that *possibility*. However, I was anything but convinced of the *probability* of that proposition as argued by Von Däniken in his book.

At this time, I was also playing around with meditation. I say "playing around with" because I was not disciplined in this exercise in any way. I was practicing a form of meditation entirely of my own design. I am sure I was seriously confusing the transcendent form of meditation derived from sources such as the Bhagavad Gita with more immanent forms of meditation more closely related to the mindfulness practices of the Buddhists. I think this confusion of the goals and specific practices of meditation was partly due to the influence of the muddled talks presented by the United Lodge of Divine Wisdom of Santa Barbara, which I was sporadically attending at the time.

I was practicing a form of meditation in which I would try to shut down all sensation and cognition and make myself identical to the void. In essence, it was a nihilistic form of meditation wherein the goal was to make one's self a nothingness. Much later in life, when discussing this form of meditation with a Buddhist mindfulness coach, he said, "I'm glad you are still with us."

To make matters even more confusing, I was also interested in the phenomenon of hypnosis. I researched this phenomenon as presented in numerous popular how-to books and was able to hypnotize some of my friends and acquaintances with acceptable results. I believed, and still do believe, that hypnosis is a real phenomenon demanding a real explanation. Whether that explanation ultimately takes the form of Freud's theories of the unconscious was not the object of careful consideration for me at the time; I was more interested in exploring the use of this tool rather than trying to understand its metaphysical underpinnings.

Let me hasten to add that I implicitly held a belief in the existence of something like an unconscious, and I never seriously questioned that assumption. I was remotely familiar with how Freud explained his success in treating hysteria using hypnosis by reference to an unconscious realm. I took for granted that ontological supposition in such a way that a fish perhaps takes for granted the existence of water. I have come to find that I was not alone in that effortless assumption. Many people will readily admit to a conviction in the existence of something like an unconscious realm. That view has become commonplace.

Along with experiments on my friends in hypnosis came experiments in self-hypnosis. I was using self-hypnosis to convince myself that I was a decent individual and that I could be an acceptable companion to my fellow high school students. That particular exercise turned out to have had a limited efficacy.

Since I have mentioned my high school colleagues, let me add that at this time in my life I had never indulged in any abuse of drugs or mind-altering substances of any kind—not even alcohol. I did don the garb of the era—a slightly suburbanized hippie style with quite long hair. But though many of my fellow classmates would not have believed it if you would have told them, I led an exceptionally clean life regarding illicit substances. Additionally, I was physically fit, participating on the school's cross-country and wrestling teams.

At this time I was reading Huston Smith's *The World's Religions*. I was especially moved by Smith's analysis of the notions of Being and Non-Being in some of the chapters of his book. What struck me in reading Smith's book is perhaps the polar opposite of what many others have said they lifted from that read. While others have said that his book led them to conclude that most religions are essentially saying the same thing, what struck me is how different they all are from one another. It fascinated me that the Abrahamic (Judeo-Christian-Islamic) notion of Being is so different from that of the Hindus, both of which are so different from the Buddhist notion, not to mention the unique treatment of Being and Non-Being by the Taoists. For example, where some systems see Being as static and permanent and hence transcendently distinct from the changing phenomenal realm around us, others see Being as a continual change and flux, and hence deny a transcendent and permanent realm. For me it was hard to impose an identity upon these disparate notions. I was like a kid in a candy store reading Smith's book, surveying the display case of varied and tempting metaphysics.

I was thinking that there could be nothing so fundamental as a notion of Being, and yet here I saw in Smith's excellent book that the belief in a particular form of that foundational structure for understanding one's life and one's place in the world is an arbitrary epiphenomenon dependent upon where and in what circumstances one happens to be born and raised. One cannot live without a metaphysics, of course, but my upbringing had been so liberal that I did not naturally gravitate to any one of these particular systems and their implied notions of Being. I felt I was literally free to give each system its due and choose according to the best algorithm I could bring to bear upon the subject.

Though that selection algorithm has undergone many transformations and refinements in the ensuing years, I have still yet to choose among the prevailing options presented by the vast menu of religious and philosophical systems. In fact, in my later musings I have come to the conclusion that all metaphysical systems—*as systems of thought*—are either self-contradictory, assume what they try to prove, or lead to infinite regresses. Such is the cynicism of an elderly mind. (Note that I did not say "a mature mind.") Of course, there is a difference between systems of thought on the one hand and experience on the other. Or, as some of us prefer to couch that distinction, there is a difference between doctrine and revelation.

At that time in my youth, facing a fire hose of different metaphysics and their derivative moral systems, I did positively respond to and adopt the one guiding principle that has consistently remained with me through the years—when I allow myself to remember and practice it. That principle was brought home to me by my readings in Christianity, Buddhism, and M. K. Gandhi, and it is rendered down to the simple injunction "Do not cause unnecessary suffering." We may quibble about what is necessary or unnecessary, yet it seems to me that once we have decided what is unnecessary, we cannot object to the notion of a general prohibition against inducing unnecessary suffering. This leads to the stance of presumptive nonviolence toward all beings capable of experiencing suffering—all sentient beings.

Be this all as it may, in '71 I was a rather pensive individual prone to taking long walks out of my neighborhood and into the adjacent hills in a solitary manner, occasioned by the remoteness of the terrain so as to promote consideration of the lofty matters of Being and Non-Being, the purpose and conduct of meditation, and other tertiary issues, such as the efficacy of hypnosis, the validity of extrasensory perception, and the existence of space aliens. This was heaven for me.

On one of these walks, I was inspired to conceive, or was somehow made acquainted with, the party-line explanation of consciousness.

It was a striking experience for me, stumbling upon that notion of consciousness. Upon conceiving (or, perhaps more appropriately, uncovering) this notion of the party-line effect of consciousness, I felt as if I had chanced upon a truth that opened my mind to a vast space of Being not previously noticed. It expanded my world by many orders of magnitude of whatever metric it is that one uses to measure one's awareness of existence. Not only was the *horizon* of my awareness expanded, but the individual *corners* and *crevices* of the world were bathed in a light that allowed me to see their contents anew, or even view them now for the very first time.

Of course that insight did not vault into an unprepared mind. I had had some experiences recently that I was contemplating and trying to understand. The cogitations upon those experiences constituted the fertile field upon which I fumbled about when first I confronted the notion of the party-line theory of consciousness. An explanation of those experiences will help explain the discovery of this unique theory.

Sometime previous to the insight of the party line, I had conceived the general form of experiments I could conduct to explore the possible existence of space aliens. These experiments were based upon a number of assumptions and conjectures derived from my musings on extrasensory perception, meditation, and some of the multifarious notions held by the United Lodge of Divine Wisdom. Looking back upon those experiments now, after having spent the brunt of my professional life participating in the design and conduct of randomized controlled trials in the field of health services, I can see that the assumptions grounding those early experiments were so hopelessly confused and interconnected that any reasonable interpretation of results would have been problematic in the extreme.

In any case, the general description of those experiments was as follows. I surmised that if space aliens had visited our planet in the past, there was no reason why there were not space aliens now in the proximity of our planet. Further, I surmised that if extrasensory perception could work between people, there is no reason why it could not work between people and other conscious organisms, including space aliens. I further supposed that if extrasensory perception worked, there is no necessity (or evidence) that it should obey a law that dictates that the intensity of the signal should attenuate as a function of the distance between the transmitter and the receiver, as is the case where the inverse square law describes the intensity of electromagnetic radiation or the force of gravity as a function of distance from the source. From all of this, I contrived to put myself in a deep meditative state so as to facilitate the contact of space aliens via extrasensory perception.

I conducted these experiments at night, when the house was quiet and was conducive to intense concentration. I cannot say what the actual mechanism of my endeavors consisted of. It is not that I do not want to say; I just cannot explain what I was literally doing. I know that I was doing something, because to my horror those efforts eventually generated specific and terrible results.

The first couple of nights when I endeavored to put myself into a deep meditative state so as to communicate with any nearby aliens, I simply fell asleep. These were not fitful sleeps. In fact, those nights when I fell asleep conducting my experiments were quite restful. Amazingly, to this day, I can put myself in a deep sleep and I awake in the morning refreshed and ready to receive the blessings of a new day. I can even fall asleep in a dentist's office awaiting a root canal. However, although I was enjoying adequate sleep, I still was not making any headway in communicating with aliens from other worlds.

I decided then to put my meditative exercise into overdrive, so to speak, and force myself not to fall asleep. I focused upon sending out a beacon of greeting and an open invitation for anything out there to contact me in the most intimate recesses of my mind. I still get goose bumps now recalling the folly of making myself unreservedly receptive to conscious influences not my own.

I believe the first inklings I had of making some sort of contact was the awareness of a series of soft voices. Though they were not physically audible, I could somehow hear those voices rising almost imperceptibly out of the dark fathomless abyss of nothingness. It was like hearing the first bars and measures of Ravel's *Bolero,* where the faint sounds of the snare drum and flute arise from silence to establish the theme developed by that great composition. But it seemed that here, if I were really hearing or experiencing anything at all, was just a cacophony of voices not unified by a guiding theme.

Further, my awareness of those hushed voices seemed unilateral. I could just faintly hear them, but there was no indication at all that they were aware of me.

This was all I perceived the first night that I attained any result from my primitive experimentations. Upon reflection the next day, I concluded that there was something real I had experienced, that it had been very faint, and that there was no danger to me in proceeding further, because it did not appear those voices paid any attention to me whatsoever. It is interesting that at that early stage in those experiments, I was even considering the possibility of danger to myself in conducting such exercises. Why did the notion of danger come up at all if I consciously believed those experiences were benign?

So, from those first tantalizing results, I decided to push ahead and see if I could make out any meaning in that mumbled hush of nonsense. After a couple weeks of prolonged concentration, I was able to turn up the volume on those voices, and I started to hear short snippets of communications from what I took to be specific sources. After a couple additional weeks, the voices grew very loud and so confusing that trying to make sense of it all was the mental and auditory equivalent of walking across Times Square in New York City and endeavoring to understand all the ambient sounds and voices as part of one great conversation. I grew weary from the effort to make sense of the buzzing jumble of signals. But one conclusion was being forced upon me as I continued these experiments—those voices did not appear to be coming from space aliens. Although never having succeeded in my initial objective, I am still open to the possibility that we can contact space aliens via some mechanism such as extrasensory perception. It is just that the content of the conversations I was then overhearing were just too mundane to be coming from superior beings from far away planets. I was deeply motivated to discover just who, or what, was behind those voices.

I decided that in subsequent exercises I would focus upon just one voice and see if I could make sense of that particular stream of consciousness. I also wanted to determine if that chosen voice could or would acknowledge me as another voice deserving of response. I had no decision procedure to use in selecting any particular voice from out of the discordant chaos. I determined to randomly pick a voice and concentrate my attention upon it.

Embarking upon this focused attention to a particular voice chosen seemingly at random from the crowd, I was soon able to discern its signal quite clearly. I found that while it maintained its unity as a single integrated voice, it itself seemed to be made up of a multitude of subvoices. In fact, it resembled nothing more than a sustained conversation of many subvoices, where the overriding conversation remained but individual subvoices came into and left the conversation. But there was something more cohesive to that conversation than just a juxtaposition of individual subvoices. It was as if the voice of the conversation itself had its own identity above and beyond the identity of the individual participating subvoices, where that integrated overall voice persisted through time. In fact, that overvoice, or conversation of subvoices, seemed to have a will all its own.

The will of that overvoice was dependent upon, but greater than, or at least different from, the simple sum of the wills of the individual subvoices constituting that integrated voice. After all, the subvoices entered and exited the conversation, but the overvoice remained intact. It turned out, though, that that first voice I chose to investigate was a bit of a humdrum affair. I do not remember what its conversation was about exactly; I could gain only a general impression of the thread of the conversation. If I remember rightly, it concerned some simple topic that did not particularly interest me. I vaguely remember that it had something to do with clothes fitting properly, but I could be misremembering this.

Again, this was a relatively benign result, but it came with the exciting discovery of the layered character of voices and subvoices. I found that visualization was useful, or even necessary, for the identification of and eventual communication with a particular voice. I think my visualizations of particular voices were not completely imposed by me upon those voices. Some deep aspect of my visualizations of the voices seemed to arise from the voices themselves. In fact, the visualization associated with the holistic conversation pertaining to the correct fitting of clothing looked remarkably like the female student from my high school who had just recently received the Betty Crocker American Homemaker of Tomorrow scholarship.

Let me assure you I have no intention to demean the Betty Crocker scholarship; nor especially do I intend to demean that particular recipient of that award. I was then the vice president of our school's chapter of the Future Farmers of America (FFA) and myself the recipient of many awards from our agricultural competitions with neighboring chapters. As it turned out, within a couple of months, the recipient of the Betty Crocker award was elected the senior class president, and by some strange celestial conjunction, I was elected the president of the entire student body. So neither of us was in a good position to call the other a nerd. In fact, I felt the visualization of the recipient of the Betty Crocker award was a rather pleasant one overall.

The visualization of the voices was a great breakthrough that allowed me to talk directly with those voices. There was one voice that had to do with boats out on the Santa Barbara Channel directly off our coast, and it was the first conversation of voices with which I was able to communicate. I chose to focus upon this voice because it seemed like a benign conversation and because my best childhood friend was an avid boater (though he called his boat a yacht). In forming my words to address this yachting voice, I felt as a toddler must feel in trying to convey her meanings to her parents. My initial forced efforts were more nonauditory phonetics rather than semantics, I am afraid. I was trying to break into the yachting conversation with something I thought might be equivalent to "Excuse me, but may I ask you a question?"

I was at first completely ignored. After trying many times, eventually the yachting voice seemed to pause, and its visualization began to gaze distractedly with annoyance in my general direction. I persisted. Finally the voice turned to me with its yachting cap jauntily perched upon its sunburned head, stared directly at me, and said, "*What?*"

"Oh, hello," I said, trying to ignore the agitation in the voice's voice. "Well, you're the first voice I've been able to successfully communicate with, and I thought I'd ask you some questions about what this is all about."

"What?" it repeated.

"Oh," I said, "I am sorry to bother you, but with you being the first voice I've been able to contact, I'm rather excited and hoping to get some answers."

"Look," the voice said, furrowing its sun-bleached eyebrows, "I'm not some *voice* you may be hearing; my name is Amateur Yachting in Santa Barbara Channel, and I don't know *you*. I'm not some encyclopedia you can reference to get answers to your questions. I'm busy. Right now I'm talking with Commercial Shipping about safety matters and rights of way in the channel shipping lanes. I don't have time to waste with your silly questions about 'what this is all about.'"

"Oh, okay." I responded. "Is there a voice, or, er, someone I can contact about how all of this works?"

"'How all of this works?' I have no idea what you are talking about. But I have been part of a discussion with Resident Teacher now and then. Maybe she can help you."

"Oh, thank you," I said with real gratitude. "Do you know how I can contact Resident Teacher?"

Again with agitation, the voice replied, "She's *Resident Teacher* for goodness' sake! Just find her." And with that Amateur Yachting in Santa Barbara Channel turned its gaze away from me, upon which our conversation was abruptly terminated.

I was stunned—not so much from the rudeness of the

conversation, but mostly from the mere fact that the conversation took place at all. I had to take a pause and think about all of this.

The next day, on one of my many solitary walks, I tried to put all of this into some sort of order. I realized that it was high time for me to have the talk with myself. Was I crazy? Hearing voices is most definitely not a good sign regarding one's mental health. I was aware, as the result of a recent double tragedy at our school, that schizophrenia begins to exhibit its horrible symptoms in the late teens and early twenties. There were two brothers, the Johansson brothers, who a year apart both came down with that debilitating disease and were removed from school, one after the other. Before each was taken away I knew they were beginning to become a bit odd, but the only real signs I saw of their disease was that just before disappearing, they both took to carrying briefcases and many varied keys on large key rings. Yet the rumors flew around the school. Both were reputed to have been receiving unsolicited advice from unseen voices that only they could hear. It was further reputed that some of that unsolicited advice was not conducive to their fitting in with society at large.

I realized that I was at a perfect time of life to begin having mental health issues if I were actually in a situation similar to that of the Johansson brothers. Again I asked myself, "Am I crazy?" On the negative side, I was most definitely hearing voices. On the positive side, those voices were not coming to me uninvited. I had control over when I contacted those voices, and I could choose to not hear them at all. (Or so I reasoned at the time.) Another positive was that the voices had no control over me that I did not allow. In fact, summoning and communicating with those voices was not dissimilar to the physical analogue of visiting my neighbors and passing the time. If I decided to engage my neighbors in conversation, it was just that—*my* decision. So it was with the voices I heard in my deep meditative state. I initiated the conversation, and it was I who could figuratively walk away from that conversation (apart from the fact, of course, that Amateur Yachting in Santa Barbara Channel was the one that so rudely terminated its conversation with me).

Further, I felt no obligation to follow any advice, if I were to receive any, from those voices. Along these lines I argued that I was not crazy and that these voices were not subjective phenomena in my mind only but were as objective as the existence of my fellow students in my mathematics class. One needs some benchmark for objectivity, and I figured the existence of my fellow math students would function perfectly well in that role.

Concluding that these voices were real, I was compelled to explain and understand them. It did not take much deep reflection to see that the voice with which I connected did not have any more information about these phenomena than I. In fact, that particular voice seemed to be annoyed by the very question regarding what these voices were all about. It seemed to be anxious to go about its business without questioning the very fundamentals that made its business possible—not unlike most of the rest of us. It also did not seem to see itself as a mere voice. Indeed, it gave itself a name—Amateur Yachting in Santa Barbara Channel—which sounded to me more like a description than a name. That confusion between names and descriptions made me wonder about the translatory efficacy of the extrasensory perception with which I was working. Or did that voice, a voice I knew from previous investigations to be made up of various subvoices all concerned with boating off our local coast, see itself as nothing more than a being whose sole raison d'être was simply interest in those affairs?

From this thought I was led to meditate upon the role of subvoices. I was particularly struck with the observation that the original voices I heard at first were themselves constructed of lower-level voices, or subvoices. That insight led me to wonder whether the subvoices were themselves constituted of voices on a level below them, and so on, in a series of lower and lower levels of voices. Of course, the possibility also struck me of voices coming together into higher and higher levels of conversations. Perhaps one conversation could became a subvoice for a higher level conversation, and so on and so on. Where did it all begin, and where did it all end? I was reminded of a joke I once heard when being introduced to the pre-Ancient Greek idea that Earth rested upon the back of a giant turtle. In the joke, one would ask, "What does the turtle stand upon?" The proper answer was "It's turtles all the way down."

This was an interesting description of how the voices could combine into levels of complexity. Still it did not answer the question pertaining to the origin of the voices in the first place. That is when the party-line theory of consciousness swept me up in a tsunami of enthusiasm the intensity of which I have never felt again. I asked myself, "What if these voices are the product of unconscious extrasensory communications between sentient beings?" Just saying the phrase "unconscious extrasensory communication" to myself filled me with hypersensitive joy, wonder, and an inexplicable humility. Contemplating the possibility of unconscious extrasensory communication made the hair on the back of my neck prickle with anticipation, mixed with a small measure of dread. I felt as if I were perched upon an astronomically elevated precipice overlooking an infinitely vast and ultimately incomprehensible meaningfulness.

If unconscious extrasensory communication were real, it would explain so much. It could account for everything from knitting circles to mob-think to war. The idea is this: Suppose that all conscious beings can, and do, partake of extrasensory communication. Suppose further that most of that extrasensory communication, if not all, occurs on an unconscious level. In that case, we are all communicating with each other to varying levels of degree, unknown to ourselves. What is more, those conversations can be joined by any number of sentient beings. In fact, the conversation itself has a persistence and identity beyond any particular participant. Further, what is to stop that conversation from itself being a participant in higher-level conversations consisting of persisting and integral conversations of their own? The base of the hierarchy of voices and conversations would broaden as conversations would become single voices in higher-level conversations leading to higher-level voices and then yet higher-level conversations. Where would it all end?

What was fascinating to me at the time—and what still fascinates me—is that these unconscious conversations get their existence, their very Being, from the individuals partaking in the conversations rather than the other way around. But those conversations take on an existence that can outlive their participants and become, for all intents and purposes, immortal. Paradoxically, their immortal existence is derivative from the very fact that we, as mortals, exist—again, rather than the other way around! This is the essence of the party-line theory of consciousness.

The party-line theory of consciousness does not explain just knitting circles and war; it also explains the existence of gods! A "conversation" at a level high enough not only has its own will but also possesses a high degree of power to influence individual voices (wills) on an unconscious basis. As such, the theory does not preclude the visual manifestation of these gods to the waking experience of the existent sentient beings. Does it explain God Himself? Is He the end of the line in an ever-expanding consolidation of unconscious extrasensory conversations—like turtles all the way up? If so, then God's existence depends upon our existence, rather than ours depending upon His!

I might break into this enthusiastic reverie to let the reader know that at this point in my studies I had not become familiar with Carl Jung's notion of the "collective unconscious." The reader may be seeing some similarity between Jung's ideas and the revelation to myself of the party-line theory of consciousness. But I assure the reader that at this time I was unfamiliar with Jung's ideas. When I did finally become acquainted with Jung's ideas, I too was first astonished by the similarities. However, I have come to see that Jung's ideas are fundamentally different from my sudden inspiration. It is my, perhaps incomplete, understanding that according to Jungian scholars, his collective unconscious is populated with archetypes, which are patterns and images that influence the unconscious realm of similar species. Above all, the dissimilarity here is that those patterns and images have an objective reality apart from the individuals experiencing them. The party-line theory of consciousness, on the other hand, sees the unconscious realm as consisting of *conversations* between individuals—not necessarily of the same species—with the existence of those conversations being derivative from the existence of the participant individuals. Again, God's existence depends upon our existence! This is a bottom-up, rather than a top-down, revelation.

It further occurred to me that I was now in a position to understand the Christ's proclamation of eternal life for those special few that had true belief and faith. We have got to hand it to Jesus of Nazareth for his bravado. The bold claim of eternal life had no direct antecedent in Judaic thought. Rather, it can be seen as only loosely connected to the Greek notion of the underworld, and a little more directly connected to the Egyptian notion of the day of resurrection of the dead. But that Christian claim of eternal life, more than most other Christian claims, was the lifeline for thousands of suffering potential converts. How in the world did the Christ come to believe in eternal life?

With the notion of the party-line theory of consciousness, the claim of eternal life makes sense. It has to do with our conception of personal identity. Where do we obtain our sense of personhood? That is, how do we come to see ourselves as who we are and not as others? Generally we do so by acting in the world and observing the results. That, coupled with memory, gives us our ideas of ourselves. In this way, I have come to think that I am a guy who likes chocolate, bodysurfing, etc., and I do not like cigarette smokers, mean dogs, etc. I am a person that gets nervous around lots of people and behaves in other specific ways given particular circumstances. Now, suppose that the world you see yourself acting in is expanded to include these extrasensory voices and conversations that are only unconscious to most. What is to stop you from identifying with some of these persistent conversations instead of your body? If you do, then you dwell more in the realm of the spirit than you do in the realm of the body. Because these conversations are immortal, you then see yourself as immortal!

At this point in my experimentations, I was insufficiently attentive to another consequence of the party-line theory of consciousness. While dazzled by the brilliance of the subject matter of God's existence and our spiritual immortality, I neglected, at my peril, to realize the fact that the party-line theory of consciousness was consistent with the fact that any particular voice could join in any number of different conversations. Unfortunately, that neglect led to lethal consequences.

I was not paying attention to the fact that for any particular level, the movement up from a voice to a conversation need not be linear. That is, one particular voice may join many conversations, just as one conversation can be composed of many voices. Thus this web of voices and conversations, where a conversation turns into its own voice and then is free to join other conversations, is not a pyramid in which all voices are more and more consolidated as conversations rise from level to level. It is perhaps more like a torn net. Some conversations can become more and more isolated from one another as they take on a larger and larger base. We see this disintegrating effect in current social media phenomena. Groups of people become disassociated from one another and more and more distinct because they reinforce their own beliefs by being confronted by more and more people similar to themselves and shunning others.

What this means for the party-line theory of consciousness is that a particular psychological impulse or interest—such as the desire to go boating, the noble desire to help others, and even the evil desire to harm another—can manifest in an increasingly isolated and powerful way. This opens the possibility of an ever increasingly powerful Evil, even as the gods were becoming more powerful. In fact, there was no assurance that the gods were good. Some might be good, and some not. I neglected the possibility of the princes of darkness existing alongside the princesses of light, with disastrous results. I was not paying attention to the fact that if the party-line theory of consciousness led to God, it also led to Satan!

To be sure, I had unexamined concerns, but I heedlessly decided to push on with my experimentation. Scientific methodology requires that empirical consequences be deduced from a theory, and then those predicted consequences are tested so as to confirm or falsify the originating theory. Therefore, as a good scientist would do when confronted with a radically new conjecture about the *physical* world, I resolved to deduce and then attempt to confirm ramifications from my conjecture about the shared *conscious* realm.

III

Traumatic Memory

Just then all began to freeze and grow dark. The ground shook with tremors of approaching enormous footsteps. I could smell a sulfur stench, mixed with an electrical element. D.'s ghost and I exchanged knowing and terrified looks. Percy groaned, "Oh no! It's coming." We saw flashes in the distance, associated with the pounding and shaking of the foundation upon which we were situated. I felt the intense burn of an instantaneous flash and lost consciousness.

My first sensation after losing consciousness—I have no way of knowing how long I was out—was that of choking and being unable to breathe. I was being tumbled about in an icy stream, with the frigid water filling my mouth and lungs. Just the intense cold of the water was almost enough to stop me from breathing. Occasionally, far too occasionally, my head would bob above the frothy surface seemingly at random and I would be given an instant to gasp for breath before I would again be drawn down into the violent turbulence of that raging watercourse. I was tumbling head over heels, my arms and legs a whirling mess of confusion.

Suddenly I smashed into a huge slippery boulder, causing me to cry out and again fill my lungs with water. I fought my way to the churning surface to spit out the water in my lungs, and I saw downstream a massive rapid. It boiled with water as it crashed against still larger boulders. Somehow I was now wearing a life vest and a protective helmet over my previously exposed skull. I was pulled down below the surface again by the sucking current. The newly emergent life vest helped propel me back to the surface of that urgent stream. The quickly approaching rapid towered over me. I was sucked down a chute of boiling water and tumbled about below the surface. I regained the surface, coughing. I had no time to attempt to rise above the aethereal realm and reenter the safety of the real world. All my attention was now being given to trying not to drown.

After being crushed against another huge rock, I bounced back into the rapidity of the central stream. I caught a glimpse of Percy standing upon a flat boulder, calling out to me. She had her arms outstretched in order to catch me as I was about to pass near her, propelled by the raging current. I kicked as hard as I could, and the motion of my efforts and the swift current combined to push me over to where Percy stood waiting. My trajectory indicated that I was going to pass where she stood, just close enough for our outstretched hands to meet with only an inch to spare. I was pushed down into the drink again, rising just in time for our hands to clench firmly around one another.

After a long struggle against the current, Percy was finally able to pull me up to the safety of the rock. Icy water swiftly swirled around us on all sides. I lay there on my stomach, slightly raised by my arms. I was shivering and coughing, retching up the water from my lungs, and trying to catch my breath. The rock felt just as cold as the water from which I had just been saved. After expelling the lion's share of the water from my lungs, I turned over on my back and looked up at the sky. It was ominously dark. I lay there shivering, stunned into silence.

But I am getting ahead of myself again. It is hard to keep these traumatic memories at bay. They force themselves upon my consciousness with an intensity rivaling that of their first appearance. Will I forever be forced to suffer these awful memories? I must will myself to return to the thread of my story, where I had resolved to deduce and then attempt to confirm ramifications from the party-line theory of consciousness.

IV

Conjecture & Confirmation (Or, Eating Cake)

Meditating upon the party-line theory of consciousness, I found that I would not be able to directly verify that theory. I would need to do so in a roundabout manner. For example, if I were to engage in a conversation again with Amateur Yachting in Santa Barbara Channel, if it were to deign to reciprocate, I would probably not have a direct observation of how the individual voices constituted that integrated being. Thus, I would not be able to directly check whether my good boyhood friend, for example, could influence that conversation—even if he were one of the conscious individuals sending out some of the unconscious extrasensory messages it comprised. I would need to confirm the mechanism of his participation with, and addition to, that conversation in a more surreptitious manner.

Fortunately I was a voracious reader of Ian Fleming's spy novels and was not unfamiliar with a few standard sleuthing maneuvers as described in the literature. I decided to plant a message with D. and see if it made its way up to the awareness of Amateur Yachting in

Santa Barbara Channel. I did not want to alert D. to my plans, so as not to confuse the findings more than they were already confused (and also, I must confess, so as not to alarm him in thinking that his good friend was becoming mentally unhinged). I needed to plant that message with D. in a devious fashion. This was my motivation for recruiting D. to my cause, unbeknownst to him, and ultimately leading to his tragic demise.

I needed to invent a wholly fictitious story—one so audacious that it could not possibly be true. But it had to be so alluring to anyone interested in yachting that he or she would desperately want it to be true. Through our many years of acquaintance, I had been repeatedly made aware of D.'s extreme interest in C. S. Forester's series on Horatio Hornblower, a British Royal Navy officer during the Napoleonic Wars. Though C. S. Forester had died in 1966—a death D. made sure we memorialized at that time as best thirteen-year-old boys could—Forester's work *The Life and Times of Horatio Hornblower* had been posthumously published in 1970. I calculated that I could fabricate a compelling story about this publication somehow.

I walked three houses over from my parents' home to visit D. Since beginning high school, we had not seen as much of each other as we had in our earlier youth, but D. graciously invited me into his backyard to catch up on events. He was working on his boat, which lay perched atop a boat trailer. I noticed that he was mending some ropes. He patiently reminded me again that these were not called ropes but instead were referred to as sheets, given that they served the nautical purpose of tying down sails. Always having been interested in knot tying, I asked him what the knot was that he was currently working upon. He said it was a halyard hitch, used to join a sheet (a.k.a. halyard) to a sail.

I asked if I could take the halyard and practice the knot. Having a talent for knots (which is probably why D. ever allowed me anywhere near his boat), I did not particularly need to concentrate on the tying as I casually said, "Oh, D., did you read in the newspaper a couple of days ago that C. S. Forester's son John is going to be at a local bookstore soon to read from *The Life and Times of Horatio Hornblower?*"

This was a complete fabrication on my part, of course, but it certainly did have the intended effect on D. D. excitedly asked me when it had been in the paper. I said that it had been a couple of days ago, maybe sometime last week, and that I thought we had already thrown away that issue. D. sadly noted that his family had thrown away their papers from last week too. He asked, "Which bookstore?"

"Oh," I said, "I think it was V—— Books; you know, that one on Main Street, down by California Street? But I could be wrong; it could be another. Jeez, maybe it wasn't even in the city. But I know it was somewhere in the area. I hope it hasn't happened already."

After catching up on areas of mutual interest (books, baseball, recent movies, rock 'n' roll, etc.) I bade him good-bye. As I left, I said, "Hey, if you figure out where and when Forester is going to be reading his dad's book, let me know. I'd like to join you."

D. waved me good-bye and said, "You got it! I can hardly wait!"

I walked home, feeling particularly proud of myself in planting the decoy that would allow me to confirm the party-line theory of consciousness. I had no idea that I had just set off a series of events that would ensnarl my dear friend in a lethal web. I have never forgiven myself. Nowhere near.

My plan was to wait a day or two, try contacting Amateur Yachting in Santa Barbara Channel again, and then see if there was any response to my false story about John Forester reading from his father's posthumously published book. I wanted to wait long enough for the false story to elicit some excitement, but not so long as to allow D. to expose it for what it was—a bold fabrication. So that night I did not try to contact Amateur Yachting in Santa Barbara Channel. Instead I went over the logic of my plan.

The outline of the logic of my plan was essentially as follows:

1) If the party-line theory of consciousness was true, then if I planted a story with D. of sufficient interest, it would become a matter of interest to Amateur Yachting in Santa Barbara Channel.
2) I did so plant that story, and it was a matter of interest to Amateur Yachting in Santa Barbara Channel (this last part was to be observed later, of course); thus,
3) the party-line theory of consciousness was true.

Having put into motion the necessary antecedents, all I had to do was check to see if Amateur Yachting in Santa Barbara Channel was interested in my story. I could then conclude that the party-line theory of consciousness was correct.

Meditating upon the overall structure of this confirmatory logic, my self-confidence was shattered. In a flash of realization, I concluded that the logical form I was using to confirm my theory was an example of fallacious reasoning. I noted with dismay that my confirmatory logic had the same form as the following:

1) If it is someone's birthday, then we are eating cake.
2) We are eating cake; therefore,
3) it is someone's birthday.

This is obviously a fallacy; we could be eating cake even though it is not someone's birthday. Thus, if I noted that Amateur Yachting in Santa Barbara Channel was interested in the fabricated story that I had planted with D., this did not prove the party-line theory of consciousness true. I was crushed.

Where had I gone wrong? How does one legitimately confirm the unobservable from the observed? How, for instance, do scientists confirm the properties of photons of light, for instance, given that no one really directly observes photons? Physicists have been confirming properties of in-principle unobservable entities based upon experiences in the observable world for centuries. What is their logic? I asked myself, "How do physical scientists avoid the birthday-cake fallacy in confirming physical theories?"

In my mind, I went over some of the reasoning I had recently read in a couple of popular books on the history of quantum mechanics and relativity to see how good science should really be conducted. I decided to concentrate on the evidence we had for the wave theory of light. In the books I had been reading, Thomas Young was credited with having proved that light was a wave phenomenon. He did this with his split-beam experiment. Young took a beam of light passing through a small hole in a window shade and split it into two parallel beams in close proximity by placing a slim card in the middle of and along the axis of the beam. When he did this, he saw that the beam projected a series of darker and lighter bands on a screen. When he blocked either of the halves of the beam, the image on the screen was a continuous blur of light, just as if he had removed the card and allowed the whole beam to shine upon the screen. The phenomenon of the bands of light appeared only when the beam had been split and both halves were allowed to travel to the screen. This was the physical, observable phenomenon calling out for explanation.

Now, Young had had plenty of experience experimenting with water and sound waves. He was familiar with a notion he called interference. In interference, a crest of a water wave meeting another crest makes a doubly high crest, a trough meeting a trough makes a doubly deep trough, and a crest meeting a trough cancel each other out to yield a flat surface with no wave. Young, applying the concept of interference to light, said that the phenomenon of the bands of light on the screen would be explained if light were a wave—the dark bands on the screen would be where the light wave crests met the wave troughs and cancelled themselves out to result in darkness. Thus he had proved that light is a wave phenomenon. This seemed pretty good to me.

Taking this as a paradigm of scientific confirmation in the physical realm, I explored the logic of Young's reasoning. I looked at that logic every which way I could. Eventually I came to the shocking conclusion that Young was using the same fallacy I had used to attempt to explain the party-line theory of consciousness! I immediately pulled myself up out of bed and ran to check the book I remembered contained Young's logic. I needed to verify that I had correctly remembered his reasoning. I found the following passage from Young's influential 1803 work, *On the Theory of Light and Colours*: "Supposing the light of any given colour to consist of undulations of a given breadth, or of a given frequency, it follows that these undulations must be liable to those effects which we have already examined in the case of the waves of water and the pulses of sound."

There it was—the word "supposing." It was the very first word in his famous paper! Young starts out his vastly influential paper by asking us to *suppose* that light is a wave, and he goes from there. And thus, there it *also* was—the birthday-cake fallacy:

1) If light is a wave, then when we perform the split-beam experiment we will see a repeating series of light and dark patches.
2) When we do perform the split-beam experiment, we do see a repeating series of light and dark patches; therefore,
3) light is a wave.

Oh no! Poor Thomas Young! How could he have committed such an obvious fallacy in confirming his theory? I decided to give Young a pass. I needed to check a more modern example of scientific methodology.

I was up from bed anyway, and I had the books right in front of me, so I hastily paged my way to Einstein's paper on the photoelectric effect. It is generally thought that Einstein's paper was the first proof that light is composed of individual particles instead of waves. Einstein published his paper in 1905, more than a century after Young's 1803 paper. Being the brilliant mathematician he was, I thought surely Einstein must have used the correct logic for confirming his theory. I figured I would lift his logic and use that logic in my attempt to confirm the party-line theory of consciousness. I thought that if Young had erred in concluding that light is a wave, then surely Einstein must have gotten it right in concluding that light is corpuscular.

Einstein's thinking in this area focused upon the previously observed phenomenon that shining light on the newly cleaned surface of a metal, say zinc, causes the surface of that metal to emit electrons. That phenomenon is what has come to be called the photoelectric effect. The more light shined on the surface, the more electrons emitted. Increasing the intensity of the light of only one frequency (color), say only a very specific frequency of ultraviolet light, increases the number of electrons emitted but not the energy of each electron. Also, even very high intensity light below a particular frequency (color) fails to cause the emission of any electrons at all. It was found that the energy of the emitted electrons is a function of the frequency (or color) of the light and is not a function of the intensity of the incident light beam. This is the phenomenon demanding explanation. This finding was at odds with Newton's dynamical and Maxwell's electrical theories, which together erroneously implied that the energy of the emitted electrons should be a function of the intensity of the light beam and not its frequency (color).

In 1905 Einstein published a paper that explained this phenomenon using the newly conceived notion of a quantum of action, as put forward by Max Planck. Regardless of having the reputation at the time of being a poor mathematician, Einstein worked out the mathematics of Planck's quantum of action as applied to light. Einstein theorized that the energy of the emitted electron was equal to the frequency of the incident light times Planck's constant for the quantum of action. Einstein showed that if light came packaged in discrete particles—particles he called photons—then shining light on a metal surface would yield the observations we indeed do observe:

the shining of light on a metal surface would show that the *energy* of individual emitted electrons is a function of the frequency and not the intensity of the incident light beam, whereas the *number* of emitted electrons is a function of the intensity of the beam.

The flow of electrons with which Einstein was working was considered to be a cathode ray, and in his 1905 paper Einstein says, "If each quantum of light were to give its energy to the electrons independently of all the others then the velocity distribution, i.e., the quality of the cathode rays produced, will be independent of the intensity of the exciting radiations; on the other hand the numbers of electrons leaving the body under equal conditions will be directly proportional to the intensity of the incident radiation."

As Young's explanation of the wave nature of light initially struck me, this reasoning of Einstein's corpuscular theory of light also sounded good to me. I was excited to see such a clear explanation of the observed phenomenon. I immediately dived into the logic of that explanation so as to find the germ of insight that allows us to use observation to confirm our theories concerning unobservables. Again I looked at this logic from every which way. I just could not believe it. Here, too, was the birthday-cake fallacy yet again!

1) If light is packaged in individual quanta, then when shining light on a metal surface we will see that the energy of the emitted electrons is a function of the frequency and not intensity of the light.
2) When we do shine light on a metal surface, we do see that the energy of the emitted electrons is a function of the frequency and not the intensity of the light; therefore,
3) light is packaged in individual quanta.

Oh no, Einstein, even you?

The problem is, of course, that it is possible that we could see the observed effect even if light were not packaged in individual quanta, just as we could be eating cake even if it were not someone's birthday. So even Einstein fell victim to the birthday-cake fallacy when "proving" that light is composed of individual corpuscles. Because Einstein's reasoning has the same form as the birthday-cake fallacy, and because the birthday-cake fallacy is indeed invalid, this means that Einstein's reasoning is, strictly speaking, invalid.

At the heart of quantum theory—the most successful physical theory of the twentieth century (and all centuries before)—where the wave and the particle theories of light are wondrously brought together and contrived to work out their differences, there lies a logical fallacy. Many people—especially laypersons with scientific interests—have claimed that quantum theory has *proved* that light is both a wave and a particle. But have we really proved that dualistic claim? If we have not even proved either that light is a wave or that light is a particle, how could we have proved it is both?

I was struck dumb. I did not only despair over the obstacles involved in proving the party-line theory of consciousness. I was also stunned into a numb state of shock in uncovering the fundamental fallacy complicit in confirming all physical theories. If all of our thinking about the physical world is based upon fallacious reasoning, then just what *is* the physical world as conventionally conceived? It may be something completely different from how we currently comprehend it. In fact, does it even exist? Maybe the physical world as conventionally envisaged is merely some fictitious story we tell ourselves to keep track of the observable realm. Perhaps it helps us hold together individual conscious experiences!

How could even Einstein have committed the birthday-cake fallacy in confirming his theories? He must have been aware of his own fallacious reasoning. I could not believe that Einstein would be ignorant of this worm eating away at the heart of Newton's apple. Then I remembered having read somewhere a passage from Einstein in which he touched upon this conundrum. Einstein is quoted as having said, "No amount of experimentation can ever prove me right; a single experiment can prove me wrong."

When I had first read that passage of Einstein's, I just passed it off as a throwaway remark verging upon mysticism. "Okay," I had said to myself, "beyond being the foremost physical scientist, Einstein is also a mystic and says some rather paradoxical things, but I should probably ignore his mysticism and concentrate on his scientific notions." But now, from the perspective of the birthday-cake fallacy, I saw that this passage is anything but mysticism. In fact, it is the product of shining a hard, stubborn logical light upon the deepest structures of scientific methodology. The first part of his quote, that no experimentation can prove a theory true, is just the acceptance of the fact that all scientific inferences to unobservables utilize the birthday-cake fallacy and thus are no real proofs at all. The second part, in which it is noted that a single experiment can prove a theory false, is again an insight about the birthday-cake fallacy, or rather a variation on that reasoning that is not itself a fallacy.

Suppose I said the following: "[1] If it is someone's birthday, then we are eating cake; [2] we are not eating cake; therefore, [3] it is not someone's birthday." If I had articulated that train of thought, then the reasoning in that train would *not* be a fallacy; in fact, that reasoning would be valid. So if light being a wave would lead to seeing dark and light bands on a screen in the split-beam experiment, and if we performed that experiment and *did not* see the dark and light bands, then (if we had conducted the experiment correctly and our data collection apparatus was accurate) we could validly infer that light is not a wave. So Einstein was saying that we cannot prove theories about the physical realm true but we can prove them *false*. Again, if that is the case, then what really *is* the physical realm? Do we really have no valid proof that it is composed of all the things science says it is? Taking this line of inquiry further, we can even ask, "What is a physical body?" Do we know? The answer struck me in the head like a sledgehammer. No, we really do not know what a physical body is. It could be something simply made up by our minds in order to hold together our conscious experiences.

How did we—a civilization so devoted to the magnificent things science can do for us (and the many successes of science are truly magnificent)—get into this mess? Why are we so blindly allowing a simple fallacy to infect the very heart and foundation of our communal body of knowledge? Is there a vaccine for that infection? How do we keep all the wonderful knowledge that science has given us and yet avoid the fallacy at the bottom of confirming scientific theories? I set myself to explore these questions. I decided to follow the data, those most certain components of science, back from theories to their geneses in observation. Where did we go wrong? Starting from the certainty of data born of observation, we then inferred uncertain theories concerning in-principle unobservables.

If Einstein's statement about not being able to prove physical theories is an accurate portrayal of our existential position as scientists, then the fault in reasoning from appearance to reality is endemic to that inference and cannot be other than mistaken. Any inference from appearance to reality—whether in science, religion, or mysticism—is similarly mistaken. It seems that the Humpty Dumpty of conceived reality via physical science cannot be put back together again once we have broken reality apart from appearance. But the distinction between appearance on the one hand and reality on the other is endemic to our culture. We can track that bifurcation back to Ancient Greece. Thank you, Ancient Greece, for breaking that egg!

So if the problem with scientific proof is due to separating reality from appearance, then maybe we should not make that separation. Maybe appearance *is* reality! It does not take more than a moment's consideration to feel the radical, almost insurgent, nature of this conjecture. From our first intercourse with our community, we are taught that the subjective realm is not quite real—only the realm beyond appearances is real. What if that basic training were mistaken? What if there was nothing beyond the veil of appearances? What if there was only the veil? In that case, it would not be a veil at all. There would be nothing behind it to hide.

Ah, but wait! I thought to myself. *In this case the cure could be worse than the disease.* By saying that appearance *is* reality, are we saying that there are no solid facts in the world—that everything is just a matter of opinion and appearances? That could be dangerous. After all, someone may say that it seems to her that God exists, and someone else may say that it seems to him that God does not exist. If appearance were reality, then God would both exist and not exist—a logical impossibility. Reality, I thought, cannot be two contradictory things at the same time. No, we must keep facts. There must be such a thing as the objective fact of the matter. Just because I believe that the girl sitting next to me in math class thinks I am cute does not mean she really does think so. Simply believing something cannot make it true. That bears repeating: simply believing something cannot make it true. Shakespeare is full of counterexamples of this silly notion, driven home by one hard lesson after another. I believed that Einstein would have agreed with this sentiment.

To solve this conundrum, I resolved to restrict facts to the directly observed. In this way, the observation of a cherry-red '61 Chevy Impala convertible parked out in the front driveway would correspond to the fact of the car's presence in the drive. But one cannot directly observe the absence of something, so there would never be the possibility of the car both being in the front drive and not being in the front drive based upon direct observation. So if someone directly observes God, then God would need to exist in that case. But nobody is going to directly observe the nonexistence of God. Thus the paradox of relative truth is avoided. Of course it is the height of spiritual materialism to claim that one directly observes God in all His infinite magnificence. If we cannot directly observe God in all His glory, then God is an in-principal unobservable, just like the stuff of scientific theories. In this case, the inference to His existence based upon what *can* be observed is likewise conformable to the birthday-cake fallacy! Using this measure, our knowledge of God and the physical world are on equally precarious foundations.

Actually, I wanted no truck with undercutting the legitimacy of science. Already at that time in our cultural history, religious fanatics were hard at work trying to cut science off at the knees. I knew in my soul that science was real, and I wanted nothing to do with sowing doubt about the scientific endeavor. I believed that science was the best we had in our search for truth. There would be nothing gained by replacing the solidity of science with the flimsy tissue of faith. But how was I to reconcile my trust in science with the presence of the birthday-cake fallacy lying at its heart? I decided that science was dealing with objective truth as long as it stayed within the certainty of appearance and did not try to rise above appearances into a realm of unobservables. As Sir Isaac Newton is often quoted as having said, "Hypotheses non Fingo." In English this famous statement means "I frame no hypotheses." I decided that to save science, we needed to make it applicable only to appearances. Science is objective because the only objective facts we have are appearances. This was enough for me at the time.

These musings on the conflation of reality and appearance gave me a new way to see the emphasis that quantum theory gave to sentient observation. Another fallout from Planck's quantum of action was the view that in quantum mechanics there is the collapse of the distinction between the observer and the observed.

Going back to the split-beam experiment, if we lower the intensity of the light going through the splitting apparatus so that single photons pass through one at a time, the target screen lights up with a scintillating flash whenever a photon strikes it. However, over time those apparently random scintillations draw out a pattern of light and dark bands. This is a testament to the dual nature of light. Individual scintillations hit the screen, leading one to think of light as corpuscular. Those scintillations taken together create a pattern of interference of light and dark bands, leading one to think of light as a wave phenomenon.

It gets interesting if we put a photomultiplier on the apparatus. In that case, if we measure when an individual photon goes through the splitting apparatus (where it gets split into one beam or the other), then the pattern of scintillations becomes a single blur—just as if there were a single beam without interference. This is wild! The conclusion physicists have drawn from this observation is that the measurement of the photon at the splitting apparatus causes the waveform of probabilities to collapse into a single quanta of light. Without that measurement—read observation—the light continues to manifest as a wave. Therefore, observation changes the experimental result. Observation is fundamental to making the world what it is. The distinction between the observer and the observed has collapsed!

From meditating upon these findings in early quantum mechanics and the birthday-cake fallacy, I was beginning to think that observation (hear "consciousness") was more fundamental than physical stuff (hear "body"). It is not that body leads to consciousness (i.e., that consciousness emerges from a configuration of brain stuff), but rather it is that consciousness leads to our populating the observation of the world with bodies. If the above was right, then the distinction between consciousness and objective reality is a false dichotomy. All is consciousness. This is a strange, radical thesis.

But the thesis that all is consciousness is not as strange as it sounds. The consciousness that is raised from being a mere mirage to its ontologically ascendant position is a peculiar sort of consciousness. It is neither more nor less than our awareness of the everyday world. The world did not disappear once I realized that all is consciousness. Rather, the experiences of the world became infused with a substantial existence they did not previously own when erroneously conceived as a mere film overlaying reality and obstructing that occult realm from our sight.

These musings on the relative dependency of body upon consciousness, rather than the traditional view that it goes the other way around, gave me a renewed allegiance to the party-line theory of consciousness. They allowed me to see that any laws of consciousness I uncovered in my meditations were not some sort of gambol in an unsubstantial realm. They were really the laws with which legitimate science had been concerned all along.

All of these thoughts, concerns, and decisions took place while I was waiting until I could determine if the lure I had planted with D. was to percolate up to Amateur Yachting in Santa Barbara Channel. I had no idea that during those exquisitely self-indulgent cogitations, the pieces were falling into place in a drama that would ultimately lead to D.'s early death. It turned out that there was a reality out there beyond my own narcissism, and it was not benign.

Lying there on the hard surface, with blood starting to drip into my left eye, my memory began to slowly return. With a flash of sheer terror, I remembered the confrontation of the two dragons, and I turned my body to witness that gruesome conflict. I was appalled at what I saw. The two dragons were dueling with such intensity that I could hardly make out one dragon from the other. All I could see was a blur of red and green, with a continual mist of blood being thrown into the void around them in pulsating cascades of glistening crimson. I could hear the snapping of sharp teeth and the rending of solid flesh. I smelled the rancid odor of burning skin and muscle, with the smoke of the sacrifice rising above the melee.

Oh my!

V

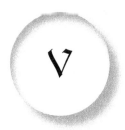

The United Lodge of Devine Wisdom

The next night, sometime in mid-April, 1971, I decided to contact Amateur Yachting in Santa Barbara Channel to determine whether the fake story I had planted with D. about C. S. Forester's book had made its way up to that rather irritating entity individuated by a description rather than a name. I was not looking forward to having a conversation with that rude voice. I was, however, keen to explore the confirmatory ground upon which the party-line theory of consciousness lay. I positioned myself in bed and began to concentrate on contacting that particular hidden conversation of consciousnesses.

I soon found that it was difficult to fix upon the signal from Amateur Yachting in Santa Barbara Channel. There was a lot of noise in the occult network of aether that night. I use the term "aether" because I am not too sure what else to call it. Additionally, my use of the term "occult" is not intended to convey any mystical connotations. I am referring to an occult network with the sense of "occult" merely meaning "hidden," not necessarily implying a mystical quality. As some readers may know, there is a common medical test for occult (hidden) blood in the stool. Undergoing that test is anything but a mystical experience. In the same way, I do not take the aether as the ground for unconscious extrasensory communications to be mystical. It is just one more fact concerning existence.

In any case, instead of receiving a clear signal from Amateur Yachting in Santa Barbara Channel, I was hearing a lot of static from many different voices and conversations. Most of those conversations were excitedly mentioning something about a new technology called a "chat room" on some ground called the "ARPANET." I had no idea at the time what there were talking about. I much later came to find that this was the rollout of the very first use of a chat room, supported by the newly developed US military network platform called the Advanced Research Projects Agency Network (ARPANET). The ARPANET later came to be the foundation of the internet as we know it today.

After intense effort, I was able to increase the signal-to-noise ratio for Amateur Yachting in Santa Barbara Channel, and I began hearing its excited conversation. A very small part of that conversation concerned the ARPANET. Most of its conversation concerned what it believed to be an upcoming reading of C. S. Forester's posthumous book. The conversation was all about endeavoring to determine when and where the reading was to take place and not wanting to miss the reading.

I was so excited that I pulled out of my connection with Amateur Yachting in Santa Barbara Channel and lay in bed, glorying in the success of confirming the party-line theory of consciousness. As I have laboriously detailed earlier, I knew these data and their resultant inference did not constitute strictly valid proof for the existence of the party-line theory, because of its reliance upon the birthday-cake fallacy for its logical structure. I thought, though, that if that line of reasoning was good enough for confirming the occult theories of twentieth century science, then it was good enough for my purposes.

As I went over the confirmatory data I had collected, I became more and more interested in a couple of implications suggested by what I had just learned. The most obvious implication was that my message about C. S. Forester had definitely gone through D. to Amateur Yachting in Santa Barbara Channel. There were only two people from whom that message could have been received. D. was one of them, and of course the other would be me. I could have unconsciously transmitted that message to Amateur Yachting in Santa Barbara Channel. But if I had been the source of that information, then it would almost assuredly have been seen for the ruse that it was, given that I was well aware that I myself had created that story out of whole cloth. Thus I could not have been the cause of all that excitement. Amateur Yachting in Santa Barbara Channel took that message as veridical. It could only have come from D. This confirmed that the unconscious network of voices was receiving messages from actually existent sentient beings—D. definitely being an existent sentient being and not a disembodied conversation floating in the aether.

Another implication from those confirmatory data was that disembodied conversations appeared to be acutely interested in, and interacting with, the embodied realm. The rumored reading, after all, was to be conducted in the realm of, and by, an existent sentient being. This was to be a real reading, at a real bookstore, by a real, live flesh-and-blood person, and the disembodied conversation did not want to miss hearing it. This last point fascinated me. I had not previously spent much time considering either this possibility or its ramifications. But it made sense and fit in with my previous discoveries concerning the hidden realm of unconscious extrasensory conversations. If, as I had reasoned earlier, the existence of those unconscious conversations were parasitic upon real existent beings in the embodied realm, then those conversations would have a vital and vested interest in the real and substantial world. Indeed, their survival would depend upon it.

Upon having the thought that nonbodied unconscious extrasensory conversations were dependent upon embodied sentient beings, I immediately had the fanciful vision of ants herding aphids around their leafy pasturage. The ants were harvesting nourishing nectar from the abdomens of those docile and unsuspecting, almost bovine, aphids. Were we the unconscious bovines? Were we unknowingly providing nourishment for those conversations in the aether? If so, then did those conversations actively manipulate our world so as to guarantee a constant supply of life-sustaining consciousness? Were these disembodied conversations husbandmen, shepherding us around in the routines of our daily lives? Again, if so, then where is our free will? Have those disembodied voices sapped our wills along with our consciousnesses?

I resolved to more fully explore this interaction between substantial sentient beings and the aethereal conversations of consciousnesses. But where to begin? I decided to back the other way around. I knew that D. had influenced Amateur Yachting in Santa Barbara Channel. I now endeavored to see if I could compel Amateur Yachting in Santa Barbara Channel to influence D. (In retrospect, I now see that this fateful decision was the fulcrum upon which D.'s continued existence as a sentient being was precariously balanced!) From my previous conversation with Amateur Yachting in Santa Barbara Channel, I had learned that that being did not particularly know me from another; nor was it much interested in me at all. So the task before me was to somehow grab the attention of Amateur Yachting in Santa Barbara Channel and alert it to some matter of interest about D. Then I could check to see if that matter made its way to D.

Thinking about what might be a matter of interest to Amateur Yachting in Santa Barbara Channel, I remembered that the first time I actually talked to that conversation in the aether, it was concerned with yachts and commercial vessels interfering with one another in shipping lanes. *Ah, shipping lanes!* This thought brought vivid images to mind of previous outings on D.'s yacht, where we were very cavalier about maneuvering around large commercial vessels. I wondered if

I could alert Amateur Yachting in Santa Barbara Channel to D.'s (and my, of course) previous proclivity to chase tankers. In this way, I might be able to nudge that disembodied conversation to cause some effect in the substantial world. I did not foresee any negative consequences to such a disclosure for D. It had been years since we had practiced such foolish maneuvers. I expected nothing more than a warning of some kind, if that. That is, of course, if those unconscious extrasensory conversations had any real efficacy in the substantial realm—which is exactly what I was trying to confirm.

At my first opportunity, I tried contacting Amateur Yachting in Santa Barbara Channel again. The initial excitement about ARPANET had subsided a bit, so the signals in the aether were not overly obscured by noise. I sent out a greeting to Amateur Yachting in Santa Barbara Channel. My greeting was ignored. I tried again. Again my invitation to converse was ignored. *What an arrogant creep,* I thought to myself.

This time, Amateur Yachting in Santa Barbara Channel reacted to my assessment of his character. It responded, keeping its sunburned nose in the air. "Arrogance is the natural and appropriate prerogative of the elevated and refined in relating to the mere hoi polloi! Stop bothering me."

"Oh," I said with a bit of surprise, "but I have some information that may interest you about yachts in shipping lanes—information about very dangerous encounters between yachts and tankers."

Amateur Yachting in Santa Barbara Channel responded in a snooty manner, "I keep my shipping lanes clear! Commercial Shipping in Santa Barbara Channel and I have a good understanding. We do not interfere with one another."

"Well," I said, using the name of D.'s yacht, which he had taken from one of the Horatio Hornblower novels, "you know, the *Lydia,* a member of the V—— Junior Yacht Club, has a history of running close to container ships and tankers. I just hope that that practice doesn't continue and cause any contention between you and Commercial Shipping in Santa Barbara Channel."

Amateur Yachting in Santa Barbara Channel snapped back, "Ah, it was the *Lydia,* was it? I knew her skipper was up to no good. Well, I'll take care of that!" And again it abruptly cut off the conversation.

I gave this revelation to Amateur Yachting in Santa Barbara Channel about a week to trickle down to the substantial world. I then went over to visit D. once more. I found him in a rather sour mood. Enthusiastically greeting him, I said, "Hey, D., how's it going?"

In a subdued manner, he simply replied, "Okay."

I sensed some disturbance in his mind. Pushing on, I enquired further. "Been out on the *Lydia* lately? She sure is looking good. You've got her all shipshape and ready to sail!"

D. replied that getting her seaworthy was about all he could do with her right now. "I've been given a two-month suspension on my yachting license," he said. "As you know, the V—— Yachting Club oversees the Junior Yacht Club, and the commodore of the yachting club somehow heard about our runs in the shipping lanes back a couple of years ago. He told me he was temporarily revoking my membership and asked the harbor patrol to give me a two-month suspension on my license."

I was aghast to hear of the strict disciplinary action taken against D. Our forays into the shipping lanes had happened years ago. But I was enthralled to hear about what could have happened only if Amateur Yachting in Santa Barbara Channel had somehow meddled in the affairs of the substantial realm. With mixed emotions, and trying hard to suppress my excitement, I said to D., "Wow. That happened years ago. How did they hear about it now?"

"I don't know," D. curtly replied. "But, you know," he continued in a more thoughtful manner, "I think I remember that a night or two before the commodore called me to suspend my membership, I dreamt about this. Yeah. In fact … I'm just remembering this now …

you were in the dream too. Uh. That's kind of funny. I guess somehow I knew I was going to get that call. Weird, huh?"

"Yeah, weird," I said in all honesty. "Well, that was kind of scary stuff we were stupidly doing back then. I'm surprised we didn't get killed."

"Yeah," he said pensively, and he added in an oddly upbeat manner and with a conspiratorial sparkle in his eye, "Well, we're young—only seventeen. We still have plenty enough time to die."

"Yeah," I said, startled by the hidden paradox in his last statement. "I guess we do. Anyway, I better get back to my math homework. Maybe I could go out on your yacht with you when they return your license? Take care!" And I left him to continue brooding over being landlocked. I did not pay any attention to his mentioning that I had been in his dream a couple of nights before his sailing license had been suspended.

After finishing my math homework that afternoon, I accompanied my sister and her boyfriend on a short ride up to Santa Barbara to attend a meeting of the United Lodge of Divine Wisdom. This quasispiritual organization met every Sunday evening on Sola Street. My sister and her boyfriend were somewhat regular attendees to the talks there. I would go along sometimes just to be around people I thought did not mind considering alternative metaphysics. They tended to believe in chakras, astral bodies, soul travel, and the like, but I gave them credit for apparently having open minds. In this regard, I thought they were one up on Unitarians, who are commonly thought to have open minds as well. However, Unitarians, to my way of thinking, paradoxically had more closed minds than most. They did not seem to stray beyond the standard steak and potatoes of mainstream American metaphysics; they simply seemed happy to profess an agnosticism related to that standard religious and metaphysical fare. I could not see that they cared to consider any other menu options available. I could not really tell what they truly believed, and I do not think they had any interest in figuring it out for themselves. At the time, I thought the members of the United Lodge of Divine Wisdom were honestly trying to figure out what to believe. So I occasionally attended some of their meetings as a guest.

Sitting in the backseat of the car on the ride up to Santa Barbara, I mused over what had just taken place with D. I was intrigued that I had apparently just demonstrated that the disembodied conversations in the aethereal realm could influence the substantial realm. While exulting in the thought that these essentially immortal foci of hidden consciousness could influence the embodied for good and just purposes, the image of Amateur Yachting in Santa Barbara Channel scuttling D.'s boating excursions seemed closer to ants tending aphids rather than the angles of our better natures coaxing us along the path of goodness.

For being just days away from the beginning of spring, the particular evening in the converted old church where the United Lodge of Divine Wisdom met was stiflingly hot. It was filled to capacity with enthusiastic devotees, adding to the ambient heat. The leader of the group was standing at the pulpit and discussing a topic that did not particularly appeal to me—something about letting the light from our astral bodies shine forth in all that we do. While I appreciated the message of doing good in one's life, the metaphysical foundation for their injunction to go forth and do good did not appeal to me. From what I could tell, the Lodge believed in an ultimate divine spiritual entity, and they further surmised that we are mere sparks derivative from that divinity. The lodge held that we all desire to part from our physical bodies and rejoin that ultimate flaming source. Apart from my questioning whether or not there really are such things as physical bodies, I was also now seriously entertaining a bottom-up form of consciousness and existence rather than the Lodge's top-down theory. With the heat of the room and my lack of interest in the subject matter being preached, my mind began to wander.

By and by, I noticed with alarm that my undisciplined mind was being caught up in a wave of unexamined devotion and adoration emanating from the devotees surrounding me and focused upon the speaker. The speaker seemed to be soaking up and luxuriating in the pulsating waves of unconditional adulation. I caught myself up and decided that this was not the right environment within which to let my mind wander with the prevailing winds. With the discipline I had been developing over the past couple of months, I wrested back control of my own consciousness. Upon regaining control of my own will, I immediately began to sense the presence of voices and conversations hostile to my instantiating my own individuality.

"Who does he think he is?" asked one voice.

"He obviously doesn't believe in the ultimate divine," accused another.

"Why is he here?" asked one paranoid voice.

"He does not belong here. All together now, push him out!" stated one voice with commanding authority, sounding very much like the speaker at the head of the chamber.

"Get him! Get him!" cried the conversation as a whole.

During the rest of the sermon in that stifling hotbox, I exerted all my will to fend off the attacking voices. For all the world, I felt like a flying intruder ducking and diving, trying to protect itself from a raucous murder of crows. The onslaught was never ending. Voices were swooping in and actually causing me mental anguish and pain. I could not take the constant swipes at my awareness, and I somehow slowly began to create some sort of mental shield around myself for protection. As before, I cannot tell you what I was actually doing in machining that shield from pure consciousness. Bit by bit, however, the wall was going up around me like a transparent bubble protecting me from the vicious attacks of the devotees. Unfortunately, building that bubble took extreme effort, and I was exhausted and sweating by the end of the sermon. When the speaker finally came to the end of his lesson and finished answering the last question from the horde of devotees, I stood up and walked out of the claustrophobic building as quickly as I could, darting around and dodging devotees as I exited. Finally I made my way back to the car. When my sister and her boyfriend caught up with me, her boyfriend asked, "Didn't you like the talk? You practically ran out of the lodge. I thought it was pretty good tonight."

I replied, "It was okay. I was just really hot," and I got into the backseat of the car.

On the ride home down the coast, I tried to make sense of it all. Quietly sitting in the back of the car, I was almost petrified with fear. If these voices could inflict that sort of pain and suffering on those of us ensconced in the solid world, then what further havoc could they wreak? I was not particularly apprehensive about the specific voices that had attacked me in the lodge; after all, I had been able to fend them off. I was more concerned with the kind of power voices and conversations further up the levels of conversations would have. It could be immense. And, for goodness' sake, what was the nature of that protective bubble? How had I been able to contrive that shield out of thin aether? As I was having these thoughts, another set of voices and conversations from the United Lodge of Divine Wisdom came swooping down upon me. They followed the car down the coast like angry seagulls. I immediately put up my bubble again, and I kept it up all the way home. I decided that a visit with Resident Teacher was long overdue.

I also concluded, belatedly as it turns out, that I needed to stop involving D. in my schemes. I had involved D. in my confirmation process without him knowing my intentions and thus not as a result of any fault of his own. It now seemed to me, however, that it was a dangerous game I was playing, and D. had been unknowingly exposed to this risk simply to satisfy my own intellectual curiosity. I resolved to extricate him from this game that unnecessarily put his safety in jeopardy. Unfortunately, I had no idea just how much danger he was already immersed in.

VI

Framing My Best Friend

The next couple of evenings—during prolonged excursions into the hidden aether—I had some unusual and disturbing experiences. I was not able to directly contact Resident Teacher, because of the distraction caused by being repeatedly harassed by individual voices from the United Lodge of Divine Wisdom. They relentlessly attacked me in my hidden wanderings and foiled my many attempts to contact Resident Teacher. These voices filled me with an ominous dread that I could not distinctly identify. It was a deep dread, though, and very concerning. Once, during a particularly bad attack, the angry voices were swooping and diving at me and causing me much suffering and pain even though I had deployed my transparent protective bubble. Just when I thought I could not take any more of this abuse, D. sailed directly at me and pulled me into his boat. Batting at the voices, which had mysteriously turned into persistent seagulls, D. dispersed the agitated flock. I was astonished that D. was there. I was also astonished that what had been previously an experience having nothing whatsoever to do with boats or the sea was now an experience of being whisked to safety on a beautiful yacht with a smugly smiling D. at its helm.

I said nothing to D.; I did not even thank him for his help. I immediately quit my excursion into the aether and resumed mundane existence in my bedroom. I was petrified with fear for myself. Mostly, however, I feared for D. How did he get there, and what kind of risk was he putting himself in by being there? And what was this "there" anyway? I decided that I needed to protect D. from any danger posed by his following me about in my aethereal excursions. After all, had I not been instrumental in involving him in that realm? And had he not just put himself in danger to protect me?

Out of a sense of loyalty and genuine caring for my friend's well-being, I realized that I needed to do something to help him. But what could I do? Should I go over to his house tomorrow immediately after school and bluntly tell him to stop joining me on my hidden excursions? What if he consciously knew nothing about these excursions? Would confronting him with all of this be somehow more detrimental to his well-being? And, conversely, what if he did consciously know about the aethereal realm of unconscious extrasensory communications? What then? How could I then protect such a strong-willed individual who had an established record of doing as he pleased rather than as advised? I needed to know which horn of the dilemma to follow. I decided to go over to his house the next day and surreptitiously scout out which game we were playing—did he consciously know of the aethereal realm, or was he unconsciously acting as my protector in that dangerous world?

As I approached D. that next day, I said, "Hey, D. How's it going? You having any more dreams about sailing the *Lydia?*"

D. rather sourly commented that dreaming about sailing was about the only sailing he was going to do these days. But he picked up interest in the conversation by adding, "Ah, actually, now that you mention it, I *have* been having some sailing dreams. God, I love to sail!

Oh, and you have been in some of them too. Don't get all weird on me. We were just sailing around like we used to do. It was loads of fun."

"Yeah," I replied, "those were good times. But aren't you going to get your license back soon? I bet you can't wait."

"Yeah," he said, "I can hardly wait. Hey, you want to go out with me on my first sail? We could make it an all-dayer, maybe go all the way out to Anacapa Island?"

"That sounds cool," I honestly replied. I then pushed a little harder. "Say, what were those dreams like? It wasn't dangerous, was it?" I asked, pretending to joke around.

"Well, not really. We did pull out of a squall once, but it was clear sailing after that. It was nice. Sailing is so relaxing! But those dreams were real lifelike," he said, breaking into a self-reflecting reverie.

"Did you learn anything from your dreams?" I asked.

"Like what?" D. enquired.

"Oh, you know. Something you could use when you actually go out on your boat ... ah, your yacht."

D. thought about it a bit on my account simply out of courtesy and said, "No, not really. It was just great to be out in the channel again." He smiled broadly.

With that reply, I decided I was about as satisfied as I was going to be with this conversation. I was not ready to go into detail with him about my excursions into the aethereal realm. I bade him good-bye and went on my way home. If only I had been more forthright with him at the time, maybe we could have avoided his catastrophic demise.

Being reluctant to confront D. consciously with my concern for his safety in the aethereal realm, I decided to try to influence him through his "dreams." That night I was extremely troubled. My excursion into the netherworld consisted mainly of struggling over huge boulders, scraping my hands and knees raw trying to scale and descend huge rocks blocking my path forward. It did not take long in this exposed position before the voices that were the crows of the

United Lodge of Divine Wisdom sought me out and swooped down upon me. I threw up my protective bubble as best I could, but it was a flimsy prophylactic given my need to concentrate on the rocky path before me. After an interminable period of this suffering, as I both desired and dreaded, D. came sailing my way and I jumped into his yacht. He smiled and tacked hard starboard, and we swiftly sailed off to safety, trailing a flock of squawking seagulls that struggled in their failure to keep up with us.

"D.," I said, "I didn't thank you last time for saving me from those seagulls."

"Oh, sure," he said, beaming with satisfaction. "You'd do the same for me."

"Yes, I would," I said. "But you know," I added, "you've got to stop doing this. It's dangerous. You could get hurt. Please tell me you won't come to my rescue like this again."

"What? Come on; you've got to be kidding," he said. Marginally raising his consciousness above a dream state in a confused manner, he continued. "It's only a dream anyway."

"No," I said with some emphasis, "it's not just a dream. And you just confirmed that."

"Ah, come on," he said, descending back into his dream. "It's a nice day. Let's just sail around and enjoy it."

"No," I emphatically continued. "I don't want you visiting me like this anymore. It's not safe. Stop this right now!"

D. looked genuinely hurt and sadly said, "I don't like you like this. Why are you trying to hurt me?"

I repeated, "Look, just don't visit me like this anymore, okay!" and I ended the conversation in anguish and reentered the mundane realm. I was shaking, thinking that I had seriously hurt the feelings of my very best friend. I needed to visit him tomorrow to see how his conscious self was taking all of this.

The next day, I walked over to D.'s house and found him in his backyard, working on his yacht as usual. "Goodness," I said, "haven't you already done about everything you can to that yacht?"

D. looked up, frowned slightly, looked away, and said, "Oh. Hi." He cleared his throat and added, "Look, I can't really talk right now. I've got to, uh … got to go pick up my mom at her work. She doesn't have her car. So I don't really have time to talk."

"Okay," I said. "Well, you should be getting your license back in a couple of days. Maybe we could take that run out to Anacapa Island?"

In a very subdued manner, D. replied, "Uh, yeah … about that. Maybe I should go out on the *Lydia* alone at first. You know, just to make sure all the work I've done on her is okay." He avoided my eyes.

"Okay. Well, see you later."

"Yeah, Maybe."

After a long, awkward pause, D. added, "Look … you know … I'll see you later."

"Yeah," I said, "I'll see you later."

I left, sadly knowing that my interference in D.'s dreams certainly was consciously manifesting for him in a hurtful manner. I hoped that my actions were efficacious enough to counterbalance the pain I was causing him and to compel him to stop following me around on my aethereal excursions. As I left his yard, I noticed that his mom's car was not parked in the driveway; maybe she did have it after all.

Now that I had taken care of the problem of D. following me around in the aethereal realm, I finally had the time and energy to try reaching Resident Teacher. But how was I to contact that aethereal conversation? I remembered that when I first contacted Amateur Yachting in Santa Barbara Channel, it told me nothing about how to contact Resident Teacher. I remember it saying, "She's *Resident Teacher* for goodness' sake! Just find her." Not much help. But that nondirection direction did contain a hidden clue, as I discovered upon reflection. Apparently Resident Teacher was not the sort of thing that had an address or any location to speak of. In fact, it finally came to me that none of these aethereal conversations with which I had been interacting, for good or for ill, had a location to them at all. They just were, without being anywhere.

Kind of like numbers, I thought to myself.

But knowing how to count did not get me any closer to knowing how to contact Resident Teacher. Reflecting upon my predicament, I came to the realization that I literally did not know how I had conducted my experiments with unconscious extrasensory communication in the first place. As well, I did not literally know how I had constructed my transparent protective bubble out of thin aether. Apparently there were a lot of things I was now doing that I did not know how I was doing them. This was very perplexing and seemed to be no help at all. I raised my arm and rubbed my eyes and forehead in frustration. At that moment, I realized that I also did not know how I had performed the mundane act of rubbing my forehead!

I raised my arm up to the ceiling and held it there. I then lowered it down to limply point at the floor. I repeated the motions again. And again. And again. No, there was no hint at all of how I was doing that. I just did it. That was all. No more to it. It was just a simple act of will.

Maybe, I thought to myself, *every volitional act is like this simple act of raising my arm! We just do it, and if nothing gets in the way, it gets done.* I went on in this vein. *There must be some sort of mechanism involved here—some sort of cause-and-effect-process that can be discerned and then used as a tool. Maybe we have been using this tool for so long that we have just forgotten what we discovered as toddlers trying to negotiate our way in the world?*

My thoughts then ran along the following lines. A neurobiologist, surely, would explain volitional acts as having a genesis in the brain, where electrochemical signals are sent out along axons to fire the requisite muscles to end up raising the arm. There seemed sense in that. But where did the first brain activity come from that resulted in the arm rising? *Here,* I thought, *is where it gets tricky for the neurobiologists; they would answer that the initial brain activity that eventually results in the arm rising is caused by other physical brain processes that came before that originating brain activity.* So in a real sense, according to this way of thinking, all of our volitions are caused and determined by prior physical processes. Those prior physical processes are caused by physical processes prior to them, and our awareness of those actions is simply emergent from the electrochemical processes. In essence, then, the neurobiologists see our volitions as not really voluntary and our consciousness as nothing more than a nonparticipatory observer; our conscious minds are just along for the ride. Objecting to this line of thinking, I raised my clenched fist in defiance.

After recovering from a short burst of laughter, I had the sobering thought that if the deterministic view of volitions were true, then there would be no place for taking responsibility for our actions. In essence this metaphysical view of the brain, where consciousness is simply a bystander to events in our lives and where there are no real volitions, is a convenient haven for sociopaths. My direct observation was that I did have real volition. I also thought that responsibility was a fundamental notion, and I was coming to the conclusion that the neurobiologist's view of the world was too laden with theory to be anything close to direct or even to indirect observation. I was reminded of my earlier decision that I was now to embark upon a program of taking only facts derived from direct observation as fundamental. If a theory—like those underpinning the neurobiologist's—conflicted with direct observation, then that theory would be falsified. Sure, there may be clever arguments that stupefy the unwary observer into falsely doubting his own direct observations of exercise of his free will, but all those clever arguments start with assuming the theory over the evidence. Which is it? Was I to stay true to direct observation or replace that solidity with wispy theories founded upon cloudy assumptions? I had previously chosen the former tack, and so I decided to maintain that heading now.

After all, had I not previously concluded from my cogitations over the ubiquity of the birthday-cake fallacy in scientific confirmation that even the simple belief in physical bodies was in jeopardy? If we have not proved that there are physical bodies as we conceive of them, then how can the neurobiologist glibly downplay direct awareness of the exercise of free will by replacing it with assumptions of electrochemical interactions of physical bodies? To me that seemed like getting the cart before the horse. At this point, recognizing that I was descending into the spouting of colloquial aphorisms with limited utility, I forced myself back from my meditations on free will and returned to my search for Resident Teacher.

I reluctantly noticed that I had a strong predilection to getting caught up in eddies of thought that distracted me from the important demands of pure existence. The above cogitations were fun to run through, of course, but they were not helping me get any closer to contacting Resident Teacher. I had a real objective before me that was due to real concerns about my and others' safety, and I was not making any headway toward that goal. Taking my cue from the arm-raising exercise, I positioned myself on the bed and immediately embarked in a conversation with Resident Teacher. It instantaneously responded to my invitation to converse. In total shock and surprise, I blurted out, "Amateur Yachting in Santa Barbara Channel suggested I contact you."

"Ah, yes," it replied, "you wanted an answer to your question, 'What is this all about?'"

"Oh," I rather sheepishly said, "since first asking that, I have somewhat narrowed down my question—or, more precisely, my questions."

It sighed and responded with some relief, "Good. I figured I was going to have problems answering your original question. But I see you are agitated. How can I help you?"

At this point I thought to myself, *How does Resident Teacher know what my original question was?*

It immediately answered, "Well, you know, you have been pretty clear about opening yourself up for inspection. It's been fascinating to watch you go through your thought processes. You're a rather interesting fellow."

Well, I'm glad I've provided you with some entertainment.

"And we are glad you have provided us the opportunity to enjoy it."

At that point I thought that if this aethereal conversation were to continue to directly read my thoughts, then it would be extremely hard to carry on a civilized conversation. Upon my having that thought, it reluctantly replied, "Okay, we'll do this your way and use your visualization of what you take to be a civilized conversation. But, again, how can I help you?" It stated this with what I would swear was an actually audible expression of concern.

"Oh, that's better," I said, realizing that the conversation up to now, except for this last interaction, had taken no time at all. *It is nice to be back in the realm of time, carrying on a normal conversation again,* I thought to myself. Out of respect, Resident Teacher did not reply and just watched me expectantly with a sympathetic look on its face. That is when I realized that Resident Teacher had a somewhat feminine appearance but was otherwise rather generic in its benevolence. It patiently continued to gaze upon me expectantly.

I confessed, "I need help. I think I've placed myself in danger. And what's worse, if that's the case, then I've placed my dear friend in danger as well."

VII

Resident Teacher

"Yes, I can see that you need help," Resident Teacher kindly responded. "Why don't you tell me about it in your own words?"

"Well," I started, "I don't know how to protect myself, or even D." Resident Teacher nodded, perfectly aware of D. and his daring exploits following me around in my excursions in the aethereal realm. My thoughts came spilling out. "These voices and conversations from the United Lodge of Divine Wisdom just won't leave me alone, and they seem to be getting more powerful. Or maybe other more powerful voices are joining in with them; I'm not even sure that they originate from the United Lodge of Divine Wisdom anymore. I don't know where they are coming from. I'm afraid. And I'm afraid they will hurt D. He keeps coming to my rescue, though I don't think he is doing so consciously—which makes it even harder to protect him. He has no idea what danger he is in. Actually, neither do I. I'm scared."

Resident Teacher did not offer much reassurance in its reply. "You should be scared. This is serious."

Jeez, thanks for the help, I thought to myself. Resident Teacher raised one of its eyebrows and looked at me. Ignoring my brief breach of etiquette, I continued. "I mean, what can I do?" I paused, hoping for a reply. "Well," I went on after realizing that Resident Teacher was not going to give me any hints on how to proceed, "I've been thinking about consciousness—how consciousness is fundamental and there is nothing but consciousness. Also, I've been thinking about how choices and volitions are just simple acts of the will. It seems that there is no mechanics to making a choice and then doing it; you just do it or you don't. So, if all of that is true, couldn't I just will this bad story away? Can't I, just by sheer willpower, change my reality to another conscious experience? Couldn't I battle these voices and conversations with pure will and protect D. and myself?"

Resident Teacher smiled, which I took as reassurance that I had stumbled upon a possible strategy to pull D. and myself out of our mutual problem. Resident Teacher took in a deep breath and said very calmly, "What, do you think you are in some sort of science fiction novel?" I was crushed. "This is not a comic book. This is real. You really need to pay attention here, pick up the cues, and take your time thinking this through."

I thought to myself, *I don't* have *time; D. could get hurt at any moment.*

Resident Teacher gave a slight but sympathetic shrug. It said, "I—we—do appreciate your pure motive. You do seem to have D.'s interest at heart. That's in your favor."

"Yes," I almost cried out, "but how do I help him? I thought that having proved that consciousness was more fundamental than the physical realm—"

"You are quick."

I was taken aback by the interruption. I unconsciously puffed up my chest and proudly confessed, "Yes, thanks for the vote of confidence concerning my mental capabilities, but—"

"No. I mean you are too quick in jumping to unwarranted conclusions based upon the evidence before you. You are *too* quick."

"Oh," I said, exhausting the breath from my inflated chest.

Resident Teacher went on. "We are very familiar with your meditations on the use of what you call the birthday-cake fallacy as the foundation for scientific confirmation. It's fun to watch a naturally skillful but as yet untrained athlete run that particular obstacle course. We agree there is no proof of scientific theories by the birthday-cake fallacy route, and further, we agree that there appears to be no other route to proving such theories." It paused and then continued with a smile. "However, by your reckoning, there would be no such thing as birthdays."

"What?" I said.

Satisfied that it now had my full attention, Resident Teacher explained. "From the fact that there is no other way to prove scientific theories about the physical world than by using the birthday-cake fallacy, and given that that methodology turns out to be no real proof at all, you then erroneously conclude that the physical world does not exist and that everything is consciousness. That would be like saying that because we are not allowed to conclude it is someone's birthday just because we are eating cake, then there are no such things as birthdays at all!" Resident Teacher paused and looked at me intently. "Does that seem right to you—that there are no birthdays—based upon that evidence?" It smiled again.

I thought about this for a moment and then asked, "So are you saying that I can't use this reasoning to call into question the existence of the physical realm?"

"Right," it said.

"But," I added quickly, "you … er, all of you … you do agree that we can't prove any theory true about the physical world, don't you? I mean, if what you are saying is true, then it's possible there is a physical world, but we'll never be able to know that what we say about it is accurate. That seems weird."

Resident Teacher then reminded me that while scientific theories about the physical realm cannot be proven true, they can be proven false. It said, "Science can always test the current theories in vogue and throw away the ones that don't work. I've heard it said that that fact that we can falsify physical theories suggests something about the reality of the physical realm."

I pondered this and offered, "So science can keep throwing away the falsified theories and eventually be left with the true model? That would be kind of like testing and testing alternative theories and asymptotically approaching the true theory."

Resident Teacher said, "Your description of the situation through the asymptote analogy reminds me of what that great sculptor Michelangelo once said in response to a question about how he was able to carve such beautiful statues. He said something like, 'I just chip away all the marble that isn't part of the statue.'"

I stared at it with an amorphous doubt growing in my thoughts. Something did not sit well with me concerning the asymptotic description of scientific progress. I was thinking to myself that to draw an asymptotic curve, you first need to know the asymptote. But here, where we were talking about using science to ferret out truth from falsity, we did not have a known place toward which that methodology was headed—we had no a priori known asymptote. Establishing that a priori unknown point is the whole purpose of scientific methodology in the first place; so how could one conceive of scientific progress as approaching that point?

But the whole idea of an asymptote analogy to scientific progress was of my invention, so I was growing quite confused. Resident Teacher continued to stare at me intently. Finally I said, "But what guarantee do we have that science is on the right path, inexorably getting closer and closer to the true theory? Couldn't we have taken a wrong turn somewhere? If so, then we could have set ourselves back by centuries or even millennia. In fact, we could be going completely in the wrong direction. We may end up converging on a local point that is far from the universal truth of the matter. This view of science seems to run into problems if you follow it out." I then wistfully added, "Maybe it's still the case that consciousness is fundamental, and maybe still consciousness is all that there is." Resident Teacher took a step back and looked at me from a different perspective.

"But," I dribbled on in a more humble manner, remembering that I had just gotten my wrist slapped for being too quick, "I could be wrong. Maybe consciousness is not the foundation of everything. If that's the case, then D. and I may be in more trouble than I thought. I thought that maybe I had a way to protect us by the use of sheer willpower. But now I fear that I'm wrong and we are left unprotected." I was confused, dejected, and losing more and more hope as I went on.

Resident Teacher shot back, "Like I said, you're quick ... too quick. There is another fallacy at work here in your thoughts. We call it the ignorance fallacy, or the fallacy from ignorance. Just because you don't know about something doesn't mean it's not true or doesn't exist. That's what you were doing when you said that because we can't know of the physical world, then it doesn't exist—the ignorance fallacy. Now you are compounding your ignorance by holding that just because this reasoning doesn't prove that the physical realm is a function of the conscious realm, then the physical realm is not a function of the conscious world. Do you see your double use of the ignorance fallacy?"

Now I see why they call you "Resident Teacher," I glumly thought to myself.

Resident Teacher shrugged again. "But look; there is another way of going about this. We call it the honeycomb argument."

"I don't think I've heard of that argument," I said.

"Oh, you may know of it by another name or description. It's been around for some time," Resident Teacher said. It then dived even deeper into teaching mode. "Suppose you take a piece of honeycomb fresh from the beehive but drained of its honey. Your senses tell you it has a certain shape (honeycombed, of course), a certain color, and a certain hardness. You can knock on it, and it emits a certain sound. It has a certain coolness and even a certain fragrance. Now suppose you put that honeycomb in a saucer and place it near a source of heat.

After a while, it has become amorphous in shape, it has lost its dark yellow color, and it is certainly no longer hard and is now a pliant liquid. You can't knock on it and generate any sound at all, it is warm where it used to be cool, and if you have let it heat up enough, it has even lost a lot of its fragrance. Do you follow this simple story?"

"Yes," I replied.

"Good," Resident Teacher said. "Now, what allows you to say that that lump of wax continues as an enduring physical body through its change from the first state to the second?"

I thought for a second or two and responded, "Well, I saw it, of course. I sensed it before and after the change, so I know it is an enduring physical object—or body, as you call it."

"And your senses are usually thought of as sensing the physical realm, are they not?" asked Resident Teacher.

"Yes, certainly, that is the way they are normally thought of."

"And if you apprehended something through some process other than the senses, would that apprehension pertain to body or to mind?"

"I'm not too sure what you are getting at," I confessed.

"Let me try to be clearer with my question."

Just then I had a vivid image of D. cringing on the ground in agonizing pain as a giant black birdlike creature pecked at his neck and head. D. was crouched down and holding his hands over his face and crying out for help as the avian monster tried to peck at his eyes. I lost all concentration on the conversation with Resident Teacher. Then the image of D. suffering crouched on the ground disappeared as quickly as it had forced itself upon my awareness. I was panting with horror as I found myself facing Resident Teacher again.

Resident Teacher said in a consoling manner, "Yes, the world suffers on as we discuss the nature of existence. Its reality unfolds and surrounds us as we struggle to learn its manifestations so as to facilitate our existence within it. It can't be helped. We hope we can learn something from our enquiries that will help alleviate the suffering of existence."

I cried, "I can't do this! This is too hard. I've got to go and help D.!"

"How?" it asked.

"I don't know!" I shouted.

"Okay," it said, "that's what we're trying to figure out. Take some deep breaths, concentrate on healing compassion, and relax; when you're calm, we can resume our discussion."

I took the deep breaths but did not know what I was supposed to think about in concentrating on healing compassion. I just wished that D. would escape from the attacking dark bird. Fortunately the image of D. escaping the clutches of that dark monster seemed to work in calming me down, and I was soon in a state where Resident Teacher could continue with its instructional dialogue.

Resident Teacher rhetorically asked, "Okay, now where were we before that unfortunate interruption?" It paused for a moment and then went on, appearing oblivious to the seriousness of the situation. "Oh yes, we were discussing the lump of wax changing all of its sensible qualities while being conceived of as the same physical object it was before the change."

I thought, *This is bullshit; D. is out there suffering right now, and I'm not doing a damn thing to help him.*

Resident Teacher said, "Now try to concentrate; this is important."

Okay, I thought, *let's do this.*

"Good," it said. "Now, you so astutely claimed that you were able to experience this piece of wax as the same physical object as it was before the change due to your sensing the object through that change. Am I right?"

"Yes," I curtly admitted.

"Right. And we agreed that the senses are thought of as the sort of thing that pertains to the physical realm. Good. Then I asked you that if we were to apprehend something through some process other than the senses, then would that apprehension pertain to body or to mind? Did I not? And then you asked for a clarification of my question. I believe I have summarized our discussion up to this point. Do you agree?"

"Yes, that seems to be a pretty good recounting of the discussion up to the point where we became aware of D.'s suffering," I said, emphasizing the word "suffering."

"Yes, the alleviation of which is the purpose of this discussion."

"Yes," I again said curtly, trying to get on with it all.

"Okay," Resident Teacher continued, "so let me restate my question in a manner that may be more familiar to you. Instances of awareness seem to have categories, or realms over which they roam. I'm thinking here of experiences of things like the color blue, the sound of a trumpet, the feeling of heat, and even the apprehension of the number four or the love you feel for a good friend. It seems that the first three examples here, having to do with color, sound, and the feeling of heat, pertain to what we commonly call our senses. In that way those experiences, what we commonly call sensations, seem to pertain to physical bodies. Are you with me so far?"

"Yes," I said.

Resident Teacher cocked its eyebrow at the repetition of my short answer to its involved questions and continued. "The other examples, apprehension of the number four or the experience of love for a good friend, do not seem to involve the senses and also don't seem to pertain to physical bodies. Rather, the apprehension of those objects, so to speak, pertains to the mind instead of the body. So, along these lines, I asked if when we apprehend something through some process other than the senses that apprehension is always of the mental sort instead of the bodily sort. Do you understand my question now?"

Inexorably, Resident Teacher had drawn me back into its conversation. I took a deep breath and admitted, "I think I understand your question. It seems natural to think that if some apprehension, as you say, is other than via the senses, then it is a mental process rather than a bodily process. But just now I'm wondering about *extrasensory* apprehension. It seems possible that extrasensory perception can be of bodily things. But extrasensory perception is not of the senses;

that's why it's called extrasensory. If it is not sensory, then maybe this is a counterexample to the claim that all apprehension not having to do with the senses is mental."

Resident Teacher smiled and said, "It's good to have you back in the conversation. But I'm wondering if extrasensory perception is really nonsensory. Yes, we call it extrasensory, but isn't it really a case of a little-used sense or senses—a sixth (or beyond) sense, as they say? In this case, the "extra" in "extrasensory" just means "other than the commonly assumed five senses." After all, the popular parlor trick is to use extrasensory perception to determine the card someone is holding in her hand. That certainly seems, for all intents and purposes, like a visual inspection of a physical body—just one that many people don't commonly use."

"Okay," I agreed, "extrasensory perception is not really *extra*sensory, and all apprehension apart from the senses pertains to mental processes rather than bodily processes. Let's continue with your argument."

"At least," Resident Teacher mused, "let's let that claim be our working hypothesis for now. Good." After a brief pause that caused me some anxiety, Resident Teacher repeated, "Good." It then went on to say, "Now pay strict attention to what you would have actually sensed and actually observed if you were in this story about the wax and you had performed that simple experiment. Isn't it the case that the sensations you had of the piece of wax before the change are very much different from the sensations you had of it after the change? Think carefully on this, and don't answer until you are satisfied with the answer you are to give."

I paused and said, "Again, I think I can see where you are going with this." I pondered for a while. "After careful thought, as you requested, I think I would say that the sensations before and after the change are quite different, even quite clearly distinct, certainly. If someone were to have one experience only—or, more correctly, the two of them separately—then she would not be able to guess that the two experiences were of the same object," I said confidently.

"Good again," said Resident Teacher. "I need you to continue to concentrate on this story. We aren't quite done yet, but we're getting close to being done. As you said, the two experiences focusing upon what is gained from the senses from before and after the change are quite different—'clear' and 'distinct,' I think you said. But we know that the lump of wax is the same physical body before and after that change. How do we know this? Our apprehension of the wax as a persisting physical body couldn't have come through the senses; otherwise, we would conclude that the object before the change is different from the object after the change. Therefore, our knowledge of the enduring physical object didn't come to us through the senses. And if that knowledge did not come to us through the senses, as we discussed above, then it must have come to us through a mental act. Thus, our apprehension of physical bodies as enduring objects is not due to the physical realm but is solely due to the mental realm—to consciousness. Enduring physical bodies are intuited and imposed upon our awareness of the world by acts of consciousness. Consciousness creates our awareness of what we take to be physical bodies. Thus, consciousness constitutes the physical!"

There was a pause while I stared at Resident Teacher.

"'Rather than the other way around,' to use one of your expressions," Resident Teacher quickly added.

I continued to stare, wondering who was being quick now. When I had collected my wits, I blinked and quietly said, "Okay."

For all the buildup, I thought Resident Teacher's argument to be quite simple. I had a feeling of being let down—though I could see that the argument was quite general and ranged over our apprehension of all physical objects, not just some inconsequential lump of beeswax. I cleared my throat and felt the strong desire to progress the program and determine a way to use these evaporating precious moments to protect D. and myself from the violence that reigned in the aethereal realm. I said, "Okay, if that honeycomb argument is correct—"

"*If* it is," it quickly inserted.

"Yes, *if* it is correct, then the physical realm is constructed as an act, or series of actions, of the mind. And if the physical world is somehow constituted from the mental world, then why can't we just will it however we want?"

"Well, first you need to be careful what you wish for, as the saying goes," said Resident Teacher.

"You mean that we may not really want what we wish for?" I asked, relying upon the trite common aphorism in attempting to understand Resident Teacher's meaning.

"Well, that too, I guess. But what I really meant was that you have to be careful that your wishes really are your own wishes," Resident Teacher warned.

"Why would something I wished for not be my own wish? Isn't that just a logical tautology—that your wishes are your own?" I asked, unconsciously putting aside my previous cogitations on ants shepherding aphids and the implications that fanciful image suggested regarding our free will.

"We did like your picture of the ants and aphids," Resident Teacher said, forcing me to confront my own previous image. "We think you should pursue the implications of that picture and ask yourself what the ants are harvesting."

"Well," I said, pausing while trying to remember my previous thoughts here. "I figured that, insofar as the actions of the ants regarding the aphids are a representation of the interactions between unconscious extrasensory conversations and the actually existent sentient beings that support those conversations, the ants, so to speak, are harvesting consciousness from the aphids,"

"You also went a bit deeper in your thinking on this topic; can you recollect your thoughts on that? According to your quick thinking process on this matter, you also had those unconscious extrasensory conversations harvesting something even more valuable than consciousness from the sentient beings," it said, nudging me to move my thinking along more quickly than I thought it wanted me to do before.

"Actually, yes. I thought that if the conversations were shepherding us around for their own gain, then that had ramifications for our free will. I jumped to the conclusion that they may be harvesting from us not only consciousness but also our wills," I hesitantly replied. I added, "I *guess* I can see why you consider will to be even more valuable than consciousness," though I was not entirely convinced of this last point.

Resident Teacher said, "You know, an old Greek once asked me an important question when we were discussing the nature of motivations for performing good and moral acts. At one point we were discussing a possible answer suggested by one of his junior colleagues that to do good is to do that which is loved by the gods. At that point, the old Greek asked us to consider whether something is good because the gods love it, or whether the gods love it because it is good. Now, we don't need to go into the full discussion of that here, because it is a *bit* different from that which I want you to consider. But taking these conversations to be godlike in their relations with existent sentient beings, my question to you is, Do sentient beings, like yourself, will something because it is something they want to do, or do the gods believe it is something good and then will you to will it? Because of the likelihood of the latter, you need to be careful what you wish for."

"How do I do that?" I asked.

"Not too sure," responded Resident Teacher.

Great, I thought to myself.

"You need to always subject your thinking and desires to critical analysis. Think through your decisions and make sure they are your own. Constant vigilance is required."

"Vigilance over what?" I asked myself.

Resident Teacher went on. "These gods—that is, these *conversations*—are continually harvesting will from individually existent sentient beings; that's how we—they—survive. The problem is that many of these gods are not so benign; some are downright mean and even, some say, evil. These evil ones stoke fear and hatred in the world so as to consume a continual banquet of evil will and consciousness provided to them for their nourishment and power from sentient beings who are themselves unaware of being manipulated. These gods have a simple will to power, and they will to use it."

Great, I thought. *Now I have something else to worry about—are my thoughts and desires my own?* Resident Teacher stared at me, hiding a flash of terror behind its benevolent demeanor. "You know," I said, confronting Resident Teacher, "you all are complicit in all of this. This is very much your fault."

Resident Teacher thoughtfully replied, "It would be sad to disintegrate into nothingness due to a lack of devotees and worshipers. I've seen it happen. It's not a pretty sight." It paused. "Anyway," it finally added, deftly steering the topic of conversation away from the possible mortality of the immortal gods and bringing the topic back to an earlier issue, "even if the honeycomb argument is good, you still can't simply will your way out of your problem."

"Really?" I said. "If everything is consciousness, or constituted by consciousness, then can't I simply will a new conscious experience and be done with it?" Again an image of D. suffering at the hands of that horrible dark bird flashed across my consciousness. I gasped, caught my breath, and, slightly losing my balance, tried to reach out for Resident Teacher. It took my hand, gave me a look of compassion, and let my hand fall. The image of D. receded, and with it the terror of the moment. I said, "As you can see, I really need to do something about D.'s suffering. Can't I just will it away?"

"The answer to your question was answered by you earlier. Can you recollect this as well? You were considering that given that all is consciousness, then the laws of physics are more correctly seen as laws of consciousness. Just because all is consciousness doesn't mean that there are no laws of that realm that unalterably exert themselves. One can't just do whatever one wants; we all must stay within the laws of consciousness—of existence. These laws are not like getting a parking ticket where it is possible to break the law. With laws of existence, we can't do anything but follow those laws. The common phrase 'Laws are made for breaking' has no meaning here. Learning those laws may help you with your problem."

At last, I thought, *Resident Teacher is going to provide me with something useful.* I enthusiastically asked, "Can you teach me these laws of consciousness so that I can use them against that horrible giant bird harassing D.? It would be wonderful to understand the laws of existence so as to avoid suffering!"

"Uh," Resident Teacher confessed, "I'm—we're—not very solid in our knowledge of those laws. Nor are many others, if there are any at all that are. That knowledge is an evolving process, as you can imagine." My heart sank. Resident Teacher tried to be more helpful. "We all know that there are three fundamental laws of consciousness, of course; we've known those three laws from the dawn of consciousness. But I'm not too sure how they fit together and can lead to the kind of knowledge that can be useful for your purposes. To me they are more of a constraint on our awareness and our will than anything else."

"Okay," I despondently said.

Resident Teacher then pronounced the first law of consciousness as if it were reciting from an elementary school textbook. "Consciousness is always conscious of something." It was obviously very proud of remembering that first law, and I stared at it, wondering if the obviousness of the first law was useful for anything at all. Resident Teacher began mumbling to itself and then said, "Oh yeah, right, the second law of consciousness is 'Consciousness is never conscious of itself.'" Again it looked very proud of itself. I continued to stare in disbelief over the banality of these so-called *fundamental* laws of consciousness. It went on. "You will probably recognize the third law of consciousness: 'Consciousness constitutes the objects of its consciousness.' There, that's them—the three fundamental laws of consciousness."

Continuing to stare at Resident Teacher, I wondered to myself if I could somehow use this last law to help my cause.

"I don't know if you *can* use that last law," offered Resident Teacher, unashamedly reading my mind again. "Maybe you should consult Sage on this matter."

Oh no, I thought, *not another less-than-helpful teacher.* Beginning to get annoyed, Resident Teacher continued to stare at me. "Right," I said. "Who ... er, what ... is this Sage? Is it a conversation a couple of levels up from you?"

"Yes and no," Resident Teacher petulantly answered. "At a certain point, counting levels up or down doesn't make much sense. It's kind of like what Einstein said about experiencing time. From one reference point, some event may take a long time, but from another reference point, that same event could take no time at all." It was my turn again to stare at Resident Teacher. It continued. "Really, though, it's quite simple. Since many voices, as you call them, can partake in many different conversations, as you call them, and since a conversation in turn can act like a single voice and enter into other conversations, the numeration of levels becomes meaningless. It's better to just think in terms of the broadness of the base of any particular conversation. Sage has a particularly broad base. But then, so do some of the evil ones, I suppose." It paused and then added proudly, "I, myself, am a frequent participant in the Sage conversation."

Not a ringing endorsement, I thought to myself. I tried hard not to think of my immediate decision to avoid Sage at all costs; I did not want to alert Resident Teacher about my thought that if this was the type of help I could expect from "knowledgeable" conversations, I might be better off without them.

"Say," I asked, trying hard to mask my background thoughts,

"couldn't I just throw that protective bubble around D. and help him that way?" I was hoping to avoid another fruitless conversation with yet another questionable teacher.

"Perhaps," Resident Teacher thoughtfully replied, "but we're not too sure what that bubble is or how you deployed it. It is quite unique."

"What?" I responded with incredulity. "Don't you know how to construct that bubble? What do you do for protection, then?"

It replied, "We've always sought protection in numbers. We have no experience with that bubble of yours. Maybe that could be another question for Sage?"

So, I thought to myself, *Resident Teacher cannot tell me how to keep my will from being stolen by the gods, cannot tell me how to use the supposed laws of consciousness to protect D. and myself, cannot explain how I managed to create my protective bubble, and cannot even tell me what that bubble is!* I felt as if I were in a deeper state of unknowing than I had been before my dialogue with Resident Teacher.

"Well," it said in a rather offended manner, "at least you now know what you don't know! I'm sorry; I have matters I really must attend to." With that it ended our conversation.

Lying in my bed and thinking back on the conversation with Resident Teacher, I concluded that I really had been quite unfair to it. It had been a treasure trove of information. I just needed time now to put a lot of what I had learned into some semblance of order. But time was not on my side. Another image of D. in all of his suffering shot through me like an electric shock. The odd thing about this image was that I was not involved in a meditative exercise; I was just lying in my bed, back in the mundane realm. This was something new—and ominous.

VIII

Death!

I was lying in bed after my rather extended dialogue with Resident Teacher when an image of D. being tortured by the dark birdlike monster again flashed through my awareness. As I mentioned, this was something new; all such experiences before had happened when I was actively roaming the aethereal realm. This flash of suffering now came unbidden and while I was fully immersed in the mundane world. I did not welcome the implications of this new reality.

Impetuously, I dived back into the aethereal realm and sought out D. Immediately the visualizations of my surroundings became very dark and I was filled with a severely cold chill. I felt the body of the birdlike monster wrap itself around me like the coils of a giant serpent while its wings enclosed me in a shroud. Its beaked face was close to my ear, and it hissed, "There you are. I've been calling you. You have certainly taken your precious time to come to your friend's aid. Being the *courageous* person you are, I can only take that delay as an indication of your respect for my immense power!"

Frightened, but being careful not to fall into my highly polished and insulting street repertoire, I said, "Look, I don't have any quarrel with the United Lodge of Divine Wisdom. Just leave D. and me alone!" I felt I was suffocating.

The dark monster replied, "The United Lodge of Divine Wisdom! It is a baby compared to my power. I could will them away in less than an instant. However, some of its participants are important components in my base. And I heartily thank them for that. Really, though, I have participants from everywhere." And then it roared, "I am the very manifestation of will to power!" At this perhaps overzealous estimate of its own exalted significance, it again roared, but this thunderous noise was a roar, hiss, squawk, squeal, cry, and laugh all at once combined into a deafening and horrifying cacophony of evil. That noise lasted far too long.

Once I was no longer cringing from the awful noise and the ringing in my ears ceased, I asked, "What do you want with D. and me? If you are so powerful, then why do you care about us?" I asked this last question with a bit of sarcasm, and I received a severe tightening of its coils about my body in return.

"You should be more careful not to exhibit a lack of respect for your superior, little man." There was a slight pause, and it continued. "I don't give a damn about D. I've only been using him to get to you. Once you and I have reached our agreement, I will no longer have a use for him; he is entirely disposable."

I did not like his use of the word "disposable," but I tried to keep my mind clear of fear and upwelling thoughts—I did not want to give too much away to this monster. It was the hardest exercise I had encountered in the aethereal realm up to that point.

"Okay," I said, "so what do you want of me, then?"

After I asked the question of what the monster wanted from me, out of fear and a sense of self-preservation, I began to construct my protective bubble. The monster popped that protective sphere like a soap bubble being attacked by an adventurous toddler. The monster squealed in delight in bursting my protective bubble. I tried again, and the monster happily played with the bubble, blowing on it and waving at it to make it quiver; the beast then poked it with a sharpened claw, causing it to disappear in a dispersing mist. I saw it was no use in trying to construct my transparent protective envelope, and I asked again, "What do you want of me!?"

At this point, it gave what could have been interpreted as a slight, albeit evil, smile. It loosened its coils around me slightly and said, "Good, now we are negotiating."

I tried hard not to think to myself, *We are doing nothing of the kind!*

"Are you sure?" it asked. "You haven't heard my offer. I have a lot to offer. I think you'll come around; they all do ... eventually." It gave another evil laugh. It continued, and its words felt like a drill boring through my skull and into the soft matter within. "You are a strong-willed kid, to say the least—more so than I've seen in a very long time. I need you to join with me; become one of my privileged participants. With your will added to mine, we could only grow stronger! We would increase our power a hundredfold!" With that it inserted a salivating proboscis into the hole in my skull and started probing my brain; no, it began probing my very mind!

"No!" I yelled, and I pushed out the proboscis and began filling the hole in my skull. With the enormity of the effort required to repair my skull, I was starting to lose my concentration—and with that, my will.

"But just look what you would have to gain," it said. "You will become immortal by becoming a part of me. We will go on indefinitely, harvesting evil and suffering to sustain myself. Oh, there will never be a dearth of that pestilence upon Earth; I will make sure of that!"

It was getting darker and colder. I was hardly able to muster the energy to shout "Forget it, you pig! I don't want anything to do with you!" With that D. was revealed about five feet away from us, cringing on the ground, in a faint and narrow beam of light that barely showed the immense pain on his face.

There was a flash of lightning with a smell of rotten eggs in the air. D. convulsed in pain and shouted, "No! No more!"

"Maybe I can compel you to join my conversation?" the monster softly asked me. "Do you really see no reason to merge with my being?" It smiled. "Or, maybe some pain on both of your parts would be more persuasive?"

D. barely whispered, addressing the monster, "Be careful of tickling this dragon's tail, fella; I've seen his bite." I was stunned to hear D. refer to me as the dragon in this situation.

"Silence!" roared the monster, and D. went into a prolonged session of violent convulsions, crying out and splattering spittle in every direction.

"Look," I yelled, "leave D. alone and I'll talk about it," not having the slightest intention of doing any such thing.

The avian-reptilian monster looked at me and said, "Well, well, you crumble more quickly than I thought you would. Maybe you aren't worth the trouble after all."

Catching his breath, D. said, "If only I had my football uniform on, I'd really show you!" I did not consider D.'s comic defiance funny this time.

The monster mused, "You two are something else. Luckily, if I get one, I get the both of you." I had no idea what it meant by this; but I did know that with his comment about the football uniform, D. was covertly signaling to me that he was ready for us to go into our evasive routine.

Just loudly enough for D. to hear, I said, "Is that a cop?" A brief wave of acknowledgment swept across D.'s face before he was returned to agony.

The beast hissed, "What are you two talking about? There are no 'cops' here!"

With all the concentration I could muster, I conjured a small spot of shining light about fifty yards away in the direction opposite from where D. lay cringing in pain on the ground. It took every ounce of will I had to kindle that weak lamp into a small sparkling ball of light. When it was flickering just strongly enough, I loudly asked, "Is that Sage?"

Upon hearing my question, the monster yelled, "Oh no!" and turned to focus upon the shiny object. Instantly a huge ax appeared in my hands, and I raised it above my head, forcibly brought it down, and violently embedded it in the monster's skull. A dark liquid splashed up from the impact. The monster gave out the most horrendous scream I have ever heard. D. got up off of the ground, and we both took off running away as fast as we could. Unfortunately, we ran in divergent directions.

As soon as I was clear from the monster, I brought myself back into the mundane realm. I could only hope that D. was able to escape from the monster in his dream and then force himself to wake up from his nightmare. I dared not reenter the aethereal realm, and I dared not fall asleep. I stayed awake the rest of the night and dropped by D.'s house on my way down the hill to school.

I knocked on D.'s front door, and his mother answered. D.'s mom was dressed smartly and was almost ready to leave the house for work. I said, "Oh, hi, I thought I'd stop by and see if D. wanted to walk down to school with me this morning."

D.'s mom was somewhat preoccupied in preparing to leave for work but expressed her delight to see me again after all this time and then said, "Actually, D. seems to be feeling unwell this morning. We're not really too sure what's wrong. I don't think he is going to school today. But if you like, I can go upstairs and ask if he wants to see you." She left me standing at the open door and went upstairs. I heard some muffled voices, and she came back down again. She said, "D. isn't really feeling well enough for you to go up to his room right now. But he is happy that you came by, and he thinks he's fine; he's just feeling a bit down today. He said he'll talk to you later. I'm sorry."

"Okay," I said, "I just thought I'd stop by. Maybe he'll be feeling better tomorrow. I sure hope so. Bye."

D.'s mom said good-bye and shut the door. I walked on down the hill to school.

On my way to school, I considered the recent events. I was relieved to hear that D. was generally okay. I had feared the worst, and the worst apparently had not happened. He seemed to have taken it pretty hard though—at least hard enough to make him want to stay home from school today. Concerning the dark monster, I was certain that the cleaving of its skull with the ax was not a permanent solution and that it still continued to lurk out there somewhere in the aethereal shadows, healing itself and making itself stronger. I feared that I had only made it angrier toward us. I decided that I would not take any excursions into the aethereal realm for a good number of days and take the time to try to collect my thoughts. I only hoped that the injury I had inflicted on the monster was severe enough to give D. and me some breathing room—time enough for me to figure a way out of this mess. I was now even more concerned for D.'s safety than I was before.

For a week, I did not conduct any excursions into the aethereal realm; and during all that time, D. never did get back to me. I did see D. once at school, in the crowded hall during the brief time students were given to go to their lockers and make their way to the next class. I saw him only from a distance, with his back to me, walking carefully in among the mass of students. As he walked along, he was carefully looking warily from side to side, as if trying to avoid some terrible calamity. From what I could tell, he never saw me; or, if he did see me, I was not aware of that fact, and he certainly did not initiate any contact. I decided to leave him alone and let him contact me when he felt comfortable enough to do so.

Reflecting upon D.'s suffering at the hands of that dark monster, I thought to myself that at least his suffering was in his dreams only and not in real life. It then struck me that there was something wrong with my reasoning here. Maybe suffering was not the sort of thing that was attenuated by the theoretical distinction between appearance and reality. D.'s suffering was just as real to him in his dreams as if it had happened to him in waking life. Generally, if one suffered, she suffered whether she suffered in her dreams or in real life. In this way suffering is very different from belief. While luckily some beliefs can occasionally turn out to be true, one can still believe many things that are false. For belief there is a certain distinction between appearance and reality. Things can appear to be different from the way they really are. But for suffering, there is no distinction between appearance and reality; for suffering, appearance *is* reality! Anyway you cut it, suffering is real. If you suffer, you suffer—end of story. Which was too bad for us. But it was an interesting realization to think that there are significantly different types of consciousness. Suffering is a special type of consciousness where seeming so is ipso facto being so. It cannot be mistaken, as with a belief. Suffering is real, and there is plenty of it! "What *is* suffering, anyway?" I asked myself.

The above cogitations on the nature of suffering made me even more desperately want to find a way out of our monster problem, and I was having no luck coming up with a solution on my own. Reluctantly I decided to approach Resident Teacher again, out of sheer desperation.

I chose that Saturday afternoon to contact Resident Teacher. Maybe I was being superstitious, but I did not want my excursion into the aether just after our encounter with the avian-reptilian monster to be conducted at night. That afternoon I had the house to myself. My younger siblings were out with my parents somewhere, and my older brother had left home only a couple of months prior to start his life on his own. So I had a good number of hours of daylight in which to converse with Resident Teacher over the aethereal medium. I positioned myself accordingly, went into my concentrated state of mind, entered the aether, and was immediately accosted by the dark monster.

"So," the dark monster roared in my ear as it coiled itself around me, "you thought you could destroy me? There is no getting away from me! I am everywhere! And I will take your will whether you want to give it to me or not! Though my consuming it without your permission will make it less valuable, its efficacy will still be useful to me. Besides, I can already feel the pleasure of wresting it away from you." With a clawed hand it rubbed its skull where I had cleaved it. The wound was very nearly healed. "You are an ignorant little boy, thinking that you could hurt me and then run away. You see, you are mine now! But while I have you, and before I incorporate your being into mine, I plan to have a bit of fun with you, making you suffer like no one has ever before!"

With that I felt my entire being get shut inside a box about two inches on each side. I was crushed to an incredible density. Obviously I could not breathe; nor could I could see or hear. I could only feel a great and heavy pressure pushing upon me from all directions. I felt myself dying. Then I was back to full form again, wrapped by the coils of the monster. It looked at me and laughed. "Hurt, did it?" it asked. Then, with real excitement and apparently with dead seriousness it said, "I live off that stuff. I can feel you making me stronger as we speak. How wonderful it feels! It's like owning the entire universe!"

"Here," it said, "you may like this," and it turned my insides outside of me. Somehow my topology was intact, just reversed so that all my organs were hanging off of me like ripe fruit hanging from a tree, blowing in the wind. The monster blew across my exposed insides, now outside, and I cried in excruciating pain as the flux hit me like a blast from a smelter. Then I was made whole again, and I was in its clutches. I was losing consciousness; my will was being sapped from me. "You liked that, did you? You enjoy my little creative vignettes? I'm sure you will enjoy this next one," the dark monster boasted, and I was imbedded in a semimolten pond of superheated basalt. I could not take the pain any longer, and I blanked out. Coming to, I found I was again wrapped by the coils of the evil monster. "No, no, no. Don't you die on me. I want your life force. It's mine, and I will take what's mine. We'll just enjoy a little respite here and make sure what's mine is mine."

With thin liquid profusely running out of my nose and blood being coughed up by the mouthful and gushing down my chin, neck, and chest, I raised the lid of one teary and puffy eye and saw D. rapidly approaching over the monster's shoulder. "Avast there, you salty dog!" D. shouted while standing upon the bow of the *Lydia*, dressed in a complete Horatio Hornblower outfit, holding on to a halyard with one hand and waving a saber over his head with the other. His newly longish blond hair was blowing in the wind, and he looked completely confident and in charge of the situation. With a terrific crash, the *Lydia* rammed the dark birdlike monster. The noise of the crash seemed to fill the entire universe and reverberated in satanic harmonies, slowly dampening down to an undulation of peaked ocean swells. I was in the churning sea, off the coast in the channel, holding on to the hull of the capsized *Lydia* with one hand and keeping D. afloat with the other. There was no sign of the avian-reptilian monster.

"D.!" I shouted, "D., can you hear me?! D., are you okay?" D. started coughing and came to. "D., are you okay?" I pleadingly asked again.

"Yeah." He wanly smiled. "Did we get that asshole?"

I looked around, saw no sign of the monster, and answered, "Yeah, I guess so. But D., you're hurt. I really, really didn't want you following me around and getting mixed up in all of this."

D. looked emotionally hurt at my statement and asked, "Well, I'm not going to let some scurvy one-eyed pirate harass my mate, am I?"

It just then dawned on me that D.'s perception and experience of the tragedy could perfectly well be entirely different than my own. I gently answered, "No, D., you're not the type of captain to let your ship and crew go down without a fight."

This apparently gave him some amount of solace. "Damn right," he said. "Besides, it's only a dream anyway, isn't it?" I was amazed again at how he could pull himself out of his dream and into reality, and then dive right back into the veil of his dream.

A wave washed over us, and I coughed and lied, "Yes, it's only a dream."

He closed his eyes, paused, opened his eyes again, looked all around frantically, and said, "But I don't feel so good." At that, he evaporated out of my arms into nothingness.

I was left crouching on a boulder-strewn plain. All was black and gray. I could not tell where the horizon, infinitely far away, merged into the greyness of the thick air above me. A powerful cry erupted from the very depths of my being. "Noooooooooooooooo!"

IX

Persephone

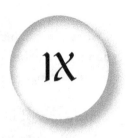

I was alone upon an endless wasteland of huge boulders packed tightly within a matrix of dry gravel and dust. It was not hot; nor was it cold. There was no light; nor was there darkness. There was only the dim illumination of dusk. I cannot say how long I lay there in the dirt, holding myself in a fetal position, softly sobbing and moaning. It must have been a long time. No one came to help me. I was on my own. Other than me, there was no sign of life whatsoever. I felt not the slightest desire to get up and find a way out. I did not even have the least motivation to wipe away the prodigious mucus dripping off of my face and providing the only dampness in this arid quarry of pain. I just lay there, acutely aware of the absence of D., my whole universe filled with a nothingness.

After the longest time, I became aware of my own breathing. I smelled the wetness of my drippings upon the dry sand and gravel, like the smell that precedes a downpour on a dry and dusty day. I wiped my mouth, my nose, and my eyes. "Ohhh," I moaned out loud, and I brought myself up into a sitting position. The memory of the tragedy of D.'s death came bolting into my awareness, and I cried, "No!" once more. I shook. The shaking was nearly uncontrollable. I breathed deeply and made the effort to relax my tense body and regain some control of my life. After I had subdued my shaking, I took a look around where I sat in that boulder-strewn wasteland and decided that I needed to get out of this desolate desert. I broke the connection to the aether and was once again lying on my bed in the dim light of early Saturday evening, in my parents' house—back in the mundane world.

After numbly lying in my bed for some time, I heard the family car pull into the driveway, bringing my parents and my two younger siblings home from their day's outing. I got up off of the bed, sneaked out the back door, and took off on a solitary walk that lasted most of the night. I walked all over town but could not find the courage to go over to D.'s house, so close to my own home. I spent a good number of hours on the end of the pier at the beach, overlooking the vast and dynamic sea. It was just days away from a full moon—what would be the first full moon after the spring equinox—and the waves were dancing in the muted luminosity of that magically suspended orb. I felt so alone, and fully responsible for D.'s tragic and painful demise. I desperately wanted to believe that D. was somehow okay—that he was snugly asleep in his own bed, having wonderful dreams of commanding the *Lydia* and its brave crew to glory. It could be true. He could still be alive in the substantial realm. I really did not know. I was in a state of limbo, waiting until it was late enough the next morning that I could go over to D.'s house to enquire about his well-being. I noted with some chagrin that tomorrow would be Sunday, meaning I would need to wait until his family would be home from Mass before I could visit him.

Late Sunday morning, I could wait no longer and absolutely needed to go over to D.'s house to determine whether or not he was well. Walking the short distance from my bedroom to the front door of D.'s house was torture. I feared that the probabilities were against

D.—against us. I wondered how a death in the aethereal realm would manifest in the real world of stuff and substance. I imagined that yesterday afternoon D. had been in his backyard, working on his beloved, yet dry-docked, *Lydia,* and had suffered some terrible accident. I wondered how it had happened. Had he fallen off the boat trailer and hit his head on the concrete? Did he feel a lot of pain? What did it sound like when his head hit the hard surface? I had heard the phenomenon described as sounding like a melon being dropped on the ground. Was his resultant pain like a terrifically horrible headache? Had he suffered for a long time? Had he cried out for help? Had he died alone?

I needed to stop dwelling on these horrible images of D.'s death and put them out of my mind. I was paralyzing myself with anticipation, and it served no purpose but to make everything much more difficult. I placed one foot in front of the other on my morbid march to D.'s house.

I found myself stationed in front of D.'s door. Things did not look right. There was a gray pickup truck in the driveway with a harbor patrol logo on its door and government plates. I tentatively knocked on the door. Immediately the front door was thrown open and D.'s mother stood there looking at me wildly; my fears were confirmed. From what I could tell from her appearance and that of the rest of the family I could spy through the open front door, there had been no Mass this morning for this family. A stranger in a uniform sat at the couch behind the coffee table. All eyes were upon me. I did not have time to say hello to D.'s mom. With hair askew, and dressed in a haphazard manner, she blurted out, "Oh, it's you!" She turned to the uniformed man and said, "This is D.'s best friend ... or used to be some years ago!" Turning to me, she pleaded, "Do you know where D. is?"

"No," I calmly stated. "I came over here this morning just to say hi to him. Is he missing?"

D.'s mother started crying, and her husband, D.'s father, came to the door and put his arm around her. "He's gone!" shouted D's mom, through her convulsive sobs, and she buried her head in her husband's shoulder.

D.'s father explained in an obviously artificial deep state of relaxation, "D. hasn't come back from his boating trip yesterday afternoon. He's been missing since then."

I thoughtlessly blurted out, "But I thought his license had been suspended!"

D.'s father continued his almost academic explanation. "It was reinstated early, on Thursday. He seemed really depressed about it all and was really happy to get it back. He took his boat out by himself on Saturday afternoon but didn't come home." Breaking from his forced calmness, he quickly said, "He shouldn't have gone out by himself!" and gave me a stern and searching look. He became calm again. "We found his car and boat trailer down at the boat ramp." D.'s father's words drifted off, and he became very interested in and focused upon the doorjamb. He flicked a speck of dust from the molding.

D.'s mother turned to me and pleaded, "Are you sure you don't know where he may be? Did he tell you anything?"

"No," I simply said. After an awkward pause, I added, in all sincerity, "But if I hear anything, I'll let you know right away. I'm sorry."

D.'s father said, "We're sorry too. The harbor patrol, here"—he gestured to the uniformed man sitting perfectly still with a forced blankness on his face—"and the coast guard are initiating a search for D. If we hear anything we'll let you know." I knew it was time for me to leave. D.'s family closed the door and then went back to conferring with the officer from the harbor patrol.

That next week at school, the week before spring break, was sheer hell for me. I am sure it was infinitely worse for poor D.'s family. I went through that week in a state of shock, being kindly reminded by some of my acquaintances about where I was supposed to be, and when. Luckily my teachers were aware of the fact that D. had gone missing, and I was given some leniency in my classroom participation. I spent a lot of those lectures staring out of the classroom windows. Oddly, I received a perfect score on my half-semester math test. I had even finished that test in half of the time allotted, well before the other students. Mortality has a sinister way of focusing one's mind.

I had refrained from any excursions into the aether during all this time, partly in fear of encountering the dark monster, but mostly just because I had lost all motivation in doing so. It just did not appeal to me. I noted with a bit of understanding that there were no unbidden flashes of evil from the monster. I explained this absence to myself by noting that the subject of those evil images, D., was no more, and also that—if I were lucky—the monster would be taking a good amount of time in licking its wounds. Hope beyond hope led me to consider that it may even be possible that the monster met its demise at the same instant that D. had passed. In any case, I spent the week after D.'s disappearance in relative peace, remaining unmolested from the world beyond.

That next Saturday morning—Holy Saturday, by the way, the day before Easter Sunday—I lay in bed looking up at the ceiling and not really thinking about anything at all. My mind was a blank, or rather was allowed to roam unfettered and unattended. I did not care where it would go. I heard the telephone ring but was unmoved. My mother answered the call, exchanged some overly polite greetings, and solemnly said, "I'll go get him." My mom knocked on my bedroom door and said, "That's D.'s dad. He wants to know if he can talk to you." That's all she said. She stepped away from my door and went back into the kitchen, staying within sight of the telephone situated in the dining room. As I approached the phone, I could see my mom watching me from the kitchen.

I picked up the phone and said, "Hello?"

D.'s father said, "We said we'd let you know when we found anything out. Well … D.'s boat has been found capsized and washed up on shore on Santa Cruz Island. The coast guard, uh … the coast guard has officially listed D. as missing at sea."

I took a deep breath in and said, "Okay."

There was a long pause; I stayed on the line. D.'s father said, "Oh, D.'s mother wants to know if you'll say a few words at his memorial. Is that okay?"

With complete sincerity, I said, "It would be a real honor."

D.'s father seemed to be listening to some discussion off-line and then came back to the conversation with me. "We think the memorial service will be next Saturday, in the mission grounds. We'll let you know the details as they firm up. You know, just a few words, only a couple of minutes. You don't have to if you don't want."

I repeated, "It would be my honor."

"Okay, then. Well, we'll be in touch. Bye."

"Okay. Bye." I quickly added, "I'm so sorry for everything." The line went dead.

I turned to my mom, and she looked at me sympathetically with a questioning look. I told her, "They found D.'s boat capsized off Santa Cruz Island. The coast guard has officially listed him as missing at sea. They want me to talk at his memorial."

"Oh, that's nice," she said, both of us knowing that her assessment applied only to the last part of my statement. She continued to look at me.

I asked, "Can I borrow the car to go down to the nursery? I want to get some compost, fertilizer, and seeds and start working on my vegetable garden."

She said, "Sure. That's nice."

I walked back into my room.

The next morning, Easter Sunday, found me working in my vegetable garden. For a good number of years now, my parents had let me have this patch of our yard for my garden. It was high time that I started working on this year's garden. The narcissus, those harbingers of spring, had pushed up through the earth more than a month ago and were already beginning to lose their heavenly fragrance and looking spent. I placed a heavy layer of compost, about three to four inches, over the entire garden and began using my pitchfork to work that decaying matter into the soil.

As I mechanically toiled at this tedious task, my mind was occupied with thoughts of birth, death, and rebirth. Plants would soon arise from this garden; they would fulfill their purpose and then die. They would then be turned into compost and plowed into the ground, and their decomposition would be the foundation for the next cycle of birth and death. It was a continuous cycle. Apparently today, Easter Sunday, was a day to reflect on rebirth—on resurrection.

The story of the Greek goddess Demeter and her daughter Persephone came to mind, which in turn brought to mind the Ancient Greek rites of the Eleusinian Mysteries. I had plenty of time before me, working that dead and decaying matter deep underground with my sharpened pitchfork; so in my mind, I went over the story of Demeter and Persephone in some detail.

Demeter was one of the three sisters of Zeus, the ruler of the gods. As such, she was well placed in the heavenly hierarchy. She was the goddess of green living things and gave to humans the fruits, grains, and vegetables required for life on Earth. She was responsible for maintaining all the right conditions for bountiful harvests, year after year. Holding a role so pivotal to the survival of the mortals, she was worshipped with great devotion by them. She was smart, nice, and responsive to human needs. She had a daughter, Persephone, who was beautiful, cheerful, and full of life. Demeter and Persephone loved one another dearly. Mortals revered both goddesses.

When Persephone was just coming into the beauty of young womanhood, one of Zeus's brothers, Hades, the god of the dead underworld, was captivated with Persephone's beauty and liveliness. Hades wanted Persephone to be his wife and live with him in the underworld to bring life and light into that dreary place. Hades petitioned Zeus, and Zeus gave permission to Hades to abduct

Persephone and take her with him into the dark caverns below, by force if necessary. Persephone hated the dismal underworld to which she had been dragged against her will, and she went on a hunger strike. She knew that to accept food from Hades in the underworld doomed one to live there forever.

Demeter was devastated at the loss of Persephone and was especially incensed at Zeus for allowing her forced abduction. In her despair, she forsook her duties as the goddess of agriculture. The earth was thrown into a period of aridity, and no food would grow. Zeus was concerned but knew he had no direct control over his own sister. Zeus selfishly worried that if humans were not sufficiently cared for, then he would lose his devotees, causing his power to fade away. No god would want his or her power to vanish because of inattention from his or her base of mortal devotees. Zeus therefore decided to send Hermes—the messenger and ambassador of the gods—to visit his brother Hades in the underworld and attempt to broker some sort of deal over Persephone.

Meanwhile, poor Persephone was still stuck in the underworld and was beginning to survey her new surroundings. She began to take pity upon the confused and despairing souls who were constantly entering that nether realm in an unending stream of human suffering. She started to minister to the needs of these newcomers out of divine compassion. She was growing weary with hunger, but still she worked on for the good of the souls forever condemned to that dark place. Hades was pleased with the love and light Persephone brought to his dark domicile. As Hermes approached the underworld on his mission for Zeus, he saw Hades sitting next to the exhausted and famished Persephone. Hades was handing Persephone a pomegranate, trying to encourage her to eat. Persephone, out of severe hunger and wanting to have the strength to continue ministering to the unlucky souls in the underworld, took the pomegranate and ate six seeds. By doing so, she sealed her fate to live forever in the underworld.

Hermes, shocked to see that he was too late, tried anyway to work out a deal with Hades. In the end they agreed that because Persephone had eaten only six seeds, she would need to stay in the underworld as Hades's wife for only six months out of the year. During the other six months of the year, she could go back to the surface of the earth and be with her mother, Demeter. They agreed that Persephone would leave Hades on the first day of spring and return to Hades on the first day of fall. Demeter was delighted to see Persephone again, and all the earth was abloom with the fruits, vegetables, and grains needed by humans to survive. Zeus's devotees were happy again and resumed their sacrifices to the king of the gods. This cycle continues every year, guaranteeing Zeus his base of devotees and allowing him to maintain his power as the god king.

As I worked the dead matter into the soil with my pitchfork, I remembered that the myth of Demeter and Persephone was the basis of the Ancient Greek rites of the Eleusinian Mysteries, a secret sect whose initiates included only the most elite of the Greeks—with its origins probably dating as far back as the time of the Minoans. Because the rites were so secret, we have no good idea today what they exactly entailed. We do know, however, that the head of a stalk of barley, a widely cultivated crop, was held in especial regard as a symbol of fertility and rebirth. The idea was probably that each grain of barley is a new baby plant and gets its being from the demise of its mother plant. Therefore, each stalk of barley represents the continuance of the cycle of rebirth. It is also known that the initiates made a psychoactive drink called *Kykeon* out of barley infected with a special ergot fungus; when imbibed, it allowed the devotees to commune with the gods. There are many Eleusinian temples across the Mediterranean Greek diaspora dedicated to Demeter, sheltering statues of the goddess holding a bundle of barley stalks. I remembered that I had come across the works of more than one scholar of religious studies suggesting that the Greek emphasis upon rebirth from the underworld illustrated by the myth of Demeter and Persephone was a precursor to the Christian notion of the resurrection of Christ.

Some scholars have even suggested that there are still to this day practitioners of the Eleusinian Mystery rites, worshipping Demeter and Persephone. Of course, there have been no devotees publically coming forward to admit that they belong to that secret society—not simply because of their innate desire for secrecy, but also because of the harsh reaction of the early Church against that practice, even though the Church incorporated that myth into its core teachings in a modified form.

I was struck by a detail of the story I had just recounted to myself as I pitched the life-giving compost deep into the soil of my garden. Zeus did not want to lose his devotees out of fear of losing his power base. He was afraid of dissolving into nothingness if humans did not worship and sacrifice to him. This notion struck me as very similar to what Resident Teacher had said about unconscious extrasensory conversations—those aethereal conversations are required to tend their garden of participatory voices in order to maintain their constant nourishment of consciousness and will. It had even said that it had actually seen some conversations disintegrate owing to a lack of voices participating in those particular conversations.

Being preoccupied in my thoughts, I found that I had finished the task of working the compost into the soil. Now was the time for me to plot out my garden. Thinking about Resident Teacher's fear of conversations dispersing into nothingness, I also began plotting out my revenge upon that dark monster that had killed my best friend. But first I needed to spend some time getting my thoughts together on what I would say at D.'s memorial.

X

A Ghost

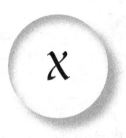

I was on spring break with no school. My only school-related activity was running practice, as I was currently participating in the long-distance events for our school's track and field team. I had plenty of free time to think about what I would say at D.'s memorial. Indeed, that topic was a major theme for the meditations I indulged upon during my training runs for the track team.

About halfway through that week of freedom from school, I was at the end of a two-mile practice race, forcing myself to the limits of my endurance with a single-minded focus on nothing but moving my body forward as quickly as possible. After crossing the finish line, I began a controlled deceleration and walked in tight circles, trying to gain back my breath and conscious awareness of the world around me. I bent over at the waist, holding my knees. I was just starting to notice the objects of the world reemerge from the altered state required for a final push when the image of the dark monster intruded upon my awareness.

The monster was much diminished from when last I apprehended that horrible specter. However, it was unquestionably the very monster. It ominously stated, "Ah, there you are. As you apprehend my glorious being, you see I'm getting stronger, gaining back my strength from that unfortunate encounter with your deluded friend. I understand he died in the clash! Good for him! And you will soon be dead too, as soon as I fully regain my strength." It then pledged, "There will be no more cat-and-mouse games with your soul. The next time I see you, I will kill you instantly. You will exist one moment, and the next you will be annihilated without warning!" It trailed off into the distance with its evil laugh echoing behind it.

It is a strange feeling, knowing that any particular moment could be your very last. With no warning, no precursor, no indication that anything is amiss, you could suddenly be turned from being into nonbeing! How could this be? I know of no terror more existentially efficacious than knowledge of the unavoidable possibility of instantaneous nonexistence. It is this existential fear that has caused men to go mad in the trenches of war. It is the fear used by dishonorable men to keep women subdued under their violent thumbs. It is the fear at the heart of the contemplation of nuclear annihilation that causes nations to go insane and start cannibalizing their own citizenry. One who wields this power to subjugate others is the ultimate bully. Its use for one's own ends is pure evil.

For me it was terrifying, of course, being told that for any moment whatsoever, that moment could be my very last—but it was paradoxically liberating. I think that monster made a momentous mistake by informing me such. I understand why it did inform me so. It identified itself as pure will to power, and as such it *needed* to know that others cowered in the penumbra of its dominance. That was its only sense of self-worth. It could not let an opportunity pass to have others cringe in the presence of its enormous and narcissistic ego. But like so many despots and dictators have found out too late, their own pathological need for others to bow to them in obeisance leads directly to their own downfall. When the monster informed me of its power over my very existence, I arose from my terror like a beautiful and proud phoenix arising from the ashes. I had nothing more to lose. I was completely freed from any other terror it could unleash upon me. I literally felt freedom down to the very core of my existence.

I was now 100 percent committed to revenging my best friend's death. Words fail me here in attempting to describe how I felt. Many similes and analogies can be used to begin to describe my complete devotion to that task, but none capture the entirety of its universe-filling dynamic. Enough said; I had a mission. I thought to myself, with goose bumps running up and down my spine, *That monster's in trouble!*

Later that night, while lying in bed, I swallowed my pride and entered the aethereal world to seek out Resident Teacher. I needed to gain any insight I could in how to kill off an unconscious extrasensory conversation. Upon entering the aethereal realm, I heard the usual white noise of voices and conversations here and there. I tried to focus upon and gain a clear signal from Resident Teacher through that static in the aether. Try as I may, a gossamer veil kept interposing itself between my goal and me. I could move around this shroud to get a better view of my objective. When I moved, it would accordingly move to intercept my gaze, yet it remained essentially hidden to my direct inspection. "What is this hidden obstacle before me?" I asked myself.

Tiring in my efforts to avoid this occult obstacle, it occurred to me that in tracking my motions, this veil was showing signs of a will of its own. I redoubled my efforts to gain a better visualization of this hindrance. For some unknown reason, my goose bumps returned. The tingling in my back and arms did not now emanate from that previously overblown sense of pride and power I had experienced when contemplating harm to the monster. In the present circumstance, my physical excitement manifested a skittishness occasioned by an unfocused sense of dread.

I could not obtain a fixed visualization of the hindrance before me. Even so, in a wave of panic, it was painfully obvious what apparition presented itself for my inspection. The specter blocking my view was an ever shifting semitransparent image of D.! I was petrified. Sometimes the specter looked as D. did as a young boy—when he and I regularly roamed our neighborhood territory—but now blown up to larger-than-full-grown proportions. Sometimes it looked like D. did when he was sailing his prized *Lydia*. Sometimes it looked like D. did when going through Confirmation in the Catholic Church. And then there was one visualization of that specter that clearly represented D. but looked more like a movie star heartthrob. The visualization was all of these images and many more, constantly shifting and merging into one another, not unlike the lava lamps that were so popular at the time. I was not prone to believing in ghosts. However, this vision scared me to my core and stopped me in my tracks. Had D. not died after all? Was he stuck somewhere and this was his unconscious plea for rescue?

When I could finally speak, I meekly asked, "D., is that you?"

It replied in a booming yet faraway voice, "I think so." Its hesitation did not inspire confidence.

I blurted out, "I thought you were dead!"

It despondently responded, "I am."

Now I was completely confused and began shaking. "How can that be? You're right here."

It asked in reply, "I am?"

Upon its nonrepetitious repetition of that simple utterance suggesting both its existence and nonexistence, I began a closer inspection of the phantom presenting itself before me. It now did not look so much like the visualization of D.'s unconscious mind with which I had become so familiar. It looked instead much more like a flimsy representation of a conversation of voices in the aether. Pieces of the puzzle began falling into place, and I excitedly said, "I think you are D.'s ghost!"

"I thought so," it said sadly, "but I didn't want to scare you. But how can this be? I don't understand."

"Me either, completely," I confessed, "but I think maybe you are an unconscious extrasensory conversation of all the people who are still alive and who have you in their hearts and keep you in their minds."

"What?" it said.

I now divulged to D.'s ghost—if that is what it was—my experimentations in the aethereal realm. I told D.'s ghost in death what I had withheld from D. in life. I explained how I had discovered a realm of unconscious extrasensory conversations. And I explained how those conversations could develop consciousnesses and wills of their own—how they could outlive their individual participant voices. As I was describing this realm to D.'s ghost, it became apparent to me that I was describing, in essence, a realm of the gods.

"But," it asked, "how does that realm have anything to do with the realm of real, existent, people? Did you explore that interaction? I mean, how does it all work?"

I was surprised and yet not surprised to hear D.'s ghost voice the very same question that I had posed to myself early in my experimentations. Thinking over how I went about investigating an answer to that question, I became extremely self-conscious. I said, "I did it through you, or rather, through D."

It became very serious and asked, "How?"

I explained my experiments involving D. and C. S. Forester's book, and also the informing of Amateur Yachting in Santa Barbara Channel of our earlier maritime indiscretions. I told it of the monster and our encounters with that evil beast.

The specter before me grew appreciably larger and then boomed, "You killed me!"

I knew its accusation about my direct involvement in D.'s death was true. I was not, however, ready to accept full responsibility for D.'s early death. Certainly the dark avian-reptilian monster shared some culpability. D. himself shared some responsibility as well, with his unconscious insistence on continually coming to my aid.

I said, "Yeah, I guess I did," and I looked away.

There was a long pause, and I looked up again at the specter. After some spectacular shape-shifting, it finally settled down and said, "I can't even begin to believe you intentionally did me harm. What happened?"

I explained to it in detail all that had happened, including D.'s coming to my rescue and the crash of the *Lydia* and then D. being listed by the coast guard as missing at sea. "Wow, my mom must be real bummed," it said, turning into a giant-sized version of D. as a toddler.

I said, "Yeah, she is."

The phantom reverted to a version of D. sailing the *Lydia* and asked, "Did we kill the monster when we rammed it?"

I replied, "No, I don't think so," and I relayed my most recent encounter with that evil being.

"Man," it said again in its booming voice, "I want to kill that scurvy pirate!"

"Yeah, but look, we really aren't even too sure what you are, or that you have any power to do anything at all. I've got an idea. Maybe you could take a good introspective look at yourself. I mean, if you can. It may be helpful to understanding how we can kill the monster." I knew I was stretching my reasoning somewhat, but I was immensely curious to determine the mechanics of this specter presenting before me.

"You said I am D.'s ghost, so what's more to know?" it offered by way of explanatory reply.

"Yeah, maybe, but is there any way you can look inside of yourself and tell me what you see?"

"I don't see anything," it said in defiance.

"Look, D.," I demanded, feeling that I was inappropriately using D.'s name, "concentrate on yourself and tell me what you see." It flashed a series of images, gave me a grudging look, and settled down in concentration. It grew another couple of inches larger.

"Huh," it said, "I see a bunch of voices, like you said."

"Can you tell whose voices they are? Is D., uh ... are you there?" I asked.

It shook its head and said, "No. D.'s not there! He's gone! Who am I?"

"Okay," I said, trying to use a soothing voice, "look more closely and tell me who's there."

It calmed down and said, "Well, there's Mom, of course, and Dad, and the rest of the family. Oh, and ... uh, some others too."

"Who?" I pushed.

"Well, there's *you*," it told me, taking on the shape of the oversize young boy.

"What?" I sputtered in surprise. "What do you mean there's me? I'm right here talking to you, aren't I? How can I be a voice inside of you, making you what you are, when I'm standing right here in front of you?" I demanded.

"Yeah, weird. But there you are," it said. "You're actually one of the loudest voices—well, that is, after Mom and ... uh ... the other one."

"What *other* one?" I again demanded.

"Oh, there's another pretty loud voice too," it confessed, and it grew two sizes larger still.

"Who?" I asked.

It grew gravely earnest, donned the image of the movie star version of D., and said with pride and a very slight hint of embarrassment, "My girlfriend."

"*What girlfriend?*" I practically shouted. "I didn't know you had a girlfriend!"

It took slight offence and said, "Of course I have—had—a girlfriend. But you know, I never told you. You and I haven't been all that close since starting high school—well, except for lately. And anyway, she's very private. We didn't tell anybody except our families, really."

"Wow" was all I could say, calming down a bit. I was thinking, *Good for poor old D.*, and I felt even more terrible for his demise.

At that time in my life, I could not even comfortably talk to girls. Not that I did not want to, but I just could not do it. I never have been able to entirely determine what the blockage was. I loved girls—desired them greatly. I desired to hold their warm softness in my arms and smell their sweetness surrounding me. Maybe that was part of the problem. When I was talking to them, my guilt from my intense desire to know them, to be near them, and to desperately want them to like me always seemed to get in the way. It was a terrible obstacle to getting to know them as the unique individuals that they are—that each of us is.

"Who is she? How did you meet?" I asked.

Obliging my curiosity, it said, "Oh, we met in the psychology class that Mrs. Crowe in the Social Studies Department offered last summer in summer school. She's real smart, and we have … had great conversations. We started talking when we were assigned to a group project together. She's really funny! It turned out that she always went home for lunch like I did. Her mom, a single parent, works weekdays. We, uh, started spending lunches together at her house."

"Oh," I said, catching its meaning. Becoming very happy and sad for D. at the same time, I asked, "What's her name? Do I know her?"

"Oh, I don't think you know her. She just started at our school this year. For some reason, she and her mom move around a lot. I think it has something to do with her mom's work. Her name is Percy."

"Percy?" I said. "But that's usually a boy's name, isn't it?"

"Oh, yeah, that's her nickname. Her real name is kind of strange—a Greek name, I think. Persephone."

"What?" I screamed.

It looked a bit annoyed at me and said, "Yeah, kind of a strange name, like I said."

"Persephone!" I screamed again.

It looked at me defensively and said, "Well, the name's not *that* strange, is it? Anyway, I like it!"

I calmed down and reassured it that I liked the name too. I told it that I had just been thinking of the myth of Demeter and Persephone and quickly conveyed that myth to it.

"Oh. I can see why you were surprised. Cool. It's funny, but you'll like this; her mom's name is Demi."

I was speechless. *What a strange double coincidence,* I thought. It was too much for me to contemplate at the moment, and I asked, "Are there any other interesting voices in you—in the conversation that is you?"

The phantom's stature and understanding seemed to be growing even more as we conversed, and along with its size grew its introspective powers. In answer to my question about the other voices constituting its conversation, it said, "Oh, you know, others here and there: some of the students I tutor, my Catechism teachers, the priest ... oh, and the kids we played ball with."

D. and I played baseball after school with a group of neighborhood kids just about every Friday afternoon all through middle school. I reminisced about those great games and said, "I wonder if they'll be in my ghost too. Gee, I wonder if I'll be a ghost when I die."

The phantom continued to grow in understanding, took on an awesome visage of the extinct D., peered intently at me, and authoritatively boomed, "You already are a ghost."

I recoiled in horror and asked, "What do you mean, I'm already a ghost?"

"Well, you are," it solemnly pronounced. "Your identity is already populated with the unconscious voices of others. When you die, when your consciousness and will expire, it's only these voices that will continue after you in a conversation that some may call your ghost."

I was stunned by the image of all living beings carrying their own ghosts around with them, waiting for the day that those specters would be set free to carry on without their mortal coils. It was an awful image.

D.'s ghost was now becoming an awful image as well. It swelled up with rage and demanded revenge on its killer. "I will kill that monster! I'm going to find it and mash its face into the gravel of nothingness! And you are going to help me!" As it loudly demanded this, it took on the form of a colossal twelve-year-old.

"Wait. Wait!" I shouted in fear. "You can't do that. Remember: you are composed of the voices of those that love you. Just like I put you, D., in danger, you'll be putting them in danger. Think of your mom, of Persephone, for goodness' sake. You don't want to endanger them!"

It looked down at me from its growing height and sternly said, "I did not forget that they compose the conversation I have become! But maybe you have forgotten that fact yourself! It is they, through me, my ghost, who demand that vengeance. And I will have it! And you, having played such an integral role in my demise, will help me in that objective! I will make that monster suffer like no other being has suffered before!"

It shouted these last two statements with accompanying echoes in the void of the aether. Holding my ears and pronouncing the obvious, I shouted, "D., this is not you speaking!" Not being able to take the stress of seeing D., or rather his ghost, mad with vengeance, I ascended from the aethereal realm and found myself back in my bedroom, lying in my bed, covered with sweat.

XI

The Eulogy

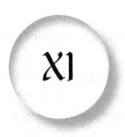

All in all, it had not been an enjoyable spring break. Not only did I have a real live monster—well, alive enough to require killing—threatening me with instant annihilation; I also had a rampaging ghost demanding my assistance in wreaking revenge against that monster. Additionally I needed to stop the ghost from putting the people that had loved D. in danger—the unwitting constituents of that raging specter. Those that were keeping D. in their hearts and minds were unconsciously putting themselves in danger through motivating the ghost they had animated out of their love for D. As if these problems were not enough to require my attention, I also planned to speak at D.'s memorial a couple of days hence.

I did not know where to start in dealing with these pressing issues. It was hard to prioritize the list. I could not let one problem be ignored by exclusively focusing upon another. If I did not deal with the threat of instant annihilation from the monster, then there was a very real possibility I would never have the opportunity to work on the other problems. On the other hand, if I did not stop D.'s ghost from rampaging through the aether, then it was a real possibility that I would have been responsible not only for D.'s death but also for the deaths of many of those that loved him in life. And if I did not have words prepared for D.'s memorial, well, then I would have failed D.'s family—and myself.

Lying there in my bed, I came to a decision to address these problems simultaneously. I would not work on each one separately at the same time—I'm no magician. Instead, I would work on a single solution that would help resolve all of these problems together. It was clear that the monster wanted to kill me. And it was clear that D.'s ghost wanted to kill the monster. It was also clear that D.'s ghost was motivated and enlivened by those who kept him in their memories. Therefore, if I wanted to recruit D.'s ghost to help protect me from the monster in a manner that did not put those that loved him in jeopardy, then I needed to guide and influence those that nourished the ghost with their unconscious thoughts. What better time to accomplish all of the above than when presenting a eulogy at D.'s memorial?

I reasoned that if what I had just learned about ghosts was true, I could have a huge influence upon D.'s ghost through those that loved him. The idea of a ghost being an unconscious extrasensory conversation of those living souls who keep the deceased in their hearts and minds fit perfectly well into my theory of unconscious extrasensory conversations having life and existence of their own. I was immediately reminded of the Japanese Shinto religion and its ancestor worship that I had read about in Huston Smith's wonderful book on the religions of the world. That now made sense to me. I noted that there are other cultures, too, throughout the world and in all ages—including certain indigenous American cultures—that hold to the notion that we must remember and pay tribute to our ancestors. The view here is that if we do not remember them, those ancestors disappear and fade away. In fact, the notion held by many indigenous Americans that the names of the deceased should not be used and that no monuments should be named in their honor now made sense as well. If ghosts were really the unconscious extrasensory conversations of those that held the deceased in their hearts, then it would be essential to keep that poor individual that has passed on clearly individuated from extraneous thoughts. We do not want to confuse the real Crazy Horse with his statue sitting nobly upon his steed. So really, the thesis of the existence of ghosts and the thesis of ancestor worship seemed to exhibit a certain consistency based upon the common explanation due to the possibility of unconscious extrasensory communication. In my estimation, there was a coherence here that lent support to both views—and to the party-line theory of consciousness.

I continued my speculative excursion by noting that the party-line theory of consciousness may even be useful in explaining rebirth—or, as some people say, reincarnation. If the ghost that survives death is powerful enough as an integral conversation of unconscious extrasensory thoughts supported by existent sentient beings, then what would stop that impressive group voice from harboring itself in a newborn manifestation of the life force? It occurred to me that the Dalai Lama—a soul supposedly reborn generation after generation—would be a very powerful conversation indeed, with its millions of supporters.

Again, if it is true that a ghost is constituted by the unconscious extrasensory thoughts of the living, then what better way to influence the behavior of that ghost than through those living souls? The eulogy presented at D.'s memorial would be another chance at confirming the existence of unconscious extrasensory communication, and hence another possible confirmation of the party-line theory of consciousness. Apparently, even after all that had been happening, I just could not control my meddling spirit. At least I was aware that this additional confirmatory exercise could have possibly lethal consequences if things went poorly or got out of hand. It was important that all went smoothly in my presentation to D.'s family and friends.

Given the dangers involved, I asked myself whether it would be moral to go about manipulating D.'s ghost in the manner I was now planning. Was I not now contemplating the very types of activities that had gotten D. killed in the first place and subsequently put all those innocent living beings in danger? What right did I have to manipulate them so? My answer to this ethical question was simple and emphatic: "I would be doing so for their own good, and therefore I have the right to do so!"

I reasoned that it was not only my right but also my *moral obligation* to influence D.'s ghost through those that had loved D. Through my previous actions, I had placed them all in danger, and now it was my moral responsibility to attempt to steer them away from that danger to which I had unintentionally exposed them. But as I had encountered in my elementary readings on moral theory, a hallmark of moral action is that one should never treat another soul as a means to an end only; each soul should be treated as an end in itself. Intentionally manipulating these beings whom I purposely kept in a state of ignorance concerning my true intentions certainly struck me as treating them as a means to an end rather than treating them as ends in themselves. I wondered, *Does this mean I should recruit those living souls as participatory moral agents, fully aware of and engaged in the project before us?* This question led directly to a moral dilemma.

If to do what is morally required here to help those innocent souls is to fully engage them in that enterprise, then the enterprise is doomed to fail, because they would not understand or believe my story and would thus feel no obligation to work toward the intended goal of their own safety. Thus, attempting to act as dictated by a moral imperative, I would have failed in my moral obligations. On the other hand, if I did not fully engage those innocent souls, then I would be treating them as a means to an end only and would also be failing my moral obligations. So I was unsure whether I should fully engage those innocent souls or not. Either way, it appeared that I ended up being immoral.

In consequence of these deliberations, I could see only one way out. I decided to grab one horn of the dilemma and prepare my eulogy to D. so that I did not directly tell the gathered living souls about the dark monster, about D.'s ghost's demand for vengeance, or that they, themselves, actually provided the ground that in turn constituted D.'s continuing parasitic pseudoexistence. I could not alert them to their own impending danger. The attentive mourners would consider my story highly irregular, to say the least. Besides, use of D.'s memorial for such a purpose would be most inappropriate.

Reasoning thus, I resolved to continue my hidden manipulative practices.

In this current circumstance, my manipulative actions would be perpetrated upon the many sentient beings keeping D. in their hearts and minds. My goal was to gently admonish the gathered souls to keep D. in their thoughts but to think only kind and wonderful thoughts about him. I needed a powerful but kind ghost on my side—on our sides collectively. To do all of this, I needed a eulogy that reminded the mourners that D. had been a gentle, kind, and yet willful individual, always ready to lend a helping hand and right wrongs in the face of adversity.

To write such a eulogy was a daunting task. And to tell the truth, a part of me did not want to cheapen my honest despair at D.'s passing by turning my talk into a crass recruitment exercise, as Antony had done when speaking at Caesar's memorial. D. himself, that wonderful soul that had lived and was now dead and gone forever, should not be forgotten in my coarse attempts to manipulate his ghost. Additionally I needed to remember that my first allegiance was to the protection of those living and breathing sentient beings that gave that ghost its semblance of life. To this end, I took the ancient Olympus portable typewriter out of its musty case that had been handed down to me from my grandfather through my mother, set it upon my desk, inserted a sheet of paper, and began to type. It took many drafts, but eventually I had what I considered to be an acceptable multipurpose eulogy. It read as follows:

> *Thank you for asking me to say a few words about my best friend D. And I'm so, so very sorry for his early departure from this life he so enthusiastically embraced in the springtime of his short existence on this beautiful planet. D. loved life, and he had no problem filling every moment of it with humor and an aesthetic appreciation of its constantly manifesting miracles. D. was a student of the exquisite nature of existence.*
>
> *But beyond his boundless appreciation of life, D. was also essentially a moral agent in this world of strife and suffering. You may not know this side of him, but in our adventures as young men, I was constantly struck by how deeply he recognized bullies for what they were and how hard he worked to lessen the burden of the oppressed. I could tell many stories illustrating his virtue in this regard—some less appropriate in this setting than others. But let me tell one short tale.*
>
> *We were about ten or eleven years old, and we were enjoying a hot afternoon in the public swimming pool. Two large bullies, who themselves could not swim, were going around the shallow end of the pool and dunking kids half their size. At one point, these two bullies were picking on a crying young girl of about six years old, relentlessly dunking her and splashing water in her face when she came up for air. I won't go into all the details here, but D. jumped into the pool and rescued that girl from her tormentors. This is a true story, and it shows how kind he was and exemplifies his unbounded strength*

> *of will in confronting bullies and upholding justice and fairness.*
>
> *It is natural to lament D.'s passing. It is a sad day indeed. But if there is any truth to the notion of the continuance of the soul through having a place alongside God, whom D. truly believed in, or through reincarnation or rebirth, then that truth is borne out in the memories we honor him by. D. lives on through our memories of him! Let's give this truly good soul the immortality he deserves by keeping his goodness and power uppermost in our hearts and minds. Let's do this for us, to lessen our sadness at our loss of his wonderful presence. But, most of all, let's keep his memory in our thoughts for the benefit of D. himself! Thank you.*

Once I had composed the eulogy I went back to worrying about an imminent attack from the monster. Though I still had no idea what I was doing in constructing my transparent protective bubble in the aethereal realm, I practiced that maneuver ceaselessly. I would enter the hidden world just long enough to throw up my shield, and then I would immediately return to the mundane ground. It was a risky exercise, but I required proficiency in deploying that defensive shelter. Basically I spent all of my time either running with the track team or practicing throwing up my transparent shield. I had no training in martial arts, yet I felt like a *Shaolin* monk exercising the nonviolent aggression for which those practitioners are famous.

Through practice, my shield was becoming stronger and thicker. Soon I learned to create a second shield and throw it, enclosing a space of my choosing in the aether. Then I learned to throw a third, and then I learned to toss them around like a juggler at a county fair. I then learned how to create multiple bubbles from the main one protecting me, squeezing them off my own shield like new cells budding from an original strain. I created a hundred protective bubbles, arranged them in a long chain, and drew that train of protective shields in a flowing streamer of circular motions about myself like a dancer twirling a long ribbon on a stick. While dancing with my protective bubbles at this time, I had not yet considered the possibility that the bubbles could just as well be used to keep something in as they could be used to keep something out.

I came to realize that my frolicking in the aethereal world was much too dangerous to continue; the marginal risk of instant annihilation now outweighed the marginal benefit of increased facility in deploying those shields. I had not seen the dark monster in my dance with the bubbles, and I was confident that it had not seen me. I had caught glimpses, though, of D.'s ghost hovering around in the shadows. Whenever I had even begun to sense the presence of that angry specter, I immediately returned to earth.

The morning of D.'s memorial service arrived, and I went to the old Spanish mission downtown early to make sure I was on time. Glimpsing the mission garden from the sidewalk along Main Street, I could see that only a few of the mourners were assembled at this time—people I did not recognize. On entering the mission grounds, I was immediately aware of a muffled chorus of voices seemingly clamoring for my attention. I assumed that those voices were material, not aethereal, and I curiously entered the chapel endeavoring to find the source of the noise. As I entered the door at the back of the chapel—across the extensive expanse of ancient wooden pews roughly hewn from large timbers—I directly faced the back wall holding the ornate altar draped with the whitest of silk cloth and glittering with gold. Stepping into the chapel, I was surrounded by a multitude of statues of the saints and the Holy Mother hovering above me; they had been placed into depressions in the thick adobe walls about twelve feet above the ruddy tile floor. I looked around the chapel and saw that it was empty, yet the indistinct voices within those walls had become louder and more insistent on gaining my attention. I looked up at the statues in wonder and realized that the voices were coming from those motionless likenesses created of wood and plaster and covered by fading and chipped pastel pigments. Those images gazed down upon me with permanently vigilant eyes and silently sang their chorus.

The voices were not materially emanating from those hunks of wood and plaster, of course, but they were intruding upon my consciousness from the aethereal realm, within which they belonged. The cacophony of voices became unbearable, and I whirled around on that cold tile floor. My gaze ran from one statue to the other as I became aware of the material absence of sound within the chapel smothered by the nonmaterial screeching of the saints. I tried to focus upon those voices separately and found that each statue was its own unconscious extrasensory conversation comprising the thousands upon thousands of individual voices from their devoted existent sentient beings who believed in and prayed to that beloved saint.

I considered each saint in turn. They were all essentially projecting the same command: "Pray to me!" Some seemed meek, some strong and arrogant, some pleading, some genuinely pious and otherworldly, and some a fraction too pious and otherworldly to be completely believable. Some of the saints manifested themselves as being nothing but good and moral—"saintly," if you will. Others had a much darker visage. But they all demanded—*demanded*—devotion and allegiance.

There was one voice in this saintly choir that I could not attribute to any particular statue arranged around the empty space of the chapel. This voice missing a material icon had a pitiful, suffering aspect and often spoke in an unfamiliar dialect or language. It was not Spanish; I would have recognized that language. As I focused upon this softly wailing voice, it soon became apparent to me that it was the cry of the enslaved local Native Americans, the Chumash. The Chumash population had been decimated by the arrival of the Spanish missionaries. It was literally their sweat and blood, their very lives, that had been ritually sacrificed in the building of the mission within which I now stood.

The discovery of the suffering voice of the Chumash immediately brought to mind that many of these saints composing the chorus of voices in this chapel were not good. In fact, they were each one of them complicit in mass extinction and forced slavery in the name of maintaining their base of devotees and thereby ensuring their continued existence. It further occurred to me that of course those saints were demanding that sentient beings pray to them; otherwise, they would eventually fade away into the aethereal mist. These saints had a vested interest in maintaining their power base of devotees.

The chorus of saints recognized my reluctance to see them as moral agents deserving of devotion. In the aethereal realm now coincident with the material world, they started to accost me in violent ways. They swirled about me, pushing me here and there, and struck me as they passed by. This conflating of the aethereal and material realms distressed me, and I decided to absent the chapel and enter the garden grounds, where D.'s mourners were gathering. As I left the chapel through a side door adjoining the mission garden grounds, I heard the saintly chorus sing, "Remember us in your heart, and pray to us!"

In your dreams, I thought to myself, and I walked out into the sunshine of the mission garden.

In the garden, surrounded by all those that loved D. and held him in their hearts, D.'s ghost sprang upon me. "You can't hide from me here! You will assist me in exacting revenge upon that monster!" it roared.

I should have expected D.'s ghost to be strongly present at D.'s memorial service; all those that loved him in life had gathered in this location to remember him. Of course his ghost's power would be enormous here. I was ashamed at my oversight in leaving myself unprotected. I soundlessly responded, "Sure, okay. But look; we can't talk about that here. This is neither the time nor place to plot our revenge. It just isn't right. Maybe you could stand down and keep an eye out for the monster? That would be helpful."

The saintly chorus sang, "Prey to us, and we will protect you!"

The ghost boomed a response to the chorus: "You didn't protect me when I was alive; where were you then?"

The chorus then collectively noticed the gathered crowd and turned its attention to harvesting those innocent souls and wills. It hovered about the assembly and sang in honeyed voices, "Here is a veritable garden of luscious fruit to be picked and savored. Let us sing our praises and nurture ourselves in the glory of their sustaining consciousness. Our power grows stronger, sweetened by their unconscious awareness. Pray to us, pray to us!"

"Avenge my death!" the ghost demanded.

"Pray to us!" the chorus beseeched.

Oh no, I thought, *This is not turning out well.*

It was all I could do not to wordlessly respond to the ghost and the chorus. To will myself not to hear those voices was beyond my abilities. I tried simply to minimize the distraction they were causing me. I found D.'s family and presented myself to them. I placed myself a good six feet to the side of the mourning ménage. A church official gave a nod to D.'s father, and that poor man began addressing the crowd. He talked for a couple of minutes, more than obviously choked with pain and suffering. It was a nice talk. At least those parts of it I could hear between the intrusions of the ghost and the saintly chorus seemed beautifully anguished. D.'s father introduced D.'s mother, but she could not bring herself to say her brief words. D.'s mother stood there crying, looking at the ground, looking around her at the garden and guests, and then looking up at the sky. Gazing past the low clouds, she quietly uttered through her sobs, "Why?" and went silent.

The saints sweetly sang, "Pray to us!" D.'s ghost grew about three feet and looked as if it could break in half the sheltering trees with its glowering glare.

D.'s father protectively decided that D.'s mother had exposed her suffering soul enough and had nothing further to say. He quietly led her back to the tight group of the family. He then paused in respectful silence. After an appropriate duration, he introduced D.'s girlfriend, Percy. I had not noticed this young woman in the crowd before her introduction, which seemed odd because she was extremely noticeable.

Percy was tall—much taller than me—with golden hair that curled freely down her shoulders. And those shoulders! They were muscular and feminine simultaneously. She had clear blue eyes—eyes that betrayed a cutting intelligence, with a fire in them that people should approach only at their own risk. And yet she inspired warmth and compassion by her very demeanor and fluid body language. I was instantly intrigued by this soul who had shared D.'s companionship. Percy walked to the center of the crowd, nodded to D.'s family, looked at the mourners gathered about her, momentarily let her gaze hover upon me while throwing me a sad little smile, and quietly yet powerfully spoke her loving devotion to D. D.'s ghost reverted to the image of the movie heartthrob and fell upon its knees, blubbering in deep sorrow.

I guess I could try to remember the actual words Percy spoke that day if I forced myself to do so. It was the emotion and feeling of her speech, though, that was the real message. Recalling her actual words would only distract from those deep, heartfelt emotions. I was moved. It was clear that Percy had truly loved D., and I could only imagine D.'s devotion to that lovely and loving—well, I will say it—goddess. I looked forward to introducing myself to Percy.

As Percy finished her remembrance of D., D.'s ghost moaned loudly, and the saintly chorus sang from the aether, "Pray to us! What a lovely gift that girl has given us. She has plowed the field in preparation for our bountiful harvest. Pray to us!"

D.'s ghost looked up and belched out, "Shut up, you morons! Go steal your strength from some other unsuspecting souls. The power from this gathering is mine and mine alone. With it I will kill the monster!"

Hush, both of you, I wordlessly said.

Through the distraction, I heard D.'s father introduce me as the final speaker in this sad gathering. I positioned myself next to D.'s family, looked at those around me, tried to ignore the soundless voices emanating from the aether, and began my few words in memory of D.

"Thank you for asking me to say a few words about my best friend D."

"Prepare the ground for the harvest," the chorus shouted. "Spill the wine of consciousness upon the fertile soil and let the glorious awareness arise from the depths of the earth!"

"And, I'm so, so very sorry for his early departure from this life he so enthusiastically embraced in the springtime of his short existence on this beautiful planet. D. loved life, and he had no problem filling every moment of it with humor and an aesthetic appreciation of its constantly manifesting miracles. D. was a student of the exquisite nature of existence."

"Kill the monster!" boomed D.'s ghost.

"But beyond his boundless appreciation of life, D. was also essentially a moral agent in this world of strife and suffering."

"Avenge my death!" shouted D.'s ghost.

"You may not know this side of him, but in our adventures as young men, I was constantly struck by how deeply he recognized bullies for what they were and how hard he worked to lessen the burden of the oppressed. I could tell many stories illustrating his virtue in this regard—some less appropriate in this setting than others. But let me tell one short tale."

"Pray to us! Pray to us!" The chorus chanted. "Yes, sing the praises of the departed, but they no longer require any power or awareness. We are your true guardians. Give to us the nourishment of your awareness and will. Pray to us!"

"We were about ten or eleven years old," I continued, "and we were enjoying a hot afternoon in the public swimming pool. Two large bullies, who themselves could not swim, were going around the shallow end of the pool and dunking kids half their size. At one point, these two bullies were picking on a crying young girl of about six years old, relentlessly dunking her and splashing water in her face when she came up for air. I won't go into all the details here, but D. jumped into the pool and rescued that girl from her tormentors. This is a true story, and it shows how kind he was and exemplifies his unbounded strength of will in confronting bullies and upholding justice and fairness."

"I have no knowledge or memory of this foolishness!" D's ghost said. "Are you going to continue to prattle on, or are you going to render assistance in wreaking vengeance upon the monster?"

Oh, shut up, will you? Let me finish this. It's important. I'm trying to secure your base of power, you idiot, to help you kill the monster.

"Oh, sons of light and power, do you hear this?" the chorus stated. "They conspire against our very manner of existence. We have no love of the monster; that is surely true. But he is one of us. We cannot allow others to even contemplate the killing of one of our own kind. That way lies danger to us all! They must not be allowed to pursue this path of destruction! These pagans must be stopped. The power of the devoted masses belongs to us, not to them. Pray to us!"

"It is natural to lament D.'s passing. It is a sad day indeed. But if there is any truth to the notion of the continuance of the soul, through having a place alongside God, whom D. truly believed in, or through reincarnation or rebirth, then that truth is borne out in the memories we honor him by. D. lives on through our memories of him!"

"Yes, my power lies in your memories of me!" D's ghost interjected. "Remember me so that I can kill the monster!"

"Let's give this truly good soul the immortality he deserves by keeping his goodness and power uppermost in our hearts and minds."

"Pray to us! Pray to us!" The chorus continued. "We are the only safety for you. Pray to us!"

"Let's do this for us, to lessen our sadness at our loss of his wonderful presence. But, most of all, let's keep his memory in our thoughts for the benefit of D. himself!"

"Kill the monster!" D's ghost shouted.

Okay, I'll kill the monster!

"Thank you."

With those final words of thanks, I stepped away from D.'s family and assimilated myself back into the crowd of gathered mourners. D.'s father adjourned the service with some parting thoughts.

After the ceremony, as the mourners began to depart, I expressed my final condolences to D.'s family and then sought out Percy. She was standing with a woman a little taller than herself—her mother, I assumed—who looked not much more than ten years older than Percy. She was even more stunning than her daughter. I walked over to them and introduced myself. "Hello," I said to Percy, raising my right hand to shake hers. "You must be Perseph ... uh, Percy. I'm very happy to meet you, though this is a sad occasion for it." The top of my head came up to about Percy's chin. My eyes were at the level of her powerful shoulders.

"Oh," she said with real enthusiasm, "you are D.'s childhood friend! What a wonderful talk you gave."

I replied, letting go of that soft yet firm handshake, "I really liked yours too. D. must have really been in love with you." I recoiled in horror at my social indiscretion and revelation of my inner thoughts, and I said, "Oh, I'm sorry. I know this is hard for you—for us all. I didn't mean to be indiscrete."

"No offense taken at all," she said as she shook her golden hair. "Yes, I think we really loved each other. A real love like that is to be celebrated, not mourned." I hesitantly smiled. She continued, nodding to the woman standing beside her, who had been smiling down upon us through our self-introductions. "This is my mom, Demi. She wanted to come to the service and hear all the wonderful things people had to say about D."

"Hello," I said, reaching out for Demi's strong hand in turn. Demi held out her hand as if I had intended to kiss it, noticed my confusion, and then quickly turned her gesture into an ordinary hand-shaking exercise.

As we shook hands, Demi said with a broad smile, "I too very much enjoyed your talk. But I couldn't help but feel that there was a lot going on behind that speech."

I kept a straight face and simply said, "Yes, there was. Maybe someday I could share some more stories of D. with you and your daughter?"

"That would be nice," said Demi as she dropped my hand.

Percy interjected, "But I've heard many more stories from D. of your youthful adventures than I can even remember! Really, I'm quite convinced that you were positively a bad influence upon him!" She said this in a humorous manner, but it was evident that there was some real feeling behind it.

I said, "Well, yes, maybe I was. Well, it was nice meeting you, and you. I've really got to go. Take care." I excused myself from the company of those lovely women.

As I left the mission grounds, I could hear in the background the saintly chorus admonishing the stubbornly incorrigible ghost for attempted usurpation.

XII

A Walk on the Beach

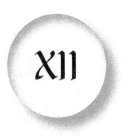

I spent the next week at school making up for being virtually absent the week before spring break. I concentrated on my studies and other school activities, and did not venture into the aethereal realm. After the disaster of D.'s memorial service, I wished for nothing more than to avoid that world of shadows. Also, I did not observe Percy walking the school halls. I went to school, went to track practice, came home, ate dinner, finished my homework, went to bed, and started all over again the next day, through the entire week. During that week, I fell asleep listening to my even then ancient LP player, letting the popular bands The Doors, Cream, Led Zeppelin, and the Who lull me to sleep with their sweet lullabies.

Saturday morning found me with nothing in particular to do. Thinking that I needed a change in pace, I decided to go for a walk along our extensive beach. About ten years earlier, the county was given permission by the state to install a series of jetties on the beach to help prevent erosion from the strong winter currents. From the pier down to the mouth of the marina, a span of about five miles, a jetty composed of huge and ragged boulders jutted out into the surf every one hundred yards. These jetties were a great success, attested to by the fact that the beach sand extended about half of the way out to the end of the jetties on their northern side, with the ocean waves coming ashore on the southern sides almost to the base of those walls of huge boulders. Depending upon the prevailing currents and the direction of swells caused by winds and offshore storms, this saw-toothed configuration of the beach almost guaranteed good waves for bodysurfing just about any time of the year, on either the northern or the southern sides of the jetties. In our childhood, D. and I had spent many days—no, *years*—bodysurfing those wonderful swells.

I parked my mother's car down by the marina, took off my shoes, and started walking up the beach toward the pier, keeping to a path on the wet sand that allowed the higher waves to periodically wash one or two inches of cold Pacific water over my bare feet. I had just passed the first jetty on my way north, up the coast, transitioning from the cold waves on the southern side of that jetty to a sea of hot, dry sand on the northern side, when I noticed Percy across that expanse of sand out by the waves. She was standing and staring over those waves, out toward the Channel Islands. I stood and watched her standing there with her back to me. I was wondering if I should approach her and say hi, which I was reluctant to do because she looked like she needed her solitude and also because of my pathological fear of talking to girls. Just as I was about to move on without bothering her, she shook her shoulders, turned around to look at me, and smiled.

Having been noticed, I knew I needed to approach and greet Percy. She stood there watching me with a sad smile on her face as I trudged through the dry sand toward her. As I approached a comfortable speaking distance, I said, "Hi. Do you remember me? I'm D.'s friend. I spoke at the memorial."

"Of course I remember you," she said with a sweet smile.

"Oh," I said, "I'm just going for a walk on the beach. Are you too?"

"Actually I was just standing here looking out at the islands," she said thoughtfully. "But if you're walking up the beach, I'd love to join you."

"Oh," I said, "okay," and I resumed my walk, now accompanied by this intriguing person. "It sure is a beautiful day."

Percy responded, "Yes, beautiful. Beautiful but sad."

I answered, "Yeah, real sad," and we continued our walk together.

We passed a lifeguard kiosk, and I noticed that it was empty. I nodded to the vacant aerie and commented that there did not seem to be anyone on guard at this early hour. I then said, "I guess you know D. was a lifeguard, right?"

"Oh yes," Percy said, "that's one of the things that drew me to him. I'm qualified as a lifeguard too."

I thought to myself, *That helps explain her strong shoulders; she is a swimmer.* "Do you work here at the state beach?" I asked.

"No," she replied. "The State doesn't like to hire women lifeguards. I do work now and then at a private pool on the Eastside." I considered this reluctance by the State to hire female lifeguards and decided not to say anything about it. Giving her head a shake, she went on. "My mom and I just moved here recently—well, six months ago now—so I haven't had time to find a full-time job. Besides, I really don't have the time to work full-time; I'm trying to do all I can to get into a program at Moorpark College."

I was relieved to have an academic pursuit to explore as a topic of conversation. It took some of the pressure off of me in trying to find something to talk about—although Percy was moving the conversation along quite nicely without any apparent effort. "What program?" I asked.

"It's really interesting," she said. "It's an animal training program."

"Oh," I replied, thinking of images of Percy in a traditional lion tamer's outfit and snapping a whip at snarling big cats.

"Right now I'm in an introductory class offered to students to give them an idea of the program, and for my project, I'm training my rat to run mazes and do tricks."

"Oh, that sounds cool."

"Yeah," she said. "But rats are real smart. They can do that sort of stuff. I'm trying to train my guinea pigs too, but they aren't doing as well. My one pig, Piglet, just sits there looking straight into the maze wall right in front of her face until I pick her up and take her out!" She laughed heartily.

"Maybe she's really smart and just sitting there meditating."

"Maybe," said Percy, continuing to smile.

As we climbed up and over the next jetty on our trek up north, Percy said, "Actually, D. was helping me in getting ready for the program. I need to do well on the SAT tests to get into the program, but I don't want to waste time taking math courses at school, because I want to focus upon biology, ecology, and zoology. So D. was tutoring me in math. He had taken me all the way from algebra through geometry, and we were just finishing up trig before ..."

I waited a short time before saying, "Wow, really? I didn't know that. He was into so many things."

Percy looked at me and said, "Yes, he was something special. He was so sweet and really didn't like to see anyone suffer. We met in a psychology class this last summer school. He told me that he wanted to be a psychologist. He would have been great."

Again I said, "I didn't know that," not wanting to reveal anything I had learned about her and D. through D.'s ghost.

Percy, still thinking about D.'s proclivity for psychology, softly said, "Yes, he would have made a great psychologist. He was really intrigued by human suffering. He couldn't abide it, and yet he would often say that there must be some beneficial purpose to it. It's so widespread; there must be some meaning to it."

I said, "Well, if not a purpose per se, then maybe at least we can search for an explanation."

Percy stopped briefly and looked at me. She continued walking and said, "Yeah, I think I get your meaning. My zoology teacher says that according to Darwin, there is no *purpose* to the spotted owl having its spots, but there is a biological explanation in that the owls that blend into the background survive to pass on their genetic information."

"Yeah," I said, "kind of like that. The owl didn't purposely camouflage itself, it just turned out that those spots helped it not get killed by predators. Likewise, I don't think that human suffering has a purpose, but I think we can learn lessons from it." Undoubtedly we both were hoping that there would be some beneficial lesson we could take away from the abject sorrow occasioned by our mutual loss of D.

"So," Percy said, pursuing this line of reasoning, "what sort of lesson do you think we can learn from our suffering?" I took it that she spoke in the general sense of "our suffering," but it could just as well have been the case that she was specifically referring to her and my suffering due to D.'s recent death. I took a second to think out my reply to Percy. Not wanting to get into all the detail regarding what I had been considering about appearance and reality and how suffering is its own reality, I jumped to another topic I mistakenly thought would be more amenable to an easy conversation. I casually said, "Oh, suffering proves that God doesn't exist."

Percy looked at me startled, looked down at her feet moving in the now wet sand and said, "D. would not have thought that that was a lesson to be learned from the existence of human suffering. He believed in God." I was given the strong impression that Percy also believed in God, and I was again ashamed for transgressing upon sacred territory.

I ineffectually tried to cover over my embarrassment by telling a story about my conversation with a young Christian. "Once, right near here on this beach, I was talking to a group of young born-again Christians and found myself debating the existence of God with one of the girls that also happened to be in my social studies class at school. The next Monday, in class, she turned around to declare to me that my arguments had been persuasive and that she had left her Christian youth group and was back on drugs! Obviously that was not my intent in debating her about God's existence." I laughed and shrugged my shoulders.

Percy did not see the humor in this story. Looking horrified, she said, "Well, I assure you that I am not a druggie and that I can perfectly well handle your arguments. Why do you say suffering proves that God does not exist?"

About this time, we reached the pier. This seemed like a good place to stop and rest or turn right around and start walking back down the beach. In any case, I thought I could use this opportunity to bring this particular topic of conversation to a halt. Percy, seeing me looking around and guessing what was going through my mind, said, "Say, there's a nice taco stand up there on the pier. Maybe we could get some lunch and continue this conversation?"

"Okay," I said.

We ascended the steep steps up to the level of the pier and walked to the taco stand. I ordered a chili relleno burrito with added beef strips and extra hot sauce, and Percy ordered two vegetarian tacos with a side of guacamole. We went Dutch. As we sat down at one of the benches on the pier overlooking the ocean, I asked if she was vegetarian. "Yes, I've been a vegetarian all of my life. My mom's pretty strict about that. I can't even imagine what it would be like to eat an animal that had been living. It seems horrible to make them suffer like that when we can just as well get all of our food from plants." I did not respond. Her reasoning seemed pretty good to me. I sat and ate my beef burrito. After a time, Percy said, "But you were going to tell me why suffering proves that God does not exist."

I balled up the wrapping of my devoured burrito, threw it into a nearby trash can from where we sat, and said, "Oh yeah. It's a simple argument. I learned it from a book on the philosophy of religion." Percy raised her eyebrows and looked at me expectantly. "Well," I said, scratching the back of my head, "it goes like this: If God exists, then He is all-good, all-knowing, and all-powerful." Percy raised her eyebrows again. "If something is all-good, all-knowing, and all-powerful, then there would be no suffering in the world. But there is suffering in the world, so God doesn't exist."

Without skipping a beat, Percy inquired, "I can see that the argument is valid, but are all of the premises true?"

I was stunned to hear a peer exhibit that casual facility regarding the mechanisms of logical analysis. I shrugged and proffered, "I think they are all true."

Percy went on. "Well, what about the second premise—that if something were all-good, all-knowing, and all-powerful, then there would be no suffering in the world? I'm not sure that is true." In response to my stunned expression, Percy said, "Do you want to start walking back?" I nodded assent. We descended the steps in silence down to the dry sand and started walking back down the beach.

"I mean, really," Percy said when we both were on the sand, "isn't that the whole point of God giving us free will—so that He can judge our moral worth? If we didn't have free will, then He couldn't judge us. But He gave us free will, and that opens the door for evil and suffering. But it's not God's doing."

I thought about Percy's reply. D. and I had had similar conversations on some of our many runs. Also, that reply was discussed in the book I had read about this argument against God's existence, so I had already begun to form a response to it. Percy patiently waited for my reply. It took the length of time necessary for two separate sets of breakers to wash over our feet before I said, "But if God is really all-good, all-knowing, and all-powerful, then He doesn't really need the bullet to slam into the child's head before He can judge the shooter. He could stop the bullet in midair. I mean, really, can't He just know what is in the shooter's mind—his intention to do harm? And can't that alone form the basis for God's judgment? Surely He can do that, and if so, then there shouldn't be any real suffering. But there is, so God doesn't exist."

Percy, in her turn, took some time formulating a reply to my reply. "So," she said, "if that were the case, then all these evildoers would know that none of their actions would be effective. So they would either be dissuaded from those actions out of a sense of futility or they would run even more amok than they would otherwise. But in that case, God would not know what was truly in their minds from the start. No, God needs to set it up so that there are consequences from our actions so as to get us to show Him who we truly are."

"Okay," I said, "but God doesn't need us to truly cause one to suffer in order to judge us. Why can't He have created us all in our own worlds, with nobody else in them, but made us think that our worlds are populated as we see it now around us? There would be no one else in these worlds that we could make suffer, just because there is no one in your separate world other than you. God could feed us a lifetime of experiences and judge each of us in his or her own world, and no one other than the one person in that world would need to suffer the consequences of what he or she thinks are his or her actions. In fact, if He were all-good, you'd think that He would be morally obligated to create individualized worlds like that. But the world's not like that; there is only one world with all of us in it, and there is suffering in this one actual world, so God doesn't exist. I mean, to keep a belief in God based upon this free will defense of the argument from suffering, we need to accept some version of existence we'd find in some second-rate science fiction novel!" Percy looked far away out over the waves, fixing her stare on the islands out beyond the channel as we continued to walk along the beach.

In time she said, "Well, maybe God's not all-good, all-knowing, and all-powerful."

"What do you mean?" I asked. "That's the very definition of God. How could God not be all-good, all-knowing, and all-powerful?"

Percy said, "Well, Zeus isn't."

I assumed that Percy brought up the topic of Zeus just as an academic example and I replied, "Yeah, but Zeus isn't God."

"That's for sure," she sighed.

We walked along like this down to the marina, occasionally

commenting upon a diving pelican or an interesting-looking seashell. Eventually she said, "That's my car over there," and she pointed to a small, red, and very inexpensive-looking foreign car, the make and model of which I had never seen. As I walked Percy to her car, she said, "I can see why D. enjoyed your company so much. You two must have been very good friends. I really enjoyed our conversation."

"Yeah, it was fun," I said in all honesty, realizing that for the first time in my life, I had just had a successful conversation with a girl. The spell of my pathological fear of girls had been broken for all time.

"Do you like to bodysurf?" she asked.

"Sure," I replied.

She said, "Some of my girlfriends are going to go bodysurfing tomorrow at the pier; would you like to join us? I'd like to introduce you to my friends—Jessica in particular. I think you two would have a lot in common."

"Sure," I said again, this time a little less enthusiastically.

"Okay," she said. "We'll be meeting up around two in the afternoon, just south of the pier."

"Okay," I said.

As I watched Percy squeeze her powerful body into her tiny car, I was thinking that this was the exact antithesis of a short wannabe masculine fella using a ladder to climb into his American-made monster truck. I laughed and waved good-bye as Percy drove away.

I walked away from our trek up the beach thinking about the lessons of suffering. Somehow our discussion about the existence of God seemed much too abstract for a phenomenon like suffering, the impact of which slams into your being like one of those monster trucks hitting a poor squirrel on the freeway. Also, I was thinking, maybe God is not the sort of thing you find at the end of an argument. Perhaps Percy was thinking the same thing.

I did meet Percy and her friends at the beach the next day and had a good time of it overall. And I did meet and talk freely with Jessica, though nothing really came of it. Jessica was nice, and I noticed I did not have any trouble conversing with her, but it was a polite conversation with no real excitement behind it. It was just wonderful being able to converse freely with a group of intelligent and interested young women—and feeling that I was being accepted as one of the group, though the only boy in that group that afternoon on that beach. As the afternoon wore on, it looked like an uncommon spring storm was beginning to move onshore. This was good for the surf, creating large breakers that were thrilling to catch and ride the long distance into shore. I kept going farther and farther out into the breakers in order to catch the increasingly large curls.

The waves were now crashing over me, towering eight feet over my head. Percy's friends thought that it was getting too rough for them, and they went ashore. Percy and I stayed in the water, catching waves that were ever larger than the ones before. I noticed a particularly well-formed curl gaining tremendous height as it moved toward us. We were out in the breakers much past the point where our feet touched the rocky bottom, so I started swimming hard to shore in order to position myself to catch that monstrous wave. I noticed out of the corner of my eye that Percy had chosen to dive under the oncoming wave and not ride it in.

With a sense of exhilaration I caught that large wave and felt its power crash over me, sending my outstretched body speeding through the water. Just then an eddy of turbulence caught me up in its rotating chaos and I was pushed down to the rocky bottom, pinned down in place by the force of the wave. Immediately I was hurled into the aethereal realm, and I saw D.'s ghost and the monster engaged in combat. It looked as if the monster was having a better time of it than D.'s ghost. The ghost broke free and vanished. The monster turned around, and before it could catch sight of me, I broke the connection to that subterranean realm, pushed up off the ocean bottom, and broke the surface, sputtering and coughing.

In trying to gain my bearings, I noticed that we had now been caught in a mighty riptide caused by the storm. It was taking us out to sea with its strong current. We could not fight against its relentless push out into the ocean. I looked around and must have had an expression of panic on my face, because Percy yelled that we were in a riptide and that we would need to swim parallel to the beach to break past the outward-flowing tide. That calmed me down somewhat, but we both simultaneously came to the conclusion that we could not swim north against the storm's current but would need to swim south. The problem was that one of the jetties lay that way, and we would need to swim around the jetty to avoid being pounded against its giant boulders by the increasingly powerful swells.

Percy was obviously the stronger swimmer of the two of us, and to her credit, she stayed near me as we navigated around our stony obstacle and glided into shore on the gentle waves occasioned by the watery shadow of the jetty. I was laughing hard and shouting in nervous agitation when we were finally able to stand up and wade the final steps onto shore. Percy looked worried.

We walked around the base of the jetty and found Percy's friends on the beach, and we all talked excitedly about what had just happened to Percy and me out in the breakers. We collectively decided to suspend our bodysurfing exploits for the day. My mind was on the scene of the monster in combat with D.'s ghost. I was very much afraid for all of those that were keeping D. in their hearts and minds.

After some more polite conversation, I excused myself from the company of Percy and her friends, explaining that I needed to get my homework done before classes tomorrow morning. Percy seemed somewhat distracted and said good-bye. On the drive home, I realized that I had long enough been absent from my responsibilities regarding the constituents of D.'s ghost. I decided that I needed to do something about that monster, once and for all.

XIII

A Dream, Maybe

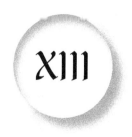

On the afternoon succeeding our experience with the riptide, I took another of my solitary sojourns subsequent to track practice. I needed clarity of mind and time and space to concentrate on how to go about killing the monster. If I were to kill the monster, I needed to know a lot more about it, what it was made of, and who animated it in its aethereal world of unconscious extrasensory conversations. It had never indulged me with the opportunity to explore its constitution. I realized with a start that I did not have the slightest idea what this monster was. I also realized with another start that I would never personally be in a position to gain that information. If I were close enough to determine its nature, then it would be close enough to instantly terminate my very existence. I needed another way to study its structure and habits.

I should be honest here; I did seriously consider the possibility of requesting D.'s ghost to explore the monster's composition for me. "If I cannot approach that monster, then maybe D.'s ghost could be my proxy," I reasoned. I calculated the pros and cons of using D.'s ghost to reconnoiter the monster's insubstantial construction. The only point in the "pro" column for making that request of D.'s ghost would be that I could gain some information on the monster without exposing myself to the risk of existential annihilation. But it turned out that there were many items in the "con" column. I could not guarantee that D.'s ghost would be levelheaded enough to be an accurate observer of the monster's inner workings. Additionally, sending D.'s ghost after the monster would be putting all those that loved him, including Percy, in direct danger. To put it bluntly, this decision procedure was a classic illustration of saving one's own skin versus the protection of many others. Even I could not ignore the obvious outcome of the calculus here. No, I absolutely needed to keep D.'s ghost out of my plans for this dangerous reconnaissance.

For some reason not entirely clear to me—maybe because of her recently having rescued me from the riptide—Percy came to mind as one to whom I could turn for help in the matter. But with a snort of derision directed at my own obviously unreasonable notion, I immediately put that consideration out of mind. Percy had no knowledge of the aethereal realm, had no reason to suspect that I had been in contact with D.'s ghost or that D.'s ghost even existed, and was entirely ignorant of that avian-reptilian monster lurking in the shadows of the nether world. It was a silly idea that Percy could be of any help in this matter. I was surprised that I even considered that possibility for a moment.

D.'s ghost was the only entity I knew of that would even be capable of helping me on my information-gathering mission in the aethereal realm, and I did not want it involved. So I reasoned that I was required to do my own dirty work. Further, I thought that if I were to be in the aethereal realm, gathering information on the monster, I had better be as efficient as possible in those endeavors. This meant that I should try to formulate my questions beforehand, enter that shadowy realm, seek out those answers, and then quickly return to the relative safety of the mundane world. So I pondered: *What do I most need to know about that monster in order to kill it?*

To answer my question, I reasoned that I should summarize what I did know about the monster, then summarize what I did not know, and then determine where there might be gaps in my knowledge. Accordingly, I made a mental note of what I knew about the monster: (1) it was evil, (2) it was a conversation in the aethereal realm, (3) it had a very strong will and was extremely powerful, (4) it wanted to kill me, (5) it had the means to seek me out and find me, (6) the monster and I could communicate, (7) it was the object of D.'s ghost's wrath, and (8) it could, at least temporally, be harmed. Oh, and (9) it was possible to distract it with the supposed presence of Sage. This last point seemed curious. I did not then sufficiently dwell upon that curiosity, beyond realizing that I had no idea what Sage was or its role in this whole saga.

I then mentally went through some relevant points I did not know about the monster: (1) why it was apparently threatened by Sage; (2) why it was angry; (3) why it sought me out; (4) what voices its being comprised; (5) as a corollary to this last point, the identities of the existent sentient beings that ultimately went into its structure and made it what it was; (6) the nature of the relationship between those existent sentient beings and the monster; (7) how strongly they were associated with the monster; (8) where it dwelled; (9) how I could find it; (10) whether it could hurt me when I was in the mundane world; (11) which conversations it was a member of; (12) whether it could identify the individual voices in D.'s ghost; (13) whether it could hurt the sentient beings that lent voices to D.'s ghost; (14) what its weaknesses were; and (15) whether it could be killed. It seemed almost hopeless. There were so many things I did not know about the monster. The gaps in my knowledge here seemed insurmountable.

It then occurred to me that I had placed myself in a position similar to a man who had been shot with a poison arrow and who did not want to remove that arrow until he knew who shot him, what sort of wood the bow was constructed of, what bird's feathers were on the arrow, whether it was a stone or iron arrowhead, why the archer had shot him, whether it was a mistake or on purpose, from what family the archer came, etc. Of course, if the poor victim had any chance of survival, he needed to remove the arrow as quickly as possible and suck out the poison—not waste time on these questions that did not lead to edification. Answers to these tertiary questions concerning the monster might have been interesting, but they would not directly lead to the cessation of my suffering at the hands of that horrible beast. The essence of what I needed to know was, Could the suffering be stopped, and if so, how? In other words, I needed to know (1) whether the monster could be killed, and (2) the best way of going about killing it.

In answer to the first question (i.e., Can the monster be killed?), it seemed that Resident Teacher had intimated that this was a distinct possibility. Resident Teacher seemed to indicate that an unconscious extrasensory conversation could be ended—dissolved—if its constituent existent sentient beings all simultaneously left the conversation. Additionally, the myth of Demeter and Persephone suggested a vulnerability of the gods—especially that part of the myth relating to Zeus's concern that his power would wane when humans were no longer devoted to him and performing sacrifices in his honor. In fact, this suggestion of the possible mortality of the immortals could be directly deduced from the party-line theory of consciousness. To kill a conversation, it was only necessary to remove the voices from that conversation. If the voices were removed, then the conversation would dissolve into nothingness—a real nothingness in this case, with no residual shadowy existence or causal continuity. So if I were to remove the voices sustaining the monster of my suffering, then that monster would cease to exist and the suffering emanating from it would simply disappear.

I had one remaining relevant question: How could I remove the voices sustaining the pseudoexistence of that monster? This was not a trivial question. I had no knowledge whatsoever of the mechanism of action of voices as constituting a conversation in the aethereal realm. So it seemed that the part of my gap analysis that identified my lack of knowledge in this regard was not entirely off track. How was I to gain just enough knowledge of this mechanism of action in order to cause the unconscious extrasensory conversation—the monster—to cease? I needed to probe the connection between conversations and their constituent voices. Yet I needed to do so in relative safety, not exposing myself to the instant annihilation threatened by that very fiend. I required a probe—an exploratory instrument that both allowed me to investigate the relationship between voices and their conversation and also provided me with some measure of safety while traversing the occult world. I also required a rather benign test subject upon which to exercise and practice using that probe.

I figured I would tackle the second issue first. I immediately discounted D.'s ghost as an adequate test subject because I did not want to risk alienating it from my efforts. It seemed a rather impetuous spirit, and it was necessary that I maintained its allegiance in reserve. I was familiar with Amateur Yachting in Santa Barbara Channel, but it did not seem to have a power base on par with the monster's and thus would be a poor proxy for that demon. Also, I did not relish becoming too intimate with that rude maritime being. I finally decided to explore the mechanism and dynamics of Resident Teacher. This last being seemed to be a relevant substitute for the monster; it apparently had a rather large power base. Also, I thought that if it were to notice my examination of its inner structure, I could present a reasonable case in my defense.

I next turned my attention to the construction of a probe to use in my investigations. I had been continuing to carefully practice making my protective shield. Now I needed a structure that was less like a bubble and more like a cavity with a small opening in one direction, allowing for interaction with aethereal beings through that aperture. Such a configuration would protect me in all directions except for the one narrow path delineating the focus of my attention. At this point in my meditation I found that I had finished my solitary afternoon foray and that I was standing on the porch of my parents' house, about to enter the front door. I resolved to begin construction of the required protective probe that very night, when the house would be peacefully wrapped in a secure veil of slumber.

That night as I lay in bed, I surreptitiously entered the aethereal realm with the real knowledge that I could be unknowingly blasted into nonexistence at any moment. To say the least, it was a stressful exercise, yet I stayed true to my previous calculus of risk versus benefit, reassured in my belief that my actions were being performed for the greater good. Upon entering that hidden realm, I instantly constructed the strongest protective bubble I had ever created. Unfortunately, the stronger I made my protective shield, the cloudier it became, with the current shield being almost entirely opaque. I conjured the visualization of lighting an acetylene torch, throwing a visor down over my face, and cutting a small hole in that solid structure enveloping me in its reassuring protection. I felt uneasy cutting a hole in my insulating shield, but I realized that interacting with beings in the occult realm required that I expose my vulnerability by breaching my serene sanctuary.

It took most of the night, but at length I was satisfied with my work. It seems almost comical now when I look back upon the design and construction of that probe. The visualization of the final product resembled nothing so much as a cigar-shaped one-person submersible, where I lay prone and looked out upon the surrounding environment through a reinforced transparent portal with an intense ray shining upon matters of interest before me. I was sorely fatigued by my engineering effort, and I decided that it was sufficient work for the night. I ascended to the mundane world and quickly descended into a much-needed sleep.

The little rest I received that night was not refreshing. Almost immediately upon falling asleep, I entered a dream state that lasted until I awoke in the morning. It was a flying dream of sorts.

In my dream, I was flying prone with my arms out in front of me, not unlike bodysurfing a wave onto shore. At first I was hovering at the foot of an immense snow-capped mountain, looking up toward its veiled heights. Reminiscing about the experience now, I would say that looking up at that mountain was similar to being in California's Owens Valley east of the High Sierras and trying to fix one's gaze upon the highest peak. I choose this analogy because at that geographical location in eastern California, the tallest mountain in the lower forty-eight states is just within an hour's drive from Death Valley, the lowest point, with the difference in elevation between these two being over fourteen thousand feet. Death Valley lives up to its name, being a dry, dusty environment frequented by blasts of superheated winds and sustaining only ghostlike vestiges of life. In my dream, it seemed that I was looking up at least fourteen thousand feet, if not more—looking up through the heat of the underworld to gaze upon the distant icy peaks of mighty Mount Olympus.

I flew up the face of the mountain. I heard voices and conversations as I soared up the tectonic mass, with each foot of ascension bringing together the voices and conversations from lower elevations into new conversations of their own. Rising still farther up the enormous and jagged stone, I noticed that the conversations created at lower altitudes were now their own voices being brought together into a new stratum of conversations. Up, up I flew, past strata of ever more integrated voices and conversations. As I ascended—it happened slowly at first—huge sections of the mountain began separating into abutments supporting two separate pinnacles at the very apices of this aggregate of stony consciousnesses. Many lower peaks came to a halt in their upward climb before reaching the two ultimate pinnacles, as is natural for a gigantic mountain, but it was clear that the majority of the mass of the mountain was separating into two major divisions as it rose in elevation, owing its allegiance to one or the other ultimate pinnacle.

As I flew above the lesser peaks, I could hear voices projecting from their spiked spires like hot volatile gasses spewing from an underwater chimney and thrown to the mercy of the cold currents. The voices evaporating from the lesser vertical points of rock were begging and pleading for attention from the mass of the mountain above. Upon noticing the voices spewed from the secondary peaks into the void above them, I also noticed that these two mountains and all their jagged peaks were not static, unmoving masses. They seemed to be alive with motion. When the voices of lower spires were answered from animated boulders above, the lower spires merged into the great mass of the mountain. Those lower crests that were conclusively ignored by the dynamic boulders above crumbled to pieces, falling down the face of the mountain in piles of scree. This dynamism of the mountain, and its two competing panicles, was incessant; they were building themselves higher and higher as I flew up their increasingly steep slopes. Indeed, my trajectory up that mountain eventually became virtually vertical.

Looking more closely at the scaffolding of these two ultimate spires as I ascended their gradients, I noticed that their constituent voices and conversations were incessantly vibrating, all a-jumble in a confused matrix of signals requesting recognition, replies of recognition and subsequent communal conjunction, and the breaking of signals between the voices. The flux of these interrelationships was ever changing, with signals being established and broken endlessly. The mountains veritably quivered with jostling voices and conversations—with the more powerful conversations perched within higher strata. Consciousness was being consolidated at ever higher levels up the mountain.

Flying so far up the mountain that I could no longer see the valley below or the mass of the mountain that supported the two ultimate pinnacles, and only able to view these two separate columns rising to the highest height, I noticed that the apices of these two final spires were active with enormous energy on a galactic scale. One was active with fire, the other with ice. The fiery peak was shooting out intensely hot blasts of lightning bolts, with the icy peak shooting out bolts of supercooled plasma chilled to absolute zero. These two peaks seemed to be dueling, where one peak blasted the other only to be met with a bolt from the other. Their beams met midway between them and annihilated one another, creating where the beams met a sphere of complete nothingness around which a spiral mist of ragged debris rotated.

As I grew nearer to this conflagration, I noticed that the two peaks as well were rotating around the common center where the bolts met and obliterated one another. In fact, it now appeared that the peaks were rotating at an incredibly fast rate—not infinitely fast in their rotation around one another, but as fast as they could possibly go. The two peaks were now removed from their supporting spires and were revolving around one another so fast that the whole whirling scene resembled a torus, or doughnut shape, in their blurred aspect. The center of the doughnut, the hole of annihilated nothingness, was where the bolts met as they were hurled from the two peaks. The doughnut itself was an illusion of solidity due to the rapidity of the rotation of the apices. For some inexplicable reason, I flew straight into the center of the doughnut hole.

The very center of the doughnut turned out to be a nothingness that gave birth to a chaos, where that nothingness itself resulted from the crashing together of the fiery and icy bolts, like the strife between love and hate. The smashing together of these opposing rays resulted in debris from their conflict. This detritus resembled nothing so much as miniscule maggots or worms wiggling in their infinitesimal proportions. It's a curious phenomenon of dreams that one can have experiences that seem so meaningful and comprehensible in the dream but that when later examined in a wakeful state are anything but understandable. However, that very phenomenon is what was happening to me when I flew into the chaotic centroid of the torus. These wiggling worms, or tiny bits of string, existed in a domain of many dimensions. I could not fix an acceptable focus upon any one minuscule string, but in my dream state it was clear they existed in ten or more dimensions. There is no analogy I can use here to make this statement make sense to our waking state; it made perfect sense in my dream.

Hovering around these tiny strings, I soon found that they were aligning in meaningful patterns. Different patterns resulted in different outcomes. From the combinations of these flitting bits of fundamental existence came time and space—and then gravity! From gravity came energy, and with energy came mass. These nearly massless particles were now arranging themselves into ornate patterns of wavelike motions. The waves collided and crashed into one another, coalescing into hunks of stuff situated in the battlefield between the two rotating peaks. That battlefield now resembled the old photos and videos of the no-man's land between the opposing armies of World War I. It was a dark and gray expanse—an endless wasteland of coalescing existence.

Just then I was caught up in a vortex created by the rotation of the peaks and with a tremendous angular momentum was thrown out of the chaos of the warring parties like a piece of gravel kicked up by the rear tire of a truck on a country road. I was thrown into a vast void, suspended between billions of immeasurably distant tiny points of light.

One point of light in that vast cosmos was beckoning me. I flew straight for it. Though my path was the shortest distance to that point of light, it turned out to be a curved and bending path. I felt like a bird swooping around obstacles while tracking a tasty flying insect. The tiny point of light of my pursuit grew larger and soon became a distant disk of fiery gas. I flew straight at that ball of fire and passed cleanly through its center, emerging on the other side. I continued on my astronomic trajectory, now keeping to a heading destined to collide with a blue-and-white ball that had been hiding itself behind the fiery sphere. I knew that this azure marbled globe had been my goal all along.

Having passed through fire, I now descended into the thin film of air surrounding this wonderful sphere. I flew over the oceans below me until I spotted my goal—a shoreline on the edge of a vast space of dry earth. But before I could land on that earth, I was required to learn the pattern of waves splashing ashore; that pattern apparently held some occult meaning. I hovered above those waves and apprehended their regular and meaningful design. Once I had discovered the order of those breakers, I dived into the water and bodysurfed a wave onto shore. Climbing out of the ocean and pulling myself up onto the sand, I noted that I had traveled through fire, upon the air, and into water, and I now stood upon solid earth. I walked the unreasonably short distance to my parents' home, entered the house, went to my bedroom, got into bed, and awoke from my dream.

It was now morning, and I was anything but refreshed from my slumber. What was worse, I was unsure if I had actually been dreaming or had somehow been dragged along on a strange tour of the aethereal realm. Had I been dreaming? I was unsure, and that uncertainty was unsettling.

XIV

Two Dragons

My dream, if that is what it was, gave me pause. I felt it held some important significance in its depiction of a backward turning circle of existence, running from a mountain of conscious voices to eternal strife between love and hate, to the genesis of the material universe as a result of that conflict, and then back to the material construction of a mountain of consciousnesses to start the cycle all over again. But I could not plumb the depths of its meaning. I was mostly concerned with the fact that I was now more uncertain than ever about the demarcation between the aethereal versus the mundane realms. What with this dream, and the fact that so many events in the aethereal realm had direct impacts upon events in the mundane realm, I was beginning to fear a dangerous mingling of the two domains. Maybe there was not a strict distinction between the mundane and the occult. Maybe a dualistic attitude was not correct and all was part of a single whole. Usually I had encountered the professing of nondualism to be accompanied with a spiritual enthusiasm. However, for me, given that the monster lived in the hidden realm, the possibility of a real nondualism was just plain scary.

On the other hand, how could that dream be a revelation of anything remotely real? Why would the mechanism of the genesis of the very universe be revealed to a lowly being like myself? Such a revelation is unthinkable—certainly undeserved. The dream could not have represented any real reality. It *must* have been merely a dream, made up by my unconscious imagination. It would be the height of audacious conceit to believe that the experience of the previous night was anything other than a fanciful hallucination brought on by the stresses of recent events. Again, it *must have been a dream*. But still I was agitated by it, as well as by my sense that I was losing a clear differentiation between the occult and mundane realms.

The disquietude generated by my "dream" gave me even more motivation to go about my business in killing the beast. As soon as practicable, I entered the aethereal realm. Safely concealed in my protective one-person probe, I sought traces of Resident Teacher. I did not want to confront Resident Teacher head on—face-to-face, so to speak. Rather, I wanted to observe the individual voices and conversations that went into the construction of Resident Teacher. In order to do this, I needed to keep Resident Teacher in my peripheral view but focus upon its trailing essence. My enterprise was more like fixing my gaze upon the tail of a comet rather than fixating upon that comet's solid icy core soaring through the void. Anyway, this is the way I visualized my effort.

I found that Resident Teacher had a rather broad base indeed. It was composed of many subconversations. Individual voices representing the unconscious extrasensory communications from separate sentient beings were in the extreme minority. I reminded myself that my plan for killing the avian-reptilian beast was to remove the voices from its power base. To this end, I realized that I did not need to know the exact mechanics of how voices and conversations constituted unconscious extrasensory conversations such as Resident Teacher. Instead I merely needed to know if I could somehow knock those constituent voices and conversations out of their overriding conversations. It struck me as ironic that in order to learn how to kill the monster of my suffering, I needed to first discover how to dismantle my teacher.

Not that I intended to actually dissolve my teacher, of course. Far from it. I just needed to know *how* to go about performing that disintegration. To this end, I decided to try knocking an unsuspecting voice from Resident Teacher's constitution. For this initial task, I chose an individual voice—not a conversation of voices—that was associated with a sentient being whose visualization appeared to represent a youngish professor of history from a community college somewhere in the US Midwest. Maneuvering my protective probe, I sidled up next to this incognizant instructor and gave it a gentle bump in a direction away from Resident Teacher. It turned, gave me an annoyed glance, and repositioned itself securely within the umbra of Resident Teacher's conversation. Even though my action here was only marginally effective, I was heartened to note that there was some effect at all. I had, ever so slightly, nudged a voice away from the overriding conversation. I considered this a success.

I now needed to determine whether I could push this lone voice out of the conversation altogether. To this end, I again positioned myself next to that solitary vocalization and gave it a momentous thrust, throwing it out of the conversation and into the void. I succeeded! It was sailing away from the conversation, and its mutterings no longer added its consciousness or will to the conversation of Resident Teacher.

Unfortunately, the diminutive yet tenacious voice of the history professor soon reappeared, took a route aimed directly at me, shook my probe about violently, and threw *me*, in my probe, out of the proximity of the overall conversation! I am ashamed to say that I took serious offence with being so rudely treated by this minor voice. I immediately returned to the conversation to confront it. It noticed me approaching it in my protective probe, and we clashed head on. In my discomposure I manhandled that voice, tossed it out of the conversation, and then threw a protective bubble around it.

This throwing of a bubble around a voice so as to isolate it was again an example of something new for me, and it was unthinkingly accomplished in the heat of the moment. What I had originally manufactured as a protective enclosure securing my own safety so many weeks ago was now being utilized as a restrictive prison. It securely restrained my competitor from wreaking vengeance upon me. I could see the lone voice inside that bubble, vainly thumping upon the inside of the shell in thinly controlled hysteria as it slowly drifted away into the void of the aether. I assumed that the shell of imprisonment I had unwittingly constructed around that voice would eventually disperse and the lone instructor would then be free again to join the conversation of Resident Teacher, none the worse for wear. I warned myself again that I did not want to cause any permanent damage to Resident Teacher's power base.

I hovered in the near vicinity of Resident Teacher, keeping a keen watch upon its constituents for what seemed in that realm to be about an hour. Sure enough, eventually that lone voice visualized as the poor community college instructor did reappear and rejoin the conversation. I felt that I was making real progress. Once more, I had no idea how I was doing what I was actually doing, but I was making great strides in becoming proficient at doing it. I then decided to exercise my will upon more powerful voices—conversations, rather—that constituted significant portions of the overall conversation denoted by "Resident Teacher." The more powerful subconversations directly adding to the powerbase of Resident Teacher included Chairperson, Endowed Chair, and Emeritus. I needed to know if I could knock these subconversations out of the Resident Teacher conversation long enough to give me time to knock its other voices and conversations out of the overall conversation if that were my goal. I was again playing the game of tickling the dragon's tail. I absolutely did not want to altogether dissolve Resident Teacher. I just wanted to demonstrate to myself that I could do so. It was a dangerous game.

I decided to take Chairperson, Endowed Chair, and Emeritus

in turn and see if I could detach them from the conversation of Resident Teacher long enough to demonstrate that I could dissolve the conversation outright if I so willed. I planned to deal with each one of these subconversations separately. I would push it out of the conversation, allow it to return to the conversation, and then move on to the next. This way I would not significantly jeopardize the continuing integrity of Resident Teacher as a whole. I realize that it sounds extremely hubristic for such a young soul as I was then to be thinking in terms of "allowing them to return to the conversation," but that was exactly what I had proposed to myself to do. As it turned out, that is exactly what I in fact did, with no lasting harm to Resident Teacher. Indeed, Resident Teacher was never the wiser concerning my efforts in probing and manipulating its constituent voices and subconversations. But it may simply be that it never gave much notice to my probing exercise because of the horrible events immediately succeeding my operating upon its internal structure.

I went about the continuation of my probe of Resident Teacher by first confronting Emeritus. I thought that, representing more aged professors, maybe Emeritus might be less energetic than Chairperson or Endowed Chair in its attachment to Resident Teacher. I was most notably wrong in that assumption. It gave me as much fight as any other conversation I had dealt with up to this time. I tried throwing it out of the conversation and enveloping it with an enshrouding bubble. It looked straight at me, popped the bubble from inside, and gave me a perfunctory shove out of the conversation as if I were of no account, not meriting a smidgen more of its attention. I should have known before I ineffectually tried to remove it from the conversation that it had one and only one focus in its pseudolife, and that was to stay in this particular conversation for as long as it could. I was filled with awe and respect for its tenacity in this undertaking. I still shiver with chills when remembering its selfless and zealous dedication to truth and learning. I needed, however, to continue in my project and to demonstrate to myself that I could remove even this stubborn voice from the conversation. I knew that if I were to dissolve the avian-reptilian beast, I would likely be confronting even more intractable opponents.

I needed to somehow distract Emeritus in order to have the time—focus of will, really—to construct an even more permanent imprisonment around it. To this end, I conjured the image of a college building named in its honor—a cheap trick, I know, but it did in fact work. Emeritus was indeed extremely interested in this shiny object dangling in front of it—interested in it long enough for me to construct an inescapable keep surrounding that respectable pseudobeing. I am absolutely certain it was sorely disappointed when it discovered that its object of attention was nothing other than a flimsy illusion. By the time it discovered my ruse, I had Emeritus securely imprisoned within my isolating dungeon, now made dark in its structural cohesion. I threw that dungeon here and there across aethereal voids, convincing myself that I could effectively restrain that subconversation from engaging in the conversation of Resident Teacher for a sufficient duration. I then carefully brought that opaque bubble back into the vicinity of Resident Teacher and lifted an escape hatch, hiding myself behind a bevy of other voices; I did not want to be bitten by my captive upon its release. It escaped its enclosure, looked around with an aggrieved presentation, stood up straight, smoothing its rumpled academic garb, and rejoined the conversation I have been calling "Resident Teacher." *Not the worse for wear,* I thought to myself.

I performed the same exercise upon Chair and Endowed Chair in turn, utilizing distractions unique to those subconversations. For Chair I dangled a shiny deanship in front of it, and for Endowed Chair I tried various distractions without success until I found that a huge private donation from a wealthy widow worked to hold its attention long enough for me to encapsulate it in its keep. I chuckled to myself about the pettiness of this all. I was jolted out of my humorous reverie upon realizing that my engagement with the evil monster was going to be anything but humorous; it promised to be a deadly serious confrontation.

Coincidentally, or maybe because I had brought that deadly evil beast to mind, I then noticed at the periphery of the portal in my protective probe that very monster prowling around in a profound rage. It seemed to sense my presence and waved its enormous horned head back and forth, searching for me, its prey. I promptly took evasive action, moving away from that beast. I did not sever my connection to the aethereal realm in self-defense as I had done before when confronted by the near presence of the beast. Instead I unwisely chose to remain in that realm to boldly test the protective properties of my probe. I moved off a good distance, keeping the beast in my outermost awareness. It grew furious with its sense of my presence, however remote I kept my distance from that monster. The spines running down the length of its back rose in anger, flashing red and purple patterns down that spiked ornamentation. It raised its beaked snout, trying to fix my location by smell, and it stomped about, shaking its obscure environment to its foundation.

At this very moment, that evil beast and Resident Teacher locked eyes, noticing each other for the first time in this corner of the aether. Both stood motionless, staring at each other for the briefest of moments. Breaking out of the momentary surprise of finding Resident Teacher here, the evil avian-reptilian beast stood up straight and became an immense, brilliantly crimson dragon many stories tall with the following huge symbol emblazoned in black upon the scarlet scales that covered its enormous chest:

I recognized the beast's emblem as an ancient Northern European rune. The very instant the beast transformed into the dragon, Resident Teacher also transformed into a fearsome dragon of similar size and terrible visage. Resident Teacher had become a gigantic green dragon, with pulses of smoke and cinders wafting up from its nostrils. The green dragon displayed what I took to be a large image of the Greek letter chi emblazoned in black upon its verdant chest. Resident Teacher's fighting emblem looked like the following:

χ

Immediately upon displaying their colors to one another, the two dragons roared, throwing blasts of superheated plasma toward one another, with the beast shouting, "Blood and soil!" and Resident Teacher shouting, "Truth and integrity!" They charged one another, meeting midway, and clashed in the chaos and fury reminiscent of a gigantic cockfight. A huge blast exploded out from the point of their impact, cracking my protective probe into useless fragments as the massive shock wave swept past me. I was thrown about, tumbling with no sense of orientation, until I came to rest upon a hard, flat surface in a crumpled mass. My ears were not ringing. In fact, there was no sound at all—just complete silence. Out of watery and stinging eyes, blurred with confusion more than with pain, I was starting to make out intense flashes instantaneously illuminating the void about me. My chest felt crushed in, but I was finally able to move my abdomen just enough to gain a quantum of relief from the sensation of asphyxiation. That is when the sharp ringing in my head began. I shook my head over and over, hitting its sides with the palms of both hands. The ringing did not stop. I could not tell where I was, what I was doing, or why I was there in the first place. I stumbled to my feet, and was immediately bowled over by another, thankfully somewhat less powerful, blast.

As I lay there on the hard surface, with blood starting to drip into my left eye, my memory began to slowly return. With a flash of sheer terror, I remembered the confrontation of the two dragons, and I turned my body to witness that gruesome conflict. I was appalled at what I saw. The two dragons were dueling with such intensity that I could hardly make out one dragon from the other. All I could see was a blur of red and green, with a continual mist of blood being thrown into the void around them in pulsating cascades of glistening crimson. I could hear the snapping of sharp teeth and the rending of solid flesh. I smelled the rancid odor of burning skin and muscle, with the smoke of the sacrifice rising above the melee.

I noticed that the combatants had kicked up the flat surface into ruts and hills in their struggle, and I had the sense to dive into a deep depression near me. I hugged my foxhole for dear life, not wanting to exit it for anything in the world. I tried to merge into the hard surface directly below me. From where I lay, I could see flashes of brilliant light, hear bellowing explosions about me through the ringing in my head, and feel the trembling of new depressions and hills produced near me by the frenetic actions of those awesome adversaries. I was right in the thick of the conflict, and I feared that an awful random blow could land upon my hole at any moment, ending my existence altogether. I am not ashamed to admit that my bowels emptied down my legs from the sheer terror of my circumstance.

I knew I needed to escape this explosive scene, but for some reason, I could not directly ascend into the mundane realm. That avenue of escape was not now working for me. I noted this failure to escape with horrified concern. If I could not escape into the comfort of my parents' home, then I needed to exit the situation hastily using some other procedure.

I cautiously raised my head out of my foxhole, looking for a path of flight. Just as I was about to jump up and attempt running away from this violent chaos, the red dragon seemed to get an advantage over its green enemy and tossed Resident Teacher on its back. The beast turned sideways to Resident Teacher and, using its immensely muscled tail, landed a powerful blow upon the neck and head of Resident Teacher. Scales and teeth flew from the blow sustained by Resident Teacher, scattering bits and pieces of the green dragon upon the area around where I lay hidden in my depression. To my amazement, many of those scales and teeth transformed back into individual voices or conversations and jumped up to rejoin Resident Teacher. Some were left quivering upon the hard surface of the dark void, moaning in pain or quietly pleading for assistance. One, I remember, was vainly yelling for its mother before its voice diminished into nothingness. Too many were left silent upon the hard ground.

One particularly large piece of the green dragon, a patch of scaly hide, was left on the ground about thirty feet in front of my foxhole. I could see it slowly turning into a faint visualization of Emeritus. That visualization flickered, and I could see that it was badly wounded. Emeritus was immobile with pain, stunned from the blow, and lay there exposed to the violence around it. I could see that in that vulnerable position, Emeritus would be crushed into nonexistence at any moment. I fought hard to calm my panic, jumped up out of my hole, dodged random blasts of hot plasma, and ran to where Emeritus lay upon the ground. I grabbed Emeritus by the shoulders of its academic garb and dragged it back into the relative safety of my den.

I have no idea when or how I came into possession of a canteen, but I opened it and splashed water over Emeritus's forehead. It looked up at me in a haze and said, "Oh, it's you. Thanks."

Emeritus then blanked out for about thirty seconds, during which time I continued to wash its forehead with cold water and yell, "Emeritus, Emeritus! Don't you leave me!"

When it came to again, it winced in pain, wiped its face, and proudly proclaimed, "Thank you so much, young man. I feel much better now. And now I shall need to rejoin the conversation to fight that evil beast!" It jumped up, looked around, yelled, "For truth and integrity!" and leaped back into the fray. It transformed itself midair into a large scale of armor and affixed itself on a particularly vulnerable portion of Resident Teacher's bare flesh. I ducked back into my foxhole just as a blast of red superheated plasma washed over my position.

I was cowering in my foxhole when I heard a loud smack and a substantial chunk of the red dragon about the size of a side of beef landed in my hole next to me. That hunk of the red dragon looked like an oversize piece of skinned raw chicken. It lay there beside me, quivering and jerking in its rawness, bloody and steaming warm vapor into the void, filling my foxhole with the stench of rotting carcass. I stared at it in amazed horror, backing as far away from it as I could get while staying in the relative safety of my sheltering burrow. I think I remember screaming incoherent curses as I rapidly moved away from it. The intensity of its jerking increased, impelling it a couple of inches off the ground with each spasm. To my horror, it pulled itself together and took on the visualization of a large muscular man wearing a well-cut but tattered military-type uniform not familiar to me. Its transformation completed with its face turned away from me. It turned and saw me cowering in the recesses of the foxhole, terrified. This warrior then quickly and expertly withdrew a bayonet from a sheath hanging at its side and lunged at me with the force of a charging bear.

I was still confused from the concussion and did not have much time to think in any case. I did not engage in any protective measures beyond simply trying to move away from the oncoming disaster. The warrior thrust the bayonet sharply, aiming to ram its lethal point up under my ribs. I turned away quickly, and the polished blade sank deeply into a wooden support joist that I had no memory of having been there before. As the attacking warrior spent the slightest moment trying to dislodge the bayonet from its woody scabbard, I picked up a large chunk of surface material and smashed it over its head. It wobbled in pain, brought itself back to its senses, and grabbed my neck, knocking us both down with me on my back and the warrior on top of, and choking the life from, my being. I pummeled the soldier frantically, to no effect. My legs kicked, and I was losing consciousness. The hostile soldier continued to suffocate me, giving a convulsive violent shake of my neck that translated down my entire spine. To gain sufficient purchase for the last neck-breaking wrench, the soldier raised its head and shoulders slightly above the level of the foxhole. Just then a powerful blast flew across the hole and knocked the violent warrior into a stunned and unconscious passivity.

I rolled away from my opponent, who now lay motionless next to me. When I finally quit coughing and could catch my breath, I used all my remaining strength to push my assailant out of the foxhole and into the risky no-man's land—all the while remaining vigilant not to expose too much of my own being to the deadly chaos ensuing all about me. Lying there in my hole, next to where I had pushed out my enemy, I could hear that enemy regain consciousness and shout "For blood and soil!" I then heard it running back to the red dragon. I assumed that it had rejoined its evil idol in its conflict with Resident Teacher, now the green dragon.

I was shaking violently. I had no control whatsoever over that frantic vibration sweeping in waves across my body. I knew I needed to make good on my immediate escape. Preparing to make a final attempt in running for my life, I popped my head up out of my hole and watched the conflict, waiting for a brief moment of calm in which I could cautiously run away to safety. That is when I noticed D.'s ghost approach the discord and join in as a third party. D.'s ghost was not fighting *alongside* Resident Teacher so much as fighting *against* the awful beast. I could not help myself; unthinkingly I shouted, "D.! No!" and the beast finally looked straight at me in recognition of its intended prey. D.'s ghost took that opportunity to strike the beast, inflicting no injury but causing the beast to refocus upon D.'s ghost's presence. It turned to face D.'s ghost and smote that angry spirit a terrific blow, throwing him back about fifty feet to my right. D.'s ghost lay where it landed, not moving. Resident Teacher took the opportunity to slash one of its sharp claws down the beast's back, severing most of the beast's awesome display of sharp dorsal spines. The beast roared, turned around, and blasted Resident Teacher with an incredibly intense ray of plasma. Resident Teacher crumbled into a singed, smoking amorphous mass.

The beast took a good look at the smoking mass that was Resident Teacher, turning its head back and forth so that each eye got a good, long look. It was apparently satisfied with its handiwork. It finally, slowly, turned to face me directly. I stared into its huge bloodshot eyes, noticing for the first time its narrow vertical pupils—jet black against an evil red. I was frozen in fear, trying to experience fully my very last moments of existence. Out of the corner of my eye, to my right, where D.'s ghost lay motionless on the ground, I noticed movement. I averted my eyes from the monster and beheld Percy!

Percy was kneeling over D.'s ghost and trying to rouse it from its blow. The beast noticed my averted gaze and turned to see what had caught my attention. The monster startled now for a second time and yelled at Percy, "So it's you!" The monster shot out a hot blast of plasma at Percy, who was hovering above D.'s crumpled ghost. Percy held out her hand before her, with her palm forward, and diverted the blast in a pattern all around her like the heat shield of a space capsule reentering the atmosphere. The cone of the deflected blast created a hellish red arc where it intersected the planar surface upon which D.'s ghost lay.

The crumpled mass that was Resident Teacher groaned loudly, reassembled itself into its original visualization of a teacher, and ran away into the covering darkness. The beast turned to find empty ground where Resident Teacher had been, whereupon Percy threw D.'s ghost over her shoulder and also ran away into the void. The beast turned and just witnessed Percy running away with D.'s ghost. I was left alone with the terrible beast. While it turned to me, letting out a horrible laugh of triumph, I tried once more to sever my ties with the occult realm. This time it worked! I found myself lying in my bed, back in the mundane world. I was sore over my entire body, and my brain pulsed with an excruciating headache. I lay there breathing heavily and twitching in pain, deeply experiencing the trauma of all that had just happened. My consciousness was a confused turmoil of terrible images, sounds, smells, and sensations of pain and suffering. I felt that my bed was spinning violently.

I tried to stop the feelings washing across me and attempted to focus my mind in rational thought. But only one thought came to mind, over and over. Given all the terrible and amazing things that had just happened, all I could ask myself was "Why was Percy there?"

XV

A Goddess?

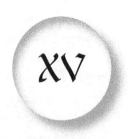

The next day, I decided that I desperately needed to contact Percy to determine the meaning of her presence at the scene of the conflict the night before. Why was she there in the middle of that melee? How did she create the heat shield that protected her and D.'s ghost from the beast's fiery blast? Why did the monster, upon first spying her, say, "Oh, it's you?" What did she know about the occult world?

I noted with some frustration that I had never gotten Percy's telephone number, did not know where she lived, and did not even know her last name. I decided to visit D.'s family and ask if they had her contact information. After breakfast and a too brief pause for a sorely needed breather, I walked the short distance from my parents' house to D.'s house.

As I walked to D.'s house, I continued my thoughts about Percy's appearance during that terrible conflict I had witnessed the night before. Had she even known I was there? She certainly had shown no awareness of my presence in that scene. And then a more serious thought arose: *Did she even know that she was there? Or was she there only unconsciously in her dreams, as D. had been when he saved me from the monster?* The seriousness of Percy's situation weighed upon me. She could be killed as her boyfriend had been killed before her. I was also very concerned for D.'s family. Given that D.'s family played a significant part in sustaining D.'s ghost—unconsciously supplying it with consciousness and will—and given that that ghost had just sustained serious injury, I was worried that D.'s family had somehow been harmed.

I found myself knocking upon what was until recently D.'s front door. After an extended period of time spent standing and waiting (indeed, I was just about to turn away), D.'s mom slowly opened the front door and peeked around it, holding most of her body behind the solid wooden structure. "Hello," I said.

"Hello," she said, trying to smile through her pain. "I'm sorry, but I won't be able to let you in. Somehow we all came down with a terrible cold during the night last night. We all feel just terrible. We don't know what it is, really. But, to be on the safe side, you probably should not come in."

"Are you guys okay?" I sincerely asked.

"I'm sure we'll all be fine," she replied, trying to keep her smile. "How can I help you?" I again relayed my condolences and then told her that I wished to contact Percy but did not know how to go about doing so. She said, "Oh, yes, it would be good for you two to talk. Stay here a second, and I'll write down her phone number." She went back into the house, leaving the door ajar, and then returned with a scrap of paper with Percy's first and last names and her telephone number written upon it. As she handed me the scrap of paper, D.'s mom said, "I don't want to pass you any germs, so I'm just giving you the piece of paper Percy used to write down her number the first time she visited here." I took the scrap of paper, thanked her, and wished her and her family well and told her I was hopeful they would all be getting better soon. I then turned and left.

"Well," I thought as I began my walk back to my parents' house, "at least they seem to be well enough, given what could have happened." I looked down at the slip of paper with Percy's name and number and read, "Persephone (Percy) Fibonacci, 1 (235) 813-2134." I stopped walking and stared at Percy's telephone number. While the number looked vaguely familiar for some reason, it struck me that this was a long-distance number for an area code nowhere near our local area. I read the numbers out loud: "One, two, three, five, eight, thirteen, twenty-one, thirty-four. Uh? No, it can't be." I turned around to go back to D.'s house to verify the number. When D.'s mother received me again I explained my confusion, "This number is long distance, for an area code not near here. Are you sure this is the right number to use to contact Percy?"

She said, "Oh yes, it's right. D. always needed to call Percy long distance. It was expensive. But it is her local number just the same. Percy told us that it is her mother's number that she uses for her work. I think she works for the government." She stated this last sentence with a slight knowing and conspiratorial air. I thanked her again and resumed my way home, continuing to think about that strange number as I walked. It vaguely struck me that there was something else strange about that number beyond being long distance; it seemed familiar somehow. Yet I could not quite place that familiarity.

That night, I called Percy. To my amazement, she answered before the end of the first ring. "Hi, Percy," I said, "This is D.'s friend. By the way, thanks again for rescuing me from that riptide; it sure was scary."

"Oh, hi!" she said. "It was nothing. Thanks for calling. What's up?"

I still did not know Percy well, but her voice sounded somewhat strained to me. I told her I had called just to say hello, see how she was doing, and so on. I did not want to bring up the events of the previous night over the phone, so I suggested we meet again down at the beach, or somewhere else of her choosing, to go for another walk. She said that she would be delighted to meet me at the beach tomorrow, a

Saturday, about noon, at the same place we had accidentally met before.

"Okay," I said, "I'm looking forward to talking with you."

She forced a cheery reply: "Me too." Then we hung up.

After hanging up the phone, I reviewed in my mind the issues I wanted to discuss with Percy when we met the next day at the beach.

Noon that next day found me standing on the beach at our designated meeting spot, looking over the waves toward the Channel Islands in the distance. What had always been a vision of inspiration and beauty now strongly reminded me of D.'s death. D.'s boat, the *Lydia,* had been found capsized upon one of the Channel Islands, with D. nowhere to be seen. The channel now reminded me of the River Styx, separating the realm of the living from the underworld—the realm of the dead—with the *Lydia* taking the place of Charon's boat, ferrying the souls of the recently deceased across the River Styx to the underworld.

I heard Percy calling me from behind, and I turned to greet her. Her long, loose curls blew golden behind her with the on-shore ocean breeze. The sight of her golden hair brought to mind her odd telephone number for some unknown reason, but I did not have the luxury to delve into that unconscious association. Her smile was subdued but sincere. "How nice for us to meet for another walk," she said. "It's a beautiful day!"

"Yes," I agreed, "shall we begin?"

"Sure," she said with a shake of her head, and we started our sojourn up the beach toward the pier. I noted that Percy looked somewhat tired or worn out. I said, turning to look at her to check her reaction, "I happened to see you the other day."

She looked genuinely surprised and said, "Did you? Where? I didn't see you."

"Yeah," I said, "I didn't think so. I was kind of hidden behind a bunch of stuff."

"But where was I when you saw me? I can't imagine where that would have been; I've been staying home so much lately—doing homework and other chores."

I stopped trudging through the loose sand and looked at her. She stopped and looked at me. I decided to reveal my story. I quietly said, looking for any reaction in her eyes, "I was watching two dragons fighting, and I saw you there." Then I intentionally gave a nervous little laugh, in case I would need to retract my statement as simply being a poor attempt at a failed joke. I knew I would need to improvise if I were to successfully retract that statement and work my way out of a tough jam. I watched Percy's face show surprise, change to shock, and then settle upon a demeanor of resignation. She was staring straight into my eyes while she proceeded through those transformations. I knew then that I had made a connection. Keeping my eyes locked with Percy's, I slightly cocked my head and waited for her reply.

At length she said, "So you were there. I didn't see you."

That was all she said, and then she resumed trudging up the beach, pushing herself through the resistant loose sand. I endeavored to follow her lengthy stride.

Catching up to and walking silently beside Percy, I realized that she knew much more than I had assumed. I could infer from her short reply that she obviously knew that she had been in the netherworld. Her presence there had not been an unconscious dream state, as it had been for D. I decided to assume that she knew at least as much about the occult realm as I. What I did not know was how she had gained this knowledge. I broke the silence. "How do you know about that other world?" Percy heaved a long sigh, looked out over the waves at the far away islands, and relayed to me her surprising tale.

According to Percy, she had been suffering greatly due to D.'s death. One night in particular, the pain was unbearable. She yearned deeply to see D. once more. She was softly sobbing in bed for D. to come back to her. At this point, D.'s ghost made a tentative appearance, not wanting to frighten Percy.

Another breach in the separation between the solid and occult realms, I thought to myself.

Percy continued her story. She said that this first hesitant visit by the specter did not present her with an awful ghost. It looked like the beautiful young boy she had loved in real life. She had not been afraid but was also not convinced that she was not suffering some sort of breakdown and experiencing a hallucination. Percy, being the critically intelligent being that she was, started quizzing the ghost on its reality. In response to these queries, D.'s ghost grew in stature, took on a more serious expression, and became a more solid manifestation. It told her all that it and I had discussed about the reality of unconscious extrasensory communications, the existence of voices and conversations in the aethereal realm, and the structure of ghosts as built up from voices and conversations contributed by those that had loved the person before it had died.

Percy relayed to me that she had asked the ghost how she could contact it in the other realm. Thereupon D.'s ghost outlined what I had told it about my meditational exercises. Percy was a quick learner and started visiting D.'s ghost in that hidden realm when she was feeling particularly depressed and lonely. Over the course of those visits, the ghost informed Percy of the avian-reptilian monster. Percy did not like the ghost's appearance and demeanor when it talked about killing the monster, and she tried desperately to convince it not to go after that evil beast. In any case, she was successful in getting the ghost to reluctantly promise not to involve me in its dangerous schemes, and to not tell me that she was communicating with it.

"Oh," I said.

There was another long pause in our conversation as we pushed through the sand and continued our trek up the beach. The cold Pacific, that River Styx, occasionally washed our feet with the waters separating the realms of life and death. Finally I broke the silence. "So that's why D.'s ghost went after the monster without me? It had promised you it would leave me out of it?"

Percy nodded and said, "Yeah. He promised me he wouldn't involve you in that. But I couldn't get him to back down on his desire to wreak vengeance upon the beast. I never saw that beast before the other night, when you were apparently there. It was horrible! And the way those two dragons fought! I've never seen anything so horrid."

After a slight pause, Percy asked, "Where were you? I didn't see you." I told her I had been hiding in a hole. She simply replied, "Good." I did not have the mental stability to describe the rest of the scene to her in great detail, but I indicated that I had been somewhat involved in the conflict.

Remembering what the beast had said when it first spied Percy, I asked, "How come the beast seemed to recognize you, if you've never seen it before? When it saw you, it said something like, 'Oh, it's you!'"

Percy averted her eyes and quickly said, "Really? I didn't hear that. Are you sure it didn't say something else?" I was no longer sure what I had heard. My mind had been extremely rattled at the time, so I conceded that I might be misremembering that portion of the awful events and I dropped this line of enquiry.

"But look," I probed. "Is D.'s ghost okay? The last I saw of that ghost, it was er, ah … dead, I guess, is the way to put it. And you were carrying it away on your shoulders."

She looked surprised and said, "Is that how you saw it? Interesting. But, yeah, D.'s okay. He was pretty shaken up there for a while. But he's starting to feel better now."

I said, "You know, if this party-line theory of consciousness is right, then if D.'s ghost gets hurt, the sentient beings keeping D. in their hearts run the risk of being hurt also. In fact, I visited D.'s family yesterday, and they were all pretty shaken up. They seem to be okay though."

"Good," she said, looking me square in the eyes. "I like D.'s family; I wouldn't want them to get hurt."

"Me too," I said.

A thought suddenly struck me, and I asked her, "How did you

form that heat shield thing to protect you and D.'s ghost from the hot plasma? It was pretty cool."

"Is that how you saw that too?" she asked. "I don't know. *My* memory is that I was just kneeling there, protecting D."

"Okay." Slightly raising my voice, I demanded, "But how did you do it?"

"I don't know. I just did it," she replied, slightly irritated by my insistence. I got the feeling that there was a lot Percy was not telling me.

There was another in a long series of lengthy pauses. A strange thought entered my mind that I could not shake, and I made a decision. I asked Percy, "Look, I'm going to ask you a crazy question. I don't know. It's silly really." She gave me a quizzical look. "It's—it's kind of weird, but, uh, are you a goddess?"

Goodness knows that by this point in my adventures, given all that had happened, I was ready for her to say yes, that she was in fact a goddess, and then for her to reveal herself in all her immortal glory with me groveling before her on the dry sand. After all, I was finding the distinction between the two realms to be slowly dissolving, so she certainly could be a goddess roaming around in the mundane realm. I was ready for anything—except, perhaps, her actual reply. She looked at me with a sly smile and a slight shrug of her powerful shoulders, and said, "I'm no more a goddess than you are a god." I shivered.

Her reply seemed a trifle rote, almost as though she had repeated the same thing times before in different circumstances, but I took her reply as genuinely honest. Given that I knew I was not a god, I took her response as a denial of her own divinity. Admittedly a little disappointed, I concluded that she was not a goddess. "I just had to ask," I said with some embarrassment, and I looked away, kicking a small mound of desiccated seaweed off the dry sand before me.

"I understand," she said diplomatically. "You've—we've—been going through a lot lately."

"No kidding," I added. I then went on and unloaded my burden.

"I don't think I can take much more of this. That last fight was horrible. I'll never get those images out of my mind. I'm still shaking. It was horrible. More than once—I mean really, *more than once*—I thought I was going to die. A person can't go through that very many times and not be changed by it all."

In my mind, I did not believe that I was fishing for sympathy; I was simply stating the facts of the case. However, I was much moved by Percy's sympathetic response: "I wasn't there for most of it. It must have been terrible. You're really brave. It's too bad you had to go through that. I think you're great."

I started to silently cry, with my chest involuntarily shaking. The suffering of it all seemed overwhelming. My whole world—existence itself—was filled to its furthest extent with pain and suffering. Percy put her arm around my shoulder and gave me a quick hug. She had to stoop a bit to do so. I was embarrassed to think that in that quick embrace she had felt my restrained convulsions.

I cleared my throat and took out my handkerchief from my back pants pocket and wiped my nose. After another pause I said, "But, ah, getting back to D.'s family, we've got to keep D.'s ghost out of trouble with that monster. If the ghost gets seriously hurt, that could hurt all those who are unconsciously sustaining the ghost with their consciousnesses and wills."

"I agree, that would be terrible," Percy responded. "What can we do?" she asked, more rhetorically than literally.

"Well," I said, taking the response literally, "we've got to do something." In a more pensive mood, I went on. "Did D.'s ghost tell you about how we, the living sentient beings, are carrying our ghosts around with us even before we die?"

"Yeah, he mentioned something about that," she said. "It makes me wonder about who we really are."

"What do you mean?" I asked, thinking to myself I already had a pretty good idea what she meant by that statement.

Percy went on to explain that if the ghost in all of us living sentient beings is constituted by the images, thoughts, desires, etc. that others have of us, then we are all connected in a vast interrelated web. She said that I am in her conscious self-identity just as she is in mine—I took this to be a rather intimate revelation on her part—as are all of our acquaintances in any degree with one another. If that is the case, she went on, then this is the polar opposite of what I had mentioned the other day in discussing the argument against God's existence based upon the reality of evil and suffering in the world. She reminded me that the logical end of that discussion about the existence of God resulted in supposing that God *could* have created all of us in our own universes, unaffected by one another, where God fed us experiences and judged us on our actions in those worlds, where we mistakenly believed that others besides ourselves existed. She said this would be a metaphysical view where we all lived in our own little monads, so to speak. She said that I had stated that we do not live in those separated worlds, so therefore God does not exist.

"But," she went on, "What if it were just the opposite? What if, instead of us all in our own unconnected universes, we were all essentially interconnected? In that case our essence is just that—to be connected to others. That is all we are—just connections to others. If the ghost-in-all-of-us idea is right, then we are very strongly connected to one another indeed. In that case, whose consciousness or whose will are we manifesting at any one time? It could be anyone's. In fact, the idea of an individual seems to dissolve, and we are left with just a holistic web of connections. There would be just one universal consciousness and will. Anyway, that's what I've been thinking about."

"Oh," I said.

I realized that what I had originally thought she meant by her first simple statement was far too modest compared to her sophisticated thinking on the subject.

There was another in the series of pauses while I mulled over what Percy had just said. We had reached the pier, and not wanting lunch, we had decided just to return the way we had come. I grew even more serious and said, "That's cool. A lot of what you've just said makes sense to me. I agree, as you know, that the view that we are all in our own separate universes seems far-fetched. And I like the notion that we are all interconnected in a web of consciousnesses, and maybe even wills. But those interconnections can't be all there is to it. I mean, interconnections between what?"

I paused again, and Percy remained silent, letting me collect my thoughts. I went on. "If we *are* carrying our ghosts around with us as we live our lives in the form of unconscious extrasensory connections to others, and if those connections survive our lives as disembodied conversations in the aether as our ghosts, then what is it that makes being alive any different from being dead? Our ghosts, just as ghosts, are missing something important—something vital. Something has to be missing after we die, and that is our self." At this point in our trek down the coast, we were on wet sand, and the waters from the Santa Barbara Channel, the River Styx, were washing our bare feet in rhythmic ablutions.

Percy said, "Yeah, I give you that; there is a difference between being alive and being dead. Uh! That expression is strange, isn't it—'*being* dead'?"

"Yeah," I said, "it's probably just an apparent paradox forced upon us because of the grammar of our particular language."

"Yeah," she said, not entirely convinced by my explanation. Nor was I. She then repeated herself: "*Being* dead."

"Besides," I said, "there may be other problems with the holistic explanation of the essence of our existence." I looked at Percy and blurted out in self-consciousness, "Gosh, that's a mouthful too, isn't it!"

"Yeah," she replied, "like saying '*Being* dead,'" not willing to give up on her oxymoron.

I ignored her insistence and went on. "I'm thinking about free will. I don't deny free will. I just question whether God, as traditionally conceived, *gave* it to us. The problem I'm starting to see here is that if we are all one consciousness and therefore one will, then there is no individual free will. But as articulated in your defense of the attack upon God's existence, if there is no individual free will, then there is no individual responsibility. That seems wrong. I don't know how to argue for it, but I really think there is individual responsibility. As for free will, well, it seems that we directly experience our free will all the time. And directly experiencing something seems one of the best ways, if not *the* best way, to argue for something's existence. How could anything be more directly experienced than our own free will?"

Percy replied, "Sometimes we do things unknowingly influenced by others. Lots of people do. And lots of people, beings, use that manipulation over others—that type of manipulation has been going on for millennia."

I said, "I'll give you that, but it seems almost contradictory to say that we are sometimes swayed in our decisions and then go on to deny that we ever exhibit free will at all. I mean, how can we be swayed in our decisions if we can't legitimately make decisions to start with?"

Percy said, "Actually, I agree with you. I believe that we have free will and that we are morally responsible for our actions. But I still think that we are all interconnected too. Somehow."

"Yeah," I said, "and I agree with you too. I wonder how all that works?"

She replied, "I don't know," and shook her head, opening her blue eyes widely.

Of course, I had no clue either. "But," I went on, "I guess that's one thing you lose when you die—your free will. Our disembodied ghosts are only performing the wills of others and no longer our own. That's part of what it's like to be dead, I guess."

Percy looked at me and said, "*Being* dead ... Oh, poor D."

"Well, talking about being dead," I asked a little too insensitively, "what are we going to do about D.'s ghost?"

Percy shot me a passing glance of distaste at my lack of reverence for the departed and said, "I guess we need to do something. We can't let all those that love him get hurt."

I asked, "Do you think we should go talk to it together? That way we may be more persuasive in dissuading it ... uh, him ... from attacking the monster."

She replied, "Maybe. But you and I have never met each other—uh, on purpose anyway—in the aethereal realm. How do we do that?"

"I don't know," I confessed. "But really, it shouldn't be that hard. You know how to contact D.'s ghost, and so do I. So that's where we'll meet—wherever that is."

"Okay," she said, "but we'll need to coordinate times. We should both try to contact D. at, say, eleven tonight."

"Okay," I said, "but I have a concert tonight. Better make it twelve o'clock midnight."

"You have a concert?" she asked.

"Yeah," I said, "I play oboe in the school orchestra."

"Oh," she said. "Math *and* music. You remind me of someone I once knew quite some time ago."

"Who's that?" I asked.

"Oh," she said, obviously wanting to change the subject, "it was someone I met in Samos, off the coast of Turkey, when my mom was working there. We just knew him casually, really."

I let it go and said, "So we're on for twelve o'clock midnight tonight?"

"Sure."

We still had a short distance to go in our walk, so I brought up the subject of how to ultimately deal with the monster. I said, "I guess we need to convince D.'s ghost not to attack the monster, but what *are* we going to do with that beast? We can't just let it hang around and destroy lives."

"That's for sure," Percy said. "But I don't know about killing it. You saw for yourself how horrible the violence can be. Isn't there something else we can do?"

I, too, was beginning to question the use of violence to stop violence—a feeling that betrayed and put into strong relief a formative and significant component of my childhood with D. We, D. and I, in our early youth, were prone to use violence upon itself. Violence was now beginning to me to seem simply nonefficacious in quelling violence. I was beginning to see violence as a never-ending cycle of revenge, and revenge just did not seem to equate to morality. I was starting to get a vague feeling that revenge was not a sufficiently solid foundation upon which to build the magnificent structure that is morality. In fact, revenge seemed antithetical to that modulating edifice. *No, revenge has no place in morality whatsoever,* I concluded in my own thoughts.

I hoped that my newfound views on the futility of revenge were not just a reaction of fear for my own personal safety due to the recent events. I did not feel like a coward, but I did not feel particularly brave either. Except for this last fear, I voiced these thoughts about the futility of revenge to Percy.

"Well," she said with a smile, "here we agree again. Revenge is just as bad as the original evil that spawned it."

If I had been thinking about it then, I would have thought that this last sentiment expressed by Percy virtually certified that she was no Greek goddess. The Greeks and their gods were consumed by their desire for revenge. Think of the motivation of "brave" Achilles in avenging the death of his best friend and lover Patroclus. Or consider the pathetic reason why Patroclus was led to his death in the first place—it was to seek revenge. In avenging his lover's death, "brave" Achilles killed the foremost Trojan warrior and statesman and dragged that defiled body behind his chariot around and around the gates of Troy. It was only the divinely directed arrow from Paris's bow that put an end to Achilles's hideous demonstration of his "bravery" by finding Achilles's unique vulnerability. For Paris's skilled archery, the Greeks sacked and completely destroyed the city of Troy, killing all of its men, raping all the women, enslaving all its children and burning that great cosmopolitan center of global trade to the ground. Troy never arose from its ashes. Some of the more partisan Greek gods continued this ugly cycle of vengeance by destroying the Greek navy in a terrible storm upon its fated attempt to return the "brave" Greeks home to their beloved Greece. Only Odysseus—one of the few Greeks to return to his homeland out of the tens of thousands who originally descended upon the lush Trojan shore to carry on a ten-year total war of utter destruction—was horrified by the indiscriminate Greek slaughter of the Trojans. Odysseus's odyssey home required another ten years of tribulations in reformation for his complicity in the sacking of glorious Troy. Agamemnon, another one of the very few Greeks to return home, met his own fate upon reuniting with his family. His wife, Clytemnestra, for her own vengeful reasons, promptly stabbed him in the back upon returning from his ten-year absence. Clytemnestra's children killed their own mother to avenge their father's murder, perpetuating the cycle. Overall, the Trojan expedition was not a good one for the Trojans or the Greeks.

For Percy to deny the morality of vengeance would have gone against all that the Ancient Greeks believed about morality. For the Greeks and their gods, virtue was seen as the ability to help one's friends and harm one's enemies. But if I had *really* been thinking about these issues back then, I would have also noted that successful, surviving gods (or, in this case, goddesses) were dynamic in their makeup and would represent the changing views of those truly existent sentient beings constituting the conversations sustaining the parasitic existence of their gods. After all, it was none other than an Ancient Greek who presaged this divine dynamism by expressing the notion that "if dogs and goats had gods, then those gods would look like dogs and goats!" But as it was, I was not having these thoughts when conversing and walking along the sunny beach with Percy that solemn day.

Percy continued, "But, really, what are we going to do about the monster? It is a great source of suffering, and it seems our obligation to lessen suffering if we can."

"I've been thinking about that," I said. "What if we blocked all of its voices from participating in its conversation? Then it would just disappear into the void," I suggested.

"That's not a form of violence?" she asked, raising an eyebrow.

"Not really. We just divert all of those voices and conversations, do them no lasting harm, and the beast disintegrates on its own!"

"The beast has an incredibly wide power base," protested Percy, expressing some doubt in my plan.

"Yeah," I said with some excitement. "It will take you, me, and D.'s ghost to do it. But I think it can be done. I can discuss the details of my plan when we meet with D.'s ghost, but it involves some risk on your part, and if you don't want to do it, I can totally understand."

"Let me hear your plan tonight, and I'll decide. I do want to help. But when we meet tonight, how are we going to protect ourselves from the beast? It could attack us at any moment, and you've said it will kill you on sight."

I pondered this existential question and said, "I never know what to do about that risk. I thought for a while that I had some sort of protective bubble, but that got blown to bits last night, so I guess it's not really much of a protection against the full rage of the evil beast. I guess we'll need to keep our conference with D.'s ghost as short as possible and return as quickly as we can to the solid world. Life in the hidden realm seems to always be on the edge."

"To say the least," added Percy.

We were now back at Percy's car, and she began unlocking the driver's-side door to get in. As she was squeezing herself into that tiny car, she said, "It's kind of strange, you know; we'll be talking to D. tonight, but he'll be largely us. We'll kind of be talking to ourselves."

"Yeah," I said as she shut the door and rolled down the window, "it's kind of weird. Hopefully there are no complications because of that."

Through the open car window, she said, "You're just spooked because of all that's been happening; it will be fine. We'll just need to keep level heads, and D. will be influenced by that. Good-bye, see you tonight!"

"Good-bye," I said.

I walked to my mom's car thinking that it would be a strange conversation indeed. My confidence in it going well was not as high as Percy's. *Maybe,* I thought to myself, *our conversation with D.'s ghost might turn out more like the ear-piercing screech of a microphone picking up noise from its own speaker. Besides, what about the monster?* Percy had a good point there. Maybe meeting Percy in the occult world was not such a good idea after all.

That night, at twelve o'clock midnight, I entered the aethereal realm once again and sought out D.'s ghost—and with it, Percy.

XVI

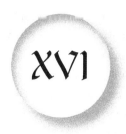

Plan For Killing the Beast

Upon entering the aethereal realm that night to meet Percy and D.'s ghost, I stumbled into a chaotic scene. My first sensation of the hidden realm that night was hearing Percy yelling, "No, D.! No! Let him go!" I looked around and saw Percy standing and shouting at D.'s ghost, who had a vile-looking creature by the throat, looking for all the world like a dog holding and shaking a skunk, not wanting to let go for fear of the skunk's noxious reprisal. "Let him go!" Percy shouted again.

D.'s ghost gave her a look as if to say, "You've got to be kidding me. Don't you know what this thing will do to us as soon as I let it go!"

I was not absolutely convinced that the best course of action *was* to release the creature, but I assumed that Percy must have had a good reason for her demand, so I also shouted "Let it go, D!"

D's ghost looked back and forth between Percy and me, shrugged its shoulders, and released the vile creature. At that moment, I realized that I had seen this creature before. It was the violent warrior that had attacked me in my foxhole. It was one of the avian-reptilian beast's more powerful minions.

As soon as D.'s ghost released the creature, the varmint turned to me, gave a hint of recognition, expelled an evil, enveloping smell, and ran away, trailing its greenish stench behind it as it vanished into the void. I assumed it was running away to rejoin its master. If so, I was sure that it would convey to that monster our whereabouts, wherever that was.

D.'s ghost gave us a nasty look through the foul-smelling green aura enveloping us, as if to say, "I told you."

Percy, after a severe bout of coughing, still holding her nose with her eyes steaming tears, said, "D., we need to talk to you about your attacking the monster."

D.'s ghost's demeanor perked up, and it excitedly asked, "You're going to help me kill it?"

Also holding my nose, I said, "Well, yes and no." D.'s ghost looked at me suspiciously. "We don't have much time; we have to make this quick. The creature you had there is one of the voices—conversations, really—of the evil beast. I recognized it just now from that fight the other night between the dragons. I think it is going to alert the monster to our presence here right now." Percy gave a sharp intake of breath and began coughing again.

D.'s ghost indignantly said, "I know it is a conversation of the beast's. I recognized it, and I ambushed it. I was going to kill it, but you two got in the way and stopped me. That was silly."

"Okay," I said, "I think we are thinking along the same lines here. We're going to kill the beast, as you want, but we're not going to attack it directly, as it seems you've figured out too."

D.'s ghost said, "So we're going to kill all of its voices and conversations! Cool! But then, why'd you make me let go of that jerk?"

Percy interjected, "No, we're not going to kill all of the beast's constituent voices and conversations." D.'s ghost looked puzzled. Percy turned to me and said, "Okay, tell us your plan."

I said, "It's going to take all three of us." Percy and the ghost looked willing but skeptical. I continued, "Percy, you were pretty impressive with that heat shield thing." She shrugged. I asked, "Do you think you could distract the monster while D. and I work on its constituent voices and conversations?"

She looked concerned and said, "Maybe. I don't know. How long will I have to be doing that?"

"I don't know," I admitted, "But if all goes well, then the power of the monster will be continually diminishing as D. and I isolate its voices and conversations. That should help. The worst part will be at the very beginning."

"Okay," she said, "I think I can do that."

I turned to D.'s ghost. "Apparently you know something about finding the beast's individual voices and conversations."

"Yeah?" replied the ghost in a drawn-out response that ended sounding like a question.

I expanded upon my observation. "I want you to identify individual voices and conversations, and then knock them out of the overall conversation of the beast and direct them to me. Think of it like when you used to hit homers in our afternoon baseball games. You'll be knocking homers to me in the outfield. Do you think you can do that?"

D.'s ghost met my last question with pride and excitement in his eyes. "You bet!"

Percy turned to me and asked, "But then what are you going to do with all of these evil voices and conversations. They'll gang up on you and kill you just as surely as the beast would. What's to stop them from coalescing again into the monster?"

"Well, that's the thing," I said. "I don't want D. to knock them out to me too quickly. We need some time between me catching each one. My idea is that when I see one coming my way, I'll throw a protective bubble around it and cast it out into the aether. That way it won't be able to rejoin its master—for a while anyway. I don't know how long those bubbles really last, so we need to be quick overall. But, we can't be too quick, 'cause I can only handle one at a time. And then again, we need to be sure you don't get tired out there in front of the beast, distracting it. It's a tight balance we'll need to find. Are you sure you're okay with that? It's kind of dangerous. I guess we can trade places if you like."

Percy thought about my plan and said, "I don't think we *can* trade places. I don't know how to create those protective bubbles of yours. That ability seems pretty unique to you. And I don't think you know how to make one of my heat shield things, as you call them."

"Yeah, that's what I was thinking," I said.

D.'s ghost said with mounting enthusiasm, "But I sure know how to knock the shit out of those voices and conversations. Man, this is gonna be fun!" Percy and I both gave D.'s ghost a concerned stare.

I said, "Okay. Well, it sounds like we've got a plan. We just need to decide when the best time to do it is."

D.'s ghost impatiently said, "Let's go right now. I'm ready to knock around some heads."

I was starting to wonder who the sentient beings were that sustained D.'s ghost. As Percy had mentioned earlier that day, her and my unconscious images of D. largely constituted D.'s ghost. I could not deny that I deeply wanted to obliterate that avian-reptilian evil beast right on the spot. Perhaps Percy thought the same way. Maybe this was an example of that feedback mechanism that I feared animated D.'s ghost. In fact, D.'s ghost turned around and started to follow the odoriferous trail of the foul-smelling minion that had recently vacated our presence.

Percy put out her hand and stopped D.'s ghost's progress. "No," she said. "We need to think this through and be rational about this."

"But," D.'s ghost protested, "we know that ugly creature was on its way to get the monster. We have no time to lose. We've got to act now, right away. It's stupid just standing around and discussing this—especially when we know what we're going to do to it."

"Well, that's the thing," I said softly, "I still don't literally know what I'm going to do to it."

Both Percy and the ghost looked at me, bewildered.

"What do you mean?" asked Percy.

"Well," I said, "I know we've been talking about me throwing protective bubbles around the individual voices and conversations that make up the substance of the monster. The thing is, I still don't know what I'm doing when I do it."

D.'s ghost shot out, "Oh, god!" Percy looked at me, terrified.

"I'll be okay," I said. "I can do it, I know. But I'd like to feel better about it all, if I could."

Percy asked me how I intended to go about getting a better feel about it. I replied, "I know we don't have much time. At any time, the monster could cause some real suffering for many people, not just us. But I think I'd like to visit Sage. Resident Teacher told me that maybe Sage could explain how I'm constructing those bubbles. Maybe with its help I could sharpen my skills and make some that really work." I paused to get their reactions.

D.'s ghost rolled its gigantic head and looked up. Percy grew pensive and calmly asked, "You plan to visit Sage?"

"Yeah," I said.

She pursed her lips and asked, "Do you mind if I come along with you?"

I was not expecting this request. I thought about it for a second and said, "No, not at all. You are welcome to join me. Have you heard of Sage somewhere?"

Percy looked evasive and said, "Oh, I think you mentioned Sage once when talking about Resident Teacher. Sage sounds interesting is all."

I could not remember having mentioned Sage to Percy, but I let that conundrum pass. "Okay," I said, addressing Percy, "You and I can discuss that visit in the relative safety of the real world soon after we return to it." Turning to D.'s ghost, I said, "And you have to promise us that you won't go off on your own and attack the monster or any of its minions. You do understand the danger here, don't you? Your family could suffer serious harm."

Percy added for emphasis, "Yeah, you really can't do that. Think of your family. I need you to promise me that you won't go after that beast on your own. This is serious."

D.'s ghost looked rebellious at first but then gave in. "Okay. I promise. For my family." Sweetly looking at Percy, it added, "And for you." Percy smiled broadly in return and nodded her golden head.

Just then all began to freeze and grow dark. The ground shook with tremors of approaching enormous footsteps. I could smell a sulfur stench, mixed with an electrical element. D.'s ghost and I exchanged knowing and terrified looks. Percy groaned, "Oh no! It's coming." We saw flashes in the distance, associated with the pounding and shaking of the foundation upon which we were situated. I felt the intense burn of an instantaneous flash and lost consciousness.

My first sensation after losing consciousness—I have no way of knowing how long I was out—was that of choking and being unable to breathe. I was being tumbled about in an icy stream, with the frigid water filling my mouth and lungs. Just the intense cold of the water was almost enough to stop me from breathing. Occasionally, far too occasionally, my head would bob above the frothy surface seemingly at random and I would be given an instant to gasp for breath before I would again be drawn down into the violent turbulence of that raging watercourse. I was tumbling head over heels, my arms and legs a whirling mess of confusion. Suddenly I smashed into a huge slippery boulder, causing me to cry out and again fill my lungs with water. I fought my way to the churning surface to spit out the water in my lungs, and I saw downstream a massive rapid. It boiled with water as it crashed against still larger boulders. Somehow I was now wearing a life vest and a protective helmet over my previously exposed skull. I was pulled down below the surface again by the sucking current. The newly emergent life vest helped propel me back to the surface of that urgent stream. The quickly approaching rapid towered over me. I was sucked down a chute of boiling water and tumbled about below the surface. I regained the surface, coughing. I had no time to attempt to rise above the aethereal realm and reenter the safety of the real world. All my attention was now being given to trying not to drown.

After being crushed against another huge rock, I bounced back into the rapidity of the central stream. I caught a glimpse of Percy standing upon a flat boulder, calling out to me. She had her arms outstretched in order to catch me as I was about to pass near her, propelled by the raging current. I kicked as hard as I could, and the motion of my efforts and the swift current combined to push me over to where Percy stood waiting. My trajectory indicated that I was going to pass where she stood, just close enough for our outstretched hands to meet with only an inch to spare. I was pushed down into the drink again, rising just in time for our hands to clench firmly around one another.

After a long struggle against the current, Percy was finally able to pull me up to the safety of the rock. Icy water swiftly swirled around us on all sides. I lay there on my stomach, slightly raised by my arms. I was shivering and coughing, retching up the water from my lungs, and trying to catch my breath. The rock felt just as cold as the water from which I had just been saved. After expelling the lion's share of the water from my lungs, I turned over on my back and looked up at the sky. It was ominously dark. I lay there shivering, stunned into silence.

Finally I tamed my heavy breathing and turned to Percy. She had been silently watching me through my lengthy recovery. "What happened?" I asked.

"I don't know. But I think the monster blew us up," she replied.

I looked around and asked, "Where's D.'s ghost?"

"I don't know. The last I saw of him, he was being chased by the monster. I hope he's okay."

"Maybe that's why the monster didn't finish us off. It was distracted by D.'s ghost."

"Maybe," she agreed.

"Wow, I'm really banged up," I said, feeling my body and massaging my injuries. Collecting my wits, I looked up at Percy and said, "Gee, you've saved me again! How did you do that? How did you happen to be here?"

"I don't know. I just was. Lucky, huh?" she responded.

I looked intently at her. "Boy, you bet! Lucky!" I said as I noticed that I was no longer wearing a life vest or protective helmet.

Percy asked, "Do you think you can now get back to the real world?"

"Yeah, I think so. I was just overwhelmed by the rapids. But I think I can get back."

"Good," she said. "Then I think we should do so. There's no telling when that monster will find you—us—again."

"Yeah, we can connect in the real world and discuss how we are going to seek out Sage."

"Yes. I'm curious to see what Sage has to say about the construction of those protective bubbles of yours. One may have been useful just now."

I was embarrassed by the obviousness of her suggestion and replied, "Yeah, and I also want to ask it about my dream."

"What dream?"

"I'll tell you about it in the real world," I suggested.

"Okay."

"Okay. Good-bye. I'll give you a call a little later in the real world?"

"Sure. Good-bye," she said, and I ascended back to the solid realm of my parents' home. I lay there in my bed and thought about what I needed to ask of Sage. I hoped that Percy had gotten safely out of the aethereal realm, and I was very much concerned for D.'s ghost.

XVII

Visiting Sage

As soon as I could, I gave Percy a call using that strange telephone number of hers that seemed to remind me of something I could not quite remember. She answered and immediately said, "Oh, I'm glad you called. I was worried that maybe you hadn't made it back."

I said, "How did you know this was me calling you?"

"Well," she said, "I didn't think it could be anyone else."

"How about someone from your mom's work?" I followed up, intrigued.

"It's not really the right time for someone to be calling my mom. Anyway, we need to talk about visiting Sage."

I moved on. "Okay, we need to figure out how we're both going to contact Sage together."

"First tell me about that dream of yours. I'm curious to know what you are going to be asking Sage about."

I took the time to explain my dream to her in detail. She was impressed. "Wow, that's pretty cool," she said. "Not many people get to have a dream like that. You're sure you're not making some of this up, maybe by mistake just exaggerating a little?" I attested that that was, in fact, the exact content of my dream. "Wow," she said, "What do you want to ask Sage about this dream?"

"Well, I'm intrigued by the notion that love and hate are in eternal conflict, and that that conflict is what creates the material world. Really, I'm not so much interested in how that conflict creates the material world, to tell you the truth, though that is a cool idea, but I'm more interested in knowing why love and hate are in eternal conflict. I mean, what's the point? And, isn't there some way out of that conflict? It just seems to me that that vision is extremely pessimistic. Is there no end to conflict and suffering in the world?"

"Nice question," Percy sighed.

"Let's talk about how we are going to contact Sage," I requested.

"Okay," Percy agreed. "How did you go about contacting Resident Teacher the first time?" I had to admit that I was not altogether sure how I had done that. "But you did do it," she stated. "Maybe we just do something similar for contacting Sage."

"We can try. But if we don't contact Sage right away, and we end up somewhere else in the aethereal realm, then we need to agree to immediately return to the solid world. Agreed?"

"Yes."

I went on. "What should I do if I contact Sage and you're not there? I really don't want to miss an opportunity to talk to Sage."

"I'll be there."

I thought about her sanguine response for just a moment and said, "Okay. Then let's set a time." We then set a time for late that night to contact Sage together in the occult realm.

That night, at the appointed time, when all was quiet in my parents' home, I entered the aethereal realm yet again and sought out Sage. In trying to contact Sage, I was not too sure what I was literally looking for or what to expect if I succeeded.

I found myself sitting in an open and airy one-room teahouse constructed mostly of bamboo and cedar wood. I was seated cross-legged upon a mat woven of split palm fronds on the floor across a short table from what was presented to me as a very old person. This person had long gray hair pulled back in a ponytail. It was Sage. For being so old, Sage appeared quite healthy, verging upon a robust skinniness. I could not tell if the visualization of Sage was male or female; it did not seem to matter. Percy was seated cross-legged to my right at the table, to Sage's left.

"Ah," said Sage in a very pleasant voice when it first noticed my presence before it, "I was wondering when you would pay me a visit." Sage looked to its left and said, "And you too? Interesting." Sage sat quietly for a moment and then elegantly and very formally poured us all scalding hot tea from a small teapot into tiny, rough clay teacups with no handles. The three open cups were steaming profusely with the hot tea. Sage sipped that scalding tea and asked me, "But did you not have a question for me?"

I was still trying to become adjusted to my new surroundings and did not have the wherewithal to venture an immediate answer to its question. It went on. "Oh yes, I remember the question you originally posed to that local yachtsman. You began to discuss that question with Resident Teacher as well, and then he referred you to me. You wanted to know what this is all about. Wasn't that your question—'What is this all about?'" It produced a small chuckle. Percy gave me a look of wonder, surprised at the revelation of my utter naïveté in having asked such an inane question.

I coughed, picked up my cup, and felt the hot tea through the thin clay sides. I decided not to scald my mouth and set the cup back down again. I looked at Percy with some embarrassment, turned to Sage, and said, "Uh ... I'm hoping I've refined my question a bit. I'm finding that things are, uh, more complicated than I first imagined. So, if you don't mind, I'd like to ask some other questions ... if you don't mind."

"What?" said Sage, raising its right bushy eyebrow with what I took to be mock surprise. "I think your original question is perfectly fine: 'What is it all about?' And you'll be happy to know that I can give you a very simple answer to that very complex question."

Sage smiled broadly and took another sip of its tea, watching me over its cup and causing hot steam to waft up its nose. It lowered the cup and blew the steam back out of its nose while I tried to take in what it had just told me. After a polite pause, I asked somewhat skeptically, "You can answer *that* question?"

"Sure," said Sage. "The answer to the question of what this is all about is ... nothing."

I sat in amazement. Looking around me, I wondered if I was in the right place. I felt that maybe, upon entering the hidden realm, I had found some quack instead of Sage. But Percy was there too, so I knew this must be the real Sage. In fact, Percy was staring at me as if it were now my turn to say something profound. I shook my head and blurted out, "You mean all of this is not about anything at all?"

Sage sat very quietly, looked me straight in the eyes, and said, "I didn't say that. I said that it is all about nothing." Sage smiled again and waited for my reply.

I was not sure how to take this paradoxical statement from Sage. I was beginning to feel that, as with Resident Teacher, I was again wasting precious time. Sage gave no indication that it was reading my mind. It sat patiently and turned to give Percy a warm smile. Percy returned a somewhat hesitant and bewildered smile to that ancient and venerable soul and then resumed staring straight before her.

I took the bait. "Well then, if this is all about nothing, then what are we doing? Why all the suffering, evil, violence, killing, and all? Surely that is anything but nothing!"

"Oh," said Sage, "I couldn't agree more with you on that. *Suffering* definitely is real. But suffering *really* is all about *nothing*."

"But if suffering is real, then how can you say this is all about nothing?" I demanded.

"Let me illustrate with a simple picture, if you don't mind indulging an old umbra like myself," said Sage while it took a hefty pinch of dry deep orange pigment from its calligraphy tray and spread it evenly over a large portion of the elegant black-lacquered tea table. With its right index finger, Sage drew two squares in the orange dust, one on top of the other, offset by about half the length of one side of the squares. It then connected the corners of the squares with straight lines. The figure it drew looked like this:

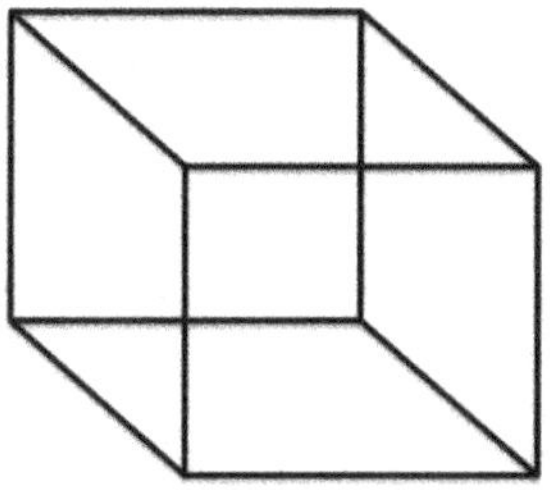

After drawing the figure, Sage seemed pleased with itself and quietly stared at the figure for some time without moving a single muscle. It finally nodded to itself in satisfaction and looked up at me. "Do you see these two squares here that I've drawn?"

"Yes," I said.

"And do you notice that by connecting these corners I've made a single cube out of the two squares?"

"Yes," I said again.

"Good. Now concentrate on that cube. I want you to see the cube so that it is coming up to the left, out of the table."

It waited patiently until I said, "Okay." I did not see the point of the exercise so far. The way Sage had drawn the cube it seemed that it of course came up out of the table, up to the left. That was the cube that Sage had drawn.

After the longest time, Sage then said, "Now I want you to change how you see the cube. Instead of seeing it coming up out of the table and to the left, I want you to see it coming up out of the table and down to the lower right." I thought that that was a strange request; the cube, as it had been drawn, was obviously coming up out of the table and up to the left. "Concentrate," said Sage.

I gave it a good try, and to my amazement I was now seeing a different cube where the first had been. The new cube was indeed coming up out of the table and down to the lower right. "Oh," I said, "I see it."

"Okay," said Sage, "now see that first cube again." I did. "Now see the other cube again," said Sage. I did that too. We went back and forth like this until Sage gave out a wonderful laugh and slapped Percy strongly on the back. Apparently Sage was happy that we were all in on the joke.

I stared at Sage. Percy collected herself, wiped some spilled tea off of her chin, and also stared at Sage. Sage, still smiling broadly, then said, "Okay, now I want you to see the cube as going *down* out of the table and to the lower right." I tried to see that image too and finally succeeded. "Now, finally," said Sage, "try seeing the cube going down out of the table and up to the left!" It laughed heartily. Percy gave a wince, expecting to be slapped on the back again. I tried and finally succeeded in seeing that image as well. I was becoming bored with the exercise and did not see its point.

Sage said, "Patience is one of the two most important of virtues," and nodded knowingly at me, opening its eyes widely. I wondered what Sage would say was the other of the two most important virtues, but he remained mute on that matter. Sage picked up the teapot and asked, "More tea?"

I declined, but Percy said, "Yes please," and sat there quietly, not moving. Sage took its time pouring out more tea for itself and for Percy. I tried to remain patient and waited to see what Sage was going to make of all of this. I was beginning to think that this was a whole lot of to-do about nothing.

Sage smiled and laughed. "Think of that first cube you saw. Let's name it cube 1. The next cube you saw we'll name cube 2. And so on. Do you understand?"

"Sure," I said.

"What are you doing when you change from seeing cube 1 to seeing cube 2?"

I figured this was some sort of trick question and a test, so I took a little time in thinking out an answer. With nothing obvious coming to mind concerning the subtlety of the question, I just went with an easy reply, "I'm changing perspectives on how I see it."

"Ah," said Sage, "but changing perspectives means that you are looking at it from a different position, and I didn't see you change your position. You were sitting right there, rather still the whole time. So this can't be a matter of simply changing between different perspectives."

"Well," I said, "not physically. But I changed perspectives mentally."

Sage smiled. "Okay, so we know that seeing cube 1 as opposed to cube 2 is not determined by anything particularly physical. After all, they are both caused by the same physical sensation. But what are you doing when you switch from seeing cube 1 to cube 2—when you are changing mental perspectives, as you say?"

I shrugged my shoulders and said, "I don't know; I'm just seeing one or the other cube."

Sage sat quietly again for some time. It finally said, "Okay. Then let me ask you another question. Where is cube 1, or cube 2, or the others?"

"Where are they?" I repeated. "Well," I reasoned, "we just demonstrated that they are not physical, so I guess they exist in my mind only. My mind imposed those cubes onto the world; they really aren't there to begin with."

"Just so," said Sage. "So they really do not exist; they are just made up. They are essentially nothings." Sage paused and then continued.

"And that is what all the suffering and violence are about—a lot of nothings." It smiled, noticed that my tea was gone, and asked me, "More tea?"

I accepted more tea and was quiet. I was not entirely satisfied with Sage's point about suffering being about nothing, or a lot of nothings. I voiced my concern. "Okay, I can see your point for simple things like cubes, but most suffering in the world is about much more important things than mere imaginary cubes. There's death, disease, depression, violence. I mean, suffering, for everyone, is *really* serious. It's not just some geometrical puzzle."

Sage gave me an appreciative look and said, "Ah, the second of the two most important virtues. Very good!" I did not know how to respond because I did not know what Sage was talking about. "Compassion," it simply said.

"Oh," I said, still not knowing exactly what it was talking about.

Sage, responding to my confusion, said, "Yes, the suffering in the world is very serious indeed. But it is still all based upon a multitude of nothings. I think you'll find that most consciousnesses are practically filled to the brim with a lot of nothingnesses." He smiled again and winked at Percy. Percy, not entirely sure what to do, smiled back. Sage, addressing Percy, said, "You are very quiet."

Percy simply replied, "Yes," and sat with her hands palms up on her lap, staring at the steam rising from her teacup, which was situated slightly in front of her on the black-lacquered table the surface of which was covered in bright orange powder. This powder seemed almost fluorescent where a beam of sunlight hit the tabletop. Dust motes quietly danced aloft in that beam of sunlight. Sage gave out a huge laugh.

I was growing fidgety. My legs were starting to ache from sitting crossed-legged on the floor. I could not see where all of this was going. Hearing crows cawing outside the teahouse, I was becoming concerned, wondering if this sanctuary was safe from the monster.

Unexpectedly, Sage abruptly inquired of me, "Do unicorns exist?"

"What?"

"Do unicorns exist? Do you understand my question?"

"No," I said. "I don't know why you are asking me if unicorns exist."

Sage patiently explained, "I didn't ask you if you knew why I was asking you that question about unicorns. I'm simply asking you if you understood what I was asking you. Do you understand the question 'Do unicorns exist'?" I thought over what Sage had just asked and had to admit that I did understand that simple question. "Well, do they?" it insisted.

"No," I said.

Sage chuckled. "Now we're getting somewhere." I did not share its optimism. "Well, you do see that my question was meaningful, had a particular meaning, and was a real question? I wasn't just spouting a series of meaningless sounds like 'blah, blah, blah, blah, blah.'"

"Okay," I reluctantly conceded, "I understood the question to be about unicorns and whether or not they really do exist".

"Good," it said. "Well, how did you know what I was asking you if, in fact, unicorns do not really exist? Don't words—especially words that function in the way 'unicorn' functions—need to refer to something in order to be meaningful? And what else would 'unicorn' refer to but unicorns? But since unicorns don't exist, then the term 'unicorn' can't possibly refer to them. Thus the term is meaningless, and thus the whole question within which that meaningless word is embedded becomes meaningless. If all of this is right, then the question would be just like saying 'blah, blah, blah, blah, blah.'" Sage loudly slapped its thigh five times in synchronicity with the "blahs" and laughed unabashedly. I stared at it.

It was Sage's turn to collect itself, and it said, "How do we even talk about nothings? How do we truly deny the existence of anything? If that thing doesn't exist in the first place, then how can we refer to it in order to deny its existence?"

"I don't know." I shrugged. "We just do."

Sage responded, "Yes, we certainly do! And that's the whole point of the matter!" At length it calmed itself down again and asked, "More tea?"

"Okay," said Sage, looking at Percy. "Take, for example, a chariot." It briefly looked me over. "Or, maybe better, a car. If you were meeting with someone and this person said he or she had arrived at the meeting in a car, you would know perfectly well what the person was talking about, yes?'

"Yes," I said.

"But," Sage said, "let's take a careful look at this car. Is it the wheels?"

"No," I said.

"Is it the fenders?"

"No."

"Is it the engine?"

"No," I said again, wondering how detailed Sage's knowledge of the engineering of cars would turn out to be and how long this line of questioning was going to continue.

"So," asked Sage, "the car is not any one of those things, or even any one of all the other things that separately make up a car?"

"No," I said, "it would be silly to think so."

"Yes," said Sage. "Is the car a pile of all of those things together?"

"No, that's silly also."

"Yes," said Sage, "It would be silly to think so. But what's not so silly is to say that the car is also not all of those parts put together in their proper positions."

"In fact, that last statement of yours *does* seem silly to me; the car most certainly *is* all of those things in the pile put together in their proper positions."

"Yes, I can see why you might say that. But consider this. What if we put all the parts together again but left out just one piece? Would it not be the car?'

"Of course it would. It would just be missing one piece," I said.

"Right," Sage said, "In fact, we could put the car together in many different ways, leaving out just this one piece, and then leaving out just this other piece, etc. In each case, we would say we ended up with the car. So the car is not *all* the pieces put together in their proper positions. Now there are a multitude of things we correctly call the car, but still there is only one car."

"Oh," I said.

Sage sat for a very long time this time and then asked, "So where is that one car?"

I also sat for a very long time before answering, "It's visiting with cube 1."

Sage shot out an explosive laugh, blowing all the orange dust off the black tabletop. It also slapped Percy again, spilling her tea all over her lap. "Yes, yes, yes!" it said excitedly. It then grew more sober. "I understand you are claiming that there is a difference between a living person and a ghost?"

I was shocked at the accuracy of its intelligence gathering but more shocked at what I took to be an abrupt change in topic. I replied, "Percy and I were discussing that, yes."

Sage was not looking at Percy but continued to stare at me and asked, "You said the difference between you as a living person and your ghost was that unique thing that made you your self. So I'd like you to look inside of yourself and find that self. Please do so now. I'll wait." I thought I was being made fun of and started to object to its request. Sage held up a hand and said, "I'm serious. Take a good look inside and tell me what you see … After all, you did ask D.'s ghost to do the very same thing." Again I was shocked at Sage's intelligence gathering, and then I began to introspect.

I do not know how long I searched; it seemed like forever. Finally I said, "I've searched and searched, and I can find no one thing that is my self."

Sage said, "Well, I'm sure you've got a lot more searching ahead of you before you can come to a definitive answer on that, but you do see my point, don't you?'

I confessed, "No, not really."

"I can understand that," it said. "But some say there is no self. What we are talking about when we refer to our selves is nothing more than something like cube 1, or that poor car we have been dismantling and haphazardly putting back together. We use the term 'self' just as a convenient designation. It gets the point across but does not really refer to any one thing, or even to a group of things, just as we use the term 'car' to refer to that car."

"Okay," I said, trying hard to make sense of all of this. I was grasping for a way to bring the discussion back to the view that suffering is due to consciousnesses being filled to the top with a lot of nothings.

"Well," added Sage, "if convenient designation is the mechanism of reference and meaning for talking about our selves, or about cars, or even in denying the existence of unicorns, then, some say, it is the mechanism we use for referring to anything. Why should the mechanism of reference differ just because the objects referred to differ?" It waited for a response from me. Not finding a timely response, it continued. "So *every* reference is empty. There is no end of the referential line for any term. They are all a bunch of nothings. Get it?"

I was starting to get the point. We all strive for happiness by grasping after one thing or another, but none of those things really exist, so we are never satisfied. The world is full of nothings. More to the point, the world is full of nothings that we have created in our own minds and then go about endlessly chasing, condemned to eternal failure in attempting to grasp those nonexistent objects of our desire!

"So," I asked, going back to one of the questions that I had originally planned to ask Sage in the first place, "If the world is just a creation of our own minds, then why can't I just make up a new world where evil and suffering don't exist?" Upon asking my question, a short stick materialized over me and gave me a sharp crack on the crown of my head. "Ow!" I cried, "What was that?" Sage just shrugged. I indignantly regained my composure and repeated my question. Again the stick came down sharply upon my head. Rubbing my crown, I figured there was something about my question that Sage thought inappropriate.

"Oh, right," I said. "There is suffering in the world, sometimes as insignificant as getting whacked on the head, and that suffering is telling us something."

Sage smiled broadly and asked, "And what is the lesson of suffering?"

I had now gained enough experience with Sage to know there was no good answer to its question, and glancing up in case I needed to dodge another stick descending upon my head, I said, "Ah—that all is not nothing; there is something after all?"

"Okay, and what is that something?" it asked with a mischievous look.

An inspiration shot through me, and I offered, "I can't say. Anything I can say, talk, or think about is a nothing. But that something that we can't talk about is there; it's real."

Sage slightly closed its eyes and rested comfortable and satisfied upon its crossed legs. It reminded me of a contented cat.

I was intrigued now and had almost entirely forgotten about the monster. I pondered and then conjectured, "So all we can really do is focus upon our direct experiences, not filtered through our concepts or impositions upon the world. We need to live in the here and now."

Sage opened its eyes and began trying to grasp the steam rising above its teacup. It would grasp a waft of steam in a clenched fist, open the fist, and look forlornly at the emptiness in its open hand. It did this over and over. After watching it for some time, I asked it what it was doing. "I'm trying to grasp the steam in my hand."

I offered, "You can't. That's impossible."

Sage smiled, quitted his ineffectual exercise and said, "Just so, you will likewise never be able to grasp the here and now. Those terms—'here' and 'now'—are convenient designators too, are they not?"

"So to live in the here and now I need to not focus upon the here and now?" I asked.

"Just so," responded Sage.

Just then I thought about the monster again. "How does all of this help with the monster?" I asked.

"I'm not sure; that's up to you," replied Sage. I groaned, and Percy looked away, scanning our surroundings outside the teahouse, worried. Sage hastily added, "But there is a little more here that may help tie all of this together for you, and it just maybe *could* be helpful in your endeavors."

I sat expectantly.

"What I have in mind," said Sage, "goes back to the meaning we give to terms and how we learn those meanings." Hearing these last words from Sage made my heart sink, but I continued to sit and listen. "Suppose someone were trying to teach you his native language. His language is as wholly unfamiliar to you as your language is wholly unfamiliar to him. To get started on the lessons, he points to a rabbit and says loudly, 'Gavagai!' What would you take the term 'gavagai' to mean in his language?"

I quickly responded, "When he says 'gavagai,' he means what we mean by the term 'rabbit.'"

"Oh," said Sage, "Couldn't he just as well have meant 'undetached rabbit parts' or even 'rabbit temporal stage?'"

"But that's just being silly again," I said. "He clearly means 'rabbit.' The meaning of the two words is the same. The spoken words are just labels attached to the same meanings."

Sage raised its eyebrows and asked, "But are the meanings just the same? How do we know that? Aren't the words just convenient designators, as we discussed before? If so, then the words could be designating very different things for the two speakers."

"Yeah, I guess," I admitted.

Sage nodded. "If that is the case, then the teacher of the new language and you could effectively be living in completely different worlds, created by completely different meanings to your words. *You'd never know that you were in those different worlds,* because you systematically mistranslate his language into your own by imposing your own ideas upon his language. One world would be composed of things like rabbits, and the other world could be composed of things like rabbit temporal stages."

"Okay," I said uneasily.

"But we can take this even further," said Sage. "Even for two speakers of the *same* language, there is no way to tell if we are referring to the same things with our use of that language. There is just our linguistic behavior to go on to help us here. That behavior, however, is not enough to guarantee that you are both talking about the same things. There is an indeterminacy of translation between speakers of the same language, just as there is an indeterminacy of translation between speakers of different languages."

"Okay," I said.

"Oh!" I said a second later. "We are all living in worlds of our own creation again!" I saw the stick reappear above my head and quickly added, "Except that we are not!" The stick disappeared without striking me.

"So," said Sage, "Maybe all of this can help you with your problem."

I was incredulous, and I demanded, "How?"

Sage calmly said, "Well, you'll have to figure that out for yourself. The monster is *your* problem, after all." I was fuming. "But I will say this, and it follows from the indeterminacy of translation. I know you are familiar with these two words I'm going to now use, but I'm not so sure you have put them together yet: ontological relativity. There is an ontological relativity between consciousnesses, even when they exist in the same universe." I did not know what to make of Sage's comment. It went on. "Two consciousnesses can be living in completely different worlds, populated with completely different things—different ontologies—while at the same time interacting relative to one another in the same universe!" Sage gave me a knowing look. I was still furious. I searched for something that would actually help me deal with my monster of suffering.

"So," I said out of frustration, "we contacted you because I wanted to ask you about what my protective bubble is and how I can make it stronger."

"Oh, good, an easier question," it said. "Your 'bubble,' as you call it, is your pure will. It just manifests to you as a bubble. By the way, its appearance to you as a bubble is a case of ontological relativity again." Noticing my frustration, it went on, "Regardless of that, you make it stronger by making your will stronger." I was not convinced this was a more easily understood answer.

"But how can I make it stronger?" I beseeched.

"You have to make your will more powerful. You need to strengthen your willpower. It's a matter of discipline. Discipline is good if for nothing else than developing your willpower."

"If I choose some discipline, any at all, then by practicing that discipline, I can strengthen my willpower and, hence, my protective bubble?" I asked.

"You'll want to choose a discipline that doesn't cause you or anyone else any suffering. Otherwise, in the long run, it will be self-defeating. There're actually not as many risk-free disciplines as you may at first think."

"Right," I said, thinking that instead of being concerned with the long run I rather needed a short-term fix to my monster problem.

I moved on. "Actually, I wanted to ask you another question also—one about a dream I had recently," I said to Sage. Percy sat up straighter.

Sage said excitedly, "Oh, good. I really liked your dream—especially that part where you learned the pattern of the waves and surfed them in to shore!"

I grimaced and wondered how it had detailed knowledge of my dream. *What* is *private in this realm anyway?* I then asked my question, not expecting any useful answer. "The part of the dream I have a question about is where love and hate are in eternal conflict. That doesn't seem right to me. Why would love and hate be continually at war with one another?"

Sage poured us all some more tea, set down the small yet eternally full and scalding teapot and asked, "And you're thinking that love is the sort of thing that shouldn't be in conflict with anything at all—not even hate?"

"That's my question! Why would love conflict with anything—even hate?" I animatedly asked.

Sage shrugged. "I don't know. It's *your* dream. Ontological relativity, remember?"

"So this dream doesn't necessarily represent the genesis of the world?" I asked, hoping for a negative response.

Sage quickly shot back, "Maybe it represents the genesis of somebody's world. It doesn't have to be *yours*." In an odd way, with this last statement, a lot of what Sage had been saying was beginning to fall together and make some sense. I was beginning to see how all of this could help in ultimately defeating the monster. Percy gave me a quizzical look, trying to discern my dawning insight.

I sat and pondered and considered our freedom of will to create our own ontological spaces while all the time living in a shared universe. Could we not choose the ontologies populating our worlds by an act of will, just like choosing to see cube 1 as opposed to seeing cube 2? Even though there was an invariant reality out there in the world somewhere—to which the existence of suffering bore witness—did we not have great license to create the world we chose to live within? Sage continued to stare at me; Percy continued to stare at the steam rising from her teacup.

It seemed it all came down to a matter of freedom of the will. But that was problematic. If the party-line theory of consciousness was true, then there were plenty of reasons to think that our wills were not entirely our own. I said out loud, "It comes down to a matter of will. But do we really have free will?"

Sage immediately responded, "Why would you think that you don't?"

"Well," I conjectured, "there are so many influences upon us: teachers, parents, the media, and so on. The messages from all of those sources get internalized, and my will gets hopelessly confused and corrupted."

Sage kindly rebuked me. "But those sources don't necessarily need to unduly influence you. You can be strong in the face of those forces and exercise your own will. The existence of these influential sources is not a decisive argument against the existence of freedom of the will. They are more a warning to you that you need to be careful in the exercise thereof. How could these corrupting sources influence your free will if your will wasn't free to begin with?" The point Sage was making sounded strikingly similar to the one I had espoused to Percy upon one of our walks.

"But," I said in exasperation, "there are other, better arguments against freedom of the will."

Sage queried, "What do you think is the single best argument against the existence of free will?"

I thought about its question for some time and replied, "I guess the best argument against free will is based upon scientific determinism. The argument is that everything in the physical universe is caused, or determined. It's based upon the notion that if we had a complete knowledge of the present, then, added to our knowledge of true causal laws, any future state is determined and can be predicted by that complete knowledge of the present. Our actions are part of the physical universe, so our actions are so determined as well. So we don't really have free will. We're doomed to follow the course of action dictated by past circumstances and causal laws."

Sage looked at me with some appreciation and said, "You can see,

I hope, that there are a couple of very important assumptions in that argument for determinism, right?"

"I guess," I said.

"The first important assumption in that argument is that we can have complete knowledge of the present. Do you see that?" Sage asked.

"Of course," I said, "and that assumption is undercut by modern ideas in physics itself, with the notion that there is a fundamental uncertainty at the very lowest levels of physical description—at the quantum level."

"Right," said Sage, "but that's not really a very good approach to questioning determinism."

"Oh," I said. After a moment, I followed up by quietly asking, "Why?"

"Uncertainty at the quantum level as a criticism of determinism fails on two counts. First, it doesn't really address free will. We can have uncertainty at a particular level of description but still not have free will. It would just be that we need to build that randomness into our physical models and predictions, but that randomness is certainly not free will."

"Oh, yeah," I said. I could certainly buy the notion that we cannot save free will by replacing it with randomness.

Sage continued. "But more importantly, the thesis about uncertainty at low levels of physical description still assumes that physical objects are real and forgets that our references to those physical objects are just convenient designations. There is an interesting point to be made here about uncertainty and all, but it gets there by fallaciously thinking there is an end of the referential line. It assumes that physical objects really exist out there and are not imputations by consciousness upon the reality of the world." I resumed my staring exercise directed upon the venerable soul seated before me. "No, there is an even deeper problem with determinism, the view that we do not exercise free will. What do you think that is?"

I thought about this for a time and hesitantly suggested, "Our understanding of causality?"

Sage sat up straight and asked, "How so?"

"Well," I improvised on my feet—or, rather, on my crossed legs or what was now presenting to me as a visualization of my crossed legs—"it seems that the determinism argument assumes that we have a good understanding of causality—that we know generally what a good causal law is."

"Go on," Sage prodded.

"But us having a good understanding of causality depends upon us having a good understanding of the objects, or sates of affairs, being asserted to be causally interacting," I ventured.

"Okay, then what?" asked Sage.

"Then that would require we have a good idea of those objects, or states of affair, being asserted to be causally related. If the notion of convenient designation, or the emptiness of reference, is right, then we don't have a good idea of those objects. Hence, we don't have a good idea of causal relations. And hence we don't have a good idea of determinism. Therefore, the best argument against free will simply evaporates, along with the things referred to by convenient designation!"

"Very good!" exclaimed Sage, whereupon Percy quickly protected the teacup she was just then raising to her mouth. Sage paused and then added, "You just took us through some very intricate logical gymnastics—and I think that is great; don't get me wrong—but you need to be careful in your use of logic. Logic can never take you beyond your own assumptions or the premises of your argument. Each logical argument is constrained to follow its own premises."

"But," I objected, "logic is the best we've got. What else is there?"

Sage looked at me and said, "I believe you already know the answer to your provocative question." Sage joined Percy in staring out over the table for some time and then added, "Using logic is like taking a train ride toward your destination. You would be foolish to get off the train too soon, but eventually you'll need to get off to finish your trip. Unless your destination is actually the train station itself, which is not very likely. Unless you're just doing math problems for the love of math itself, you'll need to disembark from the train and proceed in your travels on your own. There is something beyond logic—or, maybe more correctly, preceding logic."

Sage paused, took a sip of tea, and continued. "In this case, having to do with the demonstration of free will, there is a positive proof beyond logic."

I was thoroughly entranced by Sage's message here, and I asked, "How? What's that proof?"

It laughed again and flatly stated, "By the direct experience of the exercise of your own free will. There isn't any experience more direct than that! No cubes involved there, just direct action." I was unconvinced, but I pondered this statement and how it might fit in with the thesis of the emptiness of our references. I remembered having once raised my fist in defiance to the doctrine of determinism. It seemed that that act of defiance had taken place a long time ago. I realized that raising the cup of tea to my lips would offer a similar demonstration of my free will. After some time pondering what Sage had just said, I smiled and calmly raised my teacup to my mouth and drank deeply of my own free will. Sage asked with a wink, "Do you like the tea?"

I answered, "Oh yes, very much."

Sage sighed with contentment and asked, "Do you have any more questions, for now?"

"No," I said. "Thanks so much."

"Well," it went on, looking at both of us, "would you like some more tea?" Both Percy and I politely declined more tea.

I thanked Sage once again and turned to Percy to say, "I think we have taken enough of Sage's time. Do you think we should return?"

Percy nodded in agreement as Sage said, "No time at all, really. It was nice meeting you." Turning to Percy, it said, "And nice seeing you ag—" upon which Percy glanced at me with a flash of worry sweeping across her face and immediately disappeared before Sage could finish its sentence. "Oh," it said in surprise, "she's in a hurry. Well, take care, my young man. I'm sure all will turn out well. Diligently work out solutions to your own problems. Only you can solve them."

"Thanks, I'll work on them," I said, and then I descended back down to the solid world. Upon entering the mundane realm, I found that my legs ached like they had never ached before.

XVIII

Killing the Beast

Before calling Percy to plan the moment of our ambuscade of the monster, I needed a little time to take another look at my introductory books on Einstein's special theory of relativity. I also wanted to take another look at Lao Tzu's book, the *Tao Te Ching*.

I started by taking a look at the first line of Lao Tzu's famous book: "The Tao which can be spoken is not the constant Tao." It struck me as no accident that this was the very first line of the Tao Te Ching. A transliteration from the ancient Chinese of that line is "Tao can tao not constant Tao." I remembered having read that in the ancient Chinese language, depending upon context, "tao" can represent the Way—the mystical underpinnings of the universe ("Tao")—or it can represent the word "speak" ("tao"). In this case, the first line of the Tao Te Ching is rendered as "Tao can speak not constant Tao." In those six words, the subtlety of Sage's extensive dissertation is rendered in its essential purity. Our world, as it manifests to us, is largely a function of our spoken language. There is, however, a constant reality behind that world not captured by our words. We live in our own worlds built up from how we understand our words. Yet we relate to others and the reality preceding those words in a shared universe—a paradoxical combination of the one and the many, the one universe encompassing the many worlds.

Subtler for some, less so for others, was what I suspected to be a similar lesson hidden within Einstein's special theory of relativity. To be sure the uneducated, popular exploitation of the sophisticated theory of relativity seemed to shout, "Everything's relative, so anything goes!" But I thought I had read a different message in my youthful and naive first exposure to that complex system. I reviewed my introductory books on relativity to confirm what I had thought might be a heretical interpretation of that model of the universe. Reviewing those texts, I confirmed my interpretation, yet I found that it was anything but heretical; it was the mainstream interpretation that most scientists understood the theory to express.

Yes, Einstein argued that from different reference systems the same events can have radically different representations. Embedded within relativity theory, though, as the very foundation of that theory, is the conception of invariant objective facts. Of course the constant speed of light, regardless of reference system, is obviously the most familiar invariant fact espoused in the special theory of relativity. Another, less popularly understood, invariant in that complex theory is the distance between any two events in space-time; from the unique perspective of every reference system, that distance is equivalent. I am not talking about linear distance here, as in the length of a rigid rod, which *does* vary between the perspectives of two different reference systems according to the special theory of relativity. Instead the theory says that the "distance" between two *events* in space-time is an objective fact of the universe. That invariant distance is so important to the special theory of relativity that it is given its own special name: invariant relativistic interval. So, for Einstein, objective facts of the universe remain invariant across different observers—different consciousnesses—but each consciousness is in its own world as defined by the perspective of its unique reference system.

Here I found a certain similarity between the message Sage was attempting to convey to its sometimes reluctant pupil, me, with its notion of ontological relativity, Lao Tzu's fundamental insight that reality is unspeakable but nevertheless is the foundation of the universe for us all, and the mathematical and logical underpinnings of relativity theory with its notion of invariant facts across different reference systems. This similarity in the underlying logic between these models of the universe seemed more fundamental to me than the popular ideas then being bandied about. The then popular view asserted that Eastern mysticism—for example, Taoism—and modern science were saying the same thing; they were describing the world similarly.

The misguided popular idea of the time was that Taoism was describing the universe similarly to how science was then describing the universe. The problem with seeing this contrived similarity, of course, was that Eastern mysticism, especially Taoism, was not describing anything at all. As can be seen from the first line of the Tao Te Ching, Taoism is not in the describing game. In fact, it asserts that reality can fundamentally *not* be described. Beyond this fundamental misunderstanding of Taoism, I also doubted that Eastern mysticism and contemporary science were describing the world similarly for another reason. This doubt has borne fruition over the years. The contemporary science that was being compared to cherry-picked tidbits of Eastern mysticism was exceedingly tentative and easily prone to revision given new experimental results. How could something so hypothetical and tentatively dynamic as current scientific theories, at any time in the wonderful advance of scientific progress, be equated to enduring mystical truths—assuming for the sake of argument that there are enduring mystical truths?

No, the similarity I then saw between the theory of relativity and what Sage was teaching was something much more fundamental than a coincidental accident of the particular point we occupied in scientific progress. I was beginning to see how that lesson could be used to kill the monster. The useful teaching was simple: separate consciousnesses live in worlds of their own making, but invariant phenomena like suffering show that we all interrelate in the same universe. The question now became for me, Are there other invariant, objective facts apart from the monster of my suffering, and if so, are those invariants more positive in nature than suffering?

I called Percy. Again she answered on the first ring. I did not wait for her to say hello; I started right in. "Are you ready to go kill the monster?"

"Yes," she said, "But how are we going to find it?"

"I've been thinking about that," I offered, "We simply go join D.'s ghost. I don't think we need to actively seek out that monster; it has never had a problem finding us. Suffering has a way of doing that."

"Yeah," she said, laughing, "I guess you're right."

"Besides," I added, "that will give the three of us a little more time to go over the details of our plan while we're waiting for the monster to find us."

"Okay," she said, and she went on to ask, "What if the plan doesn't work?"

"Well," I replied, "I've been thinking about that too. I'm starting to formulate an alternative plan, but I haven't put much time into thinking it through. I've been trying to focus upon what we've decided to do. Let's stick with this first plan, since I'm pretty sure it would be easier than the alternative I'm just starting to think about."

"But our original plan doesn't really seem so easy, does it?" she offered.

"Yeah, you're right," I said, "but it is *easier* than the alternative, so let's go with that for now. Okay?"

"Okay. When do you want to go contact D.?"

"Right away. Tonight, I guess. I'm about as ready as I'm going to be. What about you?"

"Okay, tonight is good," she said. "Shall we say ten o'clock?"

"Okay, ten o'clock. I'll see you there," I replied.

"Okay, bye."

I said, "Bye," and hung up.

At ten o'clock that night, I entered the occult realm one more time. Instantly Percy, D.'s ghost, and I were standing upon a solid flat surface in a dim spotlight, surrounded by darkness. "Okay, D.," I said, "this is it. We're now going to kill the monster."

"Great!" the ghost bellowed.

"But first let's go over some details of our plan before the beast finds us here," I said.

D.'s ghost said, "It's easy. Percy is going to distract the monster, I'm going to knock its individual voices out of its conversation to you where you're waiting by the side, and you're going to surround them with that bubble thing of yours and toss them out into the void. I can hardly wait to start smashing some heads!"

I recoiled at the violence in the ghost's voice and said, "Yeah, that's the plan. But there are a couple of details we need to keep in mind."

"What's so detailed about smashing heads?" the ghost asked.

Percy said, "D., just listen for a second, okay?" The ghost sullenly looked at her and then looked back at me expectantly.

"Right," I said, "Now, we want to try to hobble the monster's power as quickly as we can, but we discussed earlier that you can't throw its voices out to me quicker than I can handle them." The ghost bit its lip, clearly expressing impatience. "But also, beyond that, we need you to knock out the stronger voices as soon as you can. So if you have a choice to knock out a stronger or a weaker voice, then always knock out the stronger first." I paused. "Got it?"

"Yeah, I can do that," said the ghost, smiling mischievously and winking at Percy.

I turned to Percy. "You have your plan down?" I asked.

"Yup," she said. "But there is one thing that bothers me about it."

"What's that?" I asked.

"The monster is interested in you, not me. How am I going to distract it and keep it away from you?"

I stood there in a panic. I thought that I had solved this problem before, but now it seemed insurmountable. I started to grow hot in the face and began to sweat. I was afraid that the monster would be along any moment, and we were obviously unprepared for its arrival. A crazy idea popped into my head. "Percy, I've been successful in a bit of conjuring in the past—uh, in this hidden realm anyway. Maybe that can help us here." Percy looked at me with curiosity. I stood there staring back at her.

Percy glanced over her shoulder, looking out for the monster, turned back to me, and said, "What?"

I breathed in. "Maybe I can conjure you to look like me, and me to look like you."

D.'s ghost moaned, "Oh, no."

I turned to the ghost and said, "Just remember: you'll be knocking voices out to me, but I'll look like Percy. Don't knock them out to Percy, who will look like me … that is, if I can conjure us to manifest in that way."

"Okay," the ghost said, "I'll knock them out to Percy, who'll be you." I was starting to see how this spontaneously improvised plan could go tragically awry.

Percy finally spoke up. "You can really do this? Make me look like you and you look like me?"

"I can try," I said. "And I can't think of anything else right at this moment. And we don't know how much time we have, so I had better get to it."

Percy simply said, "Okay," with a smile and a glint in her eye. I began with Percy. It was hard work, but eventually I was able to get her to resemble a reasonable facsimile of me.

We now had what appeared to be two of me standing before the ghost. D.'s ghost looked confused and said, "Look, don't go moving about until you're finished with the conjuring trick, would you? This is disorienting."

I was sufficiently pleased with Percy's manifestation of me, so I started conjuring me to look like her. Eventually I succeeded, and I looked like that tall, powerful woman. D.'s ghost gave out a tremendous laugh, went up to Percy, who now looked like me, bent down, and gave Percy a large kiss on the mouth. D.'s ghost whispered something into Percy's ear while giving her a big pinch. Percy blushed, and the ghost began laughing heartily, doubling over in mirth. I did not think the overall situation was conducive to comedic routines. Percy turned to me, with me now looking like her and her now looking like me, and said, "Hey, you look pretty *good!*" I began a snide retort, but just then the air around us started to flash with unmistakable signs of the approaching monster.

With the approach of the monster, the three of us sobered up immediately. Turning to my two cohorts, I said, "Okay, we all know what to do! Good luck!" Just then the monster, in all its hideous form, came into our view. Upon us seeing it, it saw us. It gave a great roar and charged us where we stood, fire streaming from its eyes, being blown back behind it in two intertwining red streamers waving in the wind created by the forward impulse of its violence.

Percy, looking like me, said, "Okay. Good luck!" and she ran away from us, causing the monster to veer off its path to pursue what it took to be its coveted prey. Running toward its supposed victim, the monster shot out a hot blast of plasma at Percy, who heard the coming of that superheated air and jumped to the side, pushing off with her right foot and avoiding all but the sparse outer penumbra of the radiant torch. D.'s ghost and I watched Percy's hasty retreat, and we simultaneously decided that it was time to begin our own maneuvers if Percy were to survive the savage onslaught of that avian-reptilian beast.

D.'s ghost ran after the beast, trying to discern individual constituent voices flowing behind that monster in a cloud reminiscent of the tail of a comet. I tried to remain slightly away from the fracas while staying within the ghost's purview. For the plan to work, D.'s ghost needed to know where I was waiting to imprison any loosened voices. I heard a gigantic smack and saw the ghost power a disheveled evil voice out to me at the side of the struggle. This first evil voice sent my way was not particularly powerful, and I quickly trapped it in an impermeable bubble and sent it on its way into the emptiness of the aether. Percy was now pinned down, with her shield held up, protecting herself from the nearly constant flow of incandescent blasts as the monster rapidly approached her.

Fortunately for Percy, but not for the ghost, when the ghost had knocked that first voice out of the monster's conversation, the ghost had given a huge satisfied laugh. Feeling its power being ever so slightly diminished from the separation of that first voice, and hearing the ghost's laugh, the monstrous beast momentarily diverted its attention to focus upon D.'s ghost. It knocked the ghost head over heels with a powerful sweep of its massive tail. Clearly the monster had the wherewithal to deal summarily with both Percy and the ghost simultaneously. But I could not join the fight. I needed to be on station to immobilize any wayward individual voices knocked loose from the evil one. I was stuck and did not know what to do to help my comrades. While I hesitated, my friends were running the serious risk of being expeditiously dispensed. I had to do something.

Without overthinking the situation, I started to conjure a hundred more images like Percy, now looking like me, all arrayed at the side of the real Percy. Each image was on its knees and holding its shield up before it. When the monster returned its attention to Percy, thinking she was me, it confronted 101 images of me. I took those images and threw them about randomly; mixing them up and then setting them back down in their kneeling, protective positions, huge shields before them on outstretched arms. The monster looked confused and became even more enraged. It randomly chose one of the images of me and threw an even more intense blast at it, obliterating it into nothingness. I hoped that that had not been the real Percy, in her disguise as me.

D.s' ghost shook, picked itself up off the surface of our battlefield, and charged back into the dense mist of voices making up the substance of our monster. The ghost was enraged and took a moment to survey the voices in its proximity and choose the most powerful voice of the lot. With a terrific crash, D.'s ghost knocked that powerful voice in a long, high arc directly to where I was standing and awaiting its arrival. I did not notice it then, but at the moment the ghost knocked that voice out of the conversation, the temperature of the beast's fiery blast diminished a significant amount owing to the loss of that powerful voice in its conversation. However, the beast continued to randomly choose images of me and blast them into nothingness. All the images of me, the real Percy included, ran around and around the monster, confusing it with a swarm of motion, counting coup by irritatingly, but ineffectually, striking at its head. Occasionally the monster would successfully disintegrate one of these swarming gnats with a powerful blast of hot plasma or a swipe of its massive yet swift arms. D.'s ghost protected itself as best it could within the conversation of the beast while it waited for me to signal that I was ready to receive another voice knocked loose from the monster.

As the evil voice that had just been knocked loose from the beast descended from the zenith of its high trajectory and came ever closer to me I noticed with terror that it was my old nemesis, the hostile soldier that had attacked me in my foxhole in the earlier battle. Apparently it recognized me as well, and with a high-pitched screech, it turned from a soldier into a huge, malevolent bird of prey with its talons stretched out before it in its descent upon my being. It crashed upon me with bewildering force, and with one of its razor-sharp talons, it slashed my chest open from my upper left shoulder to my lower right abdomen. It was a devastating blow, and I reeled, trying to regain my stability. I started bleeding profusely and became dizzy from the loss of blood. I looked down and saw Percy's chest ripped open, knowing that it was really my chest that had received the debilitating wound. Luckily my adversary had been temporarily knocked unconscious from our collision and lay motionless at my feet. In its unconscious state, it had returned to the manifestation of a foreign soldier. I felt my heart flopping out of my chest with each heartbeat, and I grabbed it with my left hand to keep it from falling out. I noticed that my lungs blew up, popping out like balloons in each attempt of my rapidly contracting diaphragm to exhaust the spent wind. My bloody hand did the best it could to hold me together.

I was starting to black out from shock when I saw that the real Percy, now standing by my side and looking like me, had left the swarm around the monster and come to my aid. She looked at me and said, "Oh what a mess you've made of me," and tore some cloth from that soldier's uniform. With this cloth she wrapped up her—my—chest and thereby held my internal organs in place. She helped steady me on my feet and said, "Are you okay now? You've got to use your willpower, right? Can you make your bubbles? I've got to get back out to the fight. D.'s out there all alone!"

"Okay," I said, feeling strange to be looking down at her into my own eyes. "I think I can make it." Percy flew off to continue her distraction maneuvers around the beast's huge head.

With effort I regained my focus and fixed a particularly strong bubble around the hostile soldier. I then threw it as far away as I could. I then signaled to D.'s ghost that I was ready for another voice to be knocked in my direction. D.'s ghost obliged and lobbed a pop-up out to where I awaited receipt of that horrible package. Except for the tremendous pain in my chest, I had no difficulty in dispatching this fly ball. The monster continued to attack the annoying images of me swarming about its head, less and less frequently scoring direct hits as D.'s ghost sent more and more voices out my way for dispatch. It seemed that we went on in this way forever. As I sent more and more voices out into the aethereal hinterlands, I noted that luckily both athletes. We certainly required that discipline now.

Percy and I, as well as D. when he had been alive, were endurance athletes. We certainly required that discipline now.

Our toils went on and on and on. From the attrition due to fiery blasts, there were fewer and fewer images of me dancing before the beast, distracting it as best as they could. D.'s ghost was growing fatigued with its effort. Some of the voices it knocked out of the conversation were now grounders, and when they came to a stop before I could run up to them, they picked themselves up and returned to rejoin the substance of the monster. Overall, though, the monster was growing more and more diminished. Soon the images of myself—among which I hoped the real Percy was included—were able to quite easily withstand the fiery blasts of the wilting beast, quite comfortable behind their protective shields. It went on like this for some time more, until I noticed that D.'s ghost was staggering around within the dwindling conversation of the monster and was no longer able to effectively knock individual voices out to my exhausted hands. What's more, there was now only one image of me hovering before that somewhat less hideous beast. Luckily I could tell it was the real Percy. She was the only me left. I did not have the energy remaining to conjure more replicas of myself to aid her now solitary mission, and D.'s ghost was being ganged up upon by the remaining voices constituting the substance of the monster. I made the decision that it was now time to take on the monster face-to-face.

I signaled to D.'s ghost that it should disengage with the monster's conversation of individual voices. Upon seeing this, Percy went right up to the monster and punched it mightily in the face, apparently in an effort to give the ghost time to withdraw. While this did give D.'s ghost just enough time to haltingly extricate itself from the monster's conversation, Percy received a sweeping blast of hot plasma across her unprotected face. She fell down to her knees, holding her eyes and crying out in excruciating pain. The monster remained fixated upon Percy, falsely believing that that poor being kneeling before it was me. D.'s ghost looked up from where it had been lying on the hard surface, perceived that Percy was in mortal peril, and charged the monster from behind while I tried to muster the strength for one last impenetrable bubble with which to surround that horrible being.

D.'s ghost violently collided with the monster from behind, knocking it to the ground beside Percy. With that great impact, two more lone voices had been loosened from the evil one, and I quickly bottled them up in their own smaller bubbles and sent them on their way, changing my plans—again—from trying for one last huge bubble. The beast turned around from where it lay on the hard surface and sent forth its last searing breath, blasting D.'s ghost into nonbeing. From the effort, the monster had severely reduced itself to just three remaining constituent voices, and I, one by one, covered them in bubbles and pushed them away to careen separately into the void. With no more voices constituting its substance, the monster simply disappeared.

I was left dangerously wounded, barely standing, slouched beside a likewise disabled kneeling Percy, who had regained just enough sight to have witnessed through her blinding tears her lover's demise.

It was just then that I realized with a shock that I had almost made a tragic mistake. I had planned to put the diminished monster in its own bubble and send it off into the void. But now I realized with horror that had I done so the monster would have survived. The only way to have killed the monster was to remove *all* of its voices from its conversation. Only in that way would the conversation constituting its identity cease to exist. Only in that way would its causal efficacy be severed and erased from the world. I stood shaking at my colossal blunder—a blunder that would have rendered Percy's heroic efforts and the ghost's noble sacrifice meaningless. They deserved much better than my impetuous blunders. I shrank and moaned with the thought of it all.

Percy slowly got up off of the hard, now cold, surface of our present world and went to stand before where D.'s ghost had last existed. She also shook all over her—my—body. She said, "D. died to save my life!"

I tried to quell my own shaking and said, "Yeah, he did the same for me before he was a ghost." We stood looking at the empty space where D.'s ghost had been—or not-been.

I looked at Percy. She had burn marks all across my face. I said, "Maybe it's time for us to manifest as ourselves?"

Percy said, "Okay," and I changed us back to looking like ourselves again. My chest was still bandaged in soaking red strips of torn cloth, and Percy, restored to her real appearance, now had burn marks on her own face, with her eyebrows completely singed off and most of her golden hair burned and damaged, except where her vulnerable face had taken the brunt of the blast, with her remaining yet damaged hair lying hidden upon the back of her skull. She looked like a burnt Mandarin with a thin golden ponytail.

Percy looked down at herself and then over at me and said, "You've got a nice body. It's actually pretty tough for being as small as it is." Then she smiled and put her arm under my right shoulder as I began to slump down to the ground. Percy looked around us and observed, "I guess we killed your monster. Poor D." I groaned assent. She continued, "Maybe it's time for us to return to the solid realm. There's nothing really left for us here. We can get together soon back in the real world."

"Okay," I said, and I did not waste time in reuniting with the mundane realm. I was again lying in my bed, in my parents' house. My heart shot hot flashes of searing pain through the core of my being with each beat. With each breath, I moaned in pain. I lay there suffering, thinking about invariant, objective facts that held together separate worlds created by their individual consciousnesses.

XIX

Commencement

The next morning, I awoke from a deep, satisfying sleep, although my heart and chest still ached tremendously. It was Sunday morning, and I had nothing in particular planned for the day; therefore, I lay in bed convalescing and thinking about all that had recently happened. I lay on my back because whenever I moved to turn on my side, the pain in my chest was unbearable. I watched a spider on the ceiling slowly descend via an unseen cord. It would drop about one foot from the ceiling and then, rewinding its cord, reascend to the ceiling. It did this a number of times as I watched it, as if it could not make up its mind where it wanted to be. I wondered what it was like to be a spider, suspended there in midair and hanging upside down. What kind of consciousness does a spider have?

Having killed the monster, for the first time in months I felt a freedom from the anxiety of instant annihilation. What's more, with D.'s ghost having met its unfortunate end, I no longer feared for those that kept D. in their hearts and minds. The demise of D.'s ghost did not cause me any great suffering—no more than I had already sustained—and I had not seen any effect on Percy with that specter's annihilation, beyond her sadness to see its death once again. So I concluded, that all those who had kept D. in their hearts and minds were probably okay as well. In destroying D.'s ghost, the monster apparently did not have time to focus upon the individuals sustaining that specter.

I felt I could finally afford to relax, and I did just that. I let my mind wander, not enforcing any adherence to the dictates of strict logical progression. I wondered if, beyond some unknowable type of consciousness, the spider indecisively dropping and rising above my head also exhibited a form of free will. Sage certainly seemed an exponent of free will, with all his tea drinking and all. He said that only I could solve my problems—that ceasing my suffering was my responsibility alone. I could not rely upon an external source to find solace in the world. I sighed and admitted that while this view gives enormous freedom to us all, it also condemns us to absolute responsibility for our actions. Along with complete freedom comes the requirement of absolute responsibility. Another paradox.

"But who, really, has that freedom if there is no self?" I asked myself. Sage had seemed to indicate that there is no self to be found via meditative introspection. No matter how hard you looked inwardly, you would never find your self. I thought that that notion made some sense, but it did not seem to square with the fact that a living person is different from its ghost. There just is the fact that the two are different. Maybe that's one of the invariant facts of the universe—that there are consciousnesses with their own perspectives, their unique reference systems. A ghost is not one of those unique perspectives; it is created of multiple preexisting perspectives. So is the self merely a unique reference system? If so, it then makes sense that one cannot directly observe one's own perspective. That perspective is what observes everything else. Was that not the second law of consciousness as espoused by Resident Teacher—consciousness can never be conscious of itself?

Softly floating in the mode of free association within which I was now obviously flowing, I considered more fully the three laws of consciousness mentioned by Resident Teacher, and how those restricting laws may fit with the doctrine of free will. I went over those three laws: (1) consciousness is always conscious of something, (2) consciousness is never conscious of itself, and (3) consciousness creates the objects of its consciousness. Given all I had been through, laws 2 and 3 now made some sort of sense. I really cannot experience my own experiencing. I am just experiencing, and that is about it. Additionally, it was becoming pretty plain to me then that we somehow create the objects we think we see in the worlds around us. It's not so much a case of "seeing is believing" as it is "believing is seeing."

But the first law seemed problematic, even though it was that first law that had originally seemed so trivial—so obviously true. It seemed to go against the invariant factors that hold together all our separate worlds. If the Tao, or the source of all things, whatever we want to call it and whatever it is, is not namable and is beyond words, then it is not, per se, an object of consciousness. Therefore, by law 1, we can never be conscious of it. That seemed like a problem. I wondered what Sage would say about these three laws. I should have asked it about them when I had the chance. In my mind, I could just hear Sage saying, "Well, you know, Resident Teacher likes numbered lists; he lives for them. Three of these, four of those, etc. But about those laws of consciousness—laws are made to be broken!" I laughed, and my chest shot a bolt of pain all the way down to my toes.

After I recovered from my painful laugh, I continued my lazy drift down the gentle wash of association. There must be some sort of consciousness or awareness of those invariant factors. If suffering was one of those, then we certainly do experience that. Is suffering an object of consciousness in the sense that law 1 is talking about objects? We certainly do have objects as the cause of our suffering; but is the experience of suffering itself an object? But why focus upon the negative all the time? Are there not more positive invariants holding together all of our separate lives ensconced in individual, imputed worlds? What about love? Does not unconditional love rise to the level of an invariant? Love is not an object of consciousness per se, yet it has objects and is directed at the beloved. Is not love telling us something at least as important as suffering?

I lay there considering the possibility that love, like suffering, can also teach us that there is something out there in the universe beyond our own separate worlds of our individual making.

I heard the phone ring and my mother answer it. Soon there was a soft knock on the door. Upon answering the knock with a "hello" from where I lay, I heard my mother say through the closed door, "There's a Percy on the phone for you, but it sounds like a girl's voice."

"Okay," I shouted to my mom, "I'll get up and get it."

I got up, pulled on my pants, went into the dining room while holding my chest, and answered the phone. "Hello," I said. My mother was watching me from the kitchen.

Percy said, "Hey, hi! Are you okay?"

"Yeah, I'm fine. You?" I asked.

"Fine" was her one-word reply. There followed an awkward silence on the phone. "Well," she said, "I just wanted to see how you were. Uh, also, I, uh ... have something I need to talk to you about."

"Okay," I said, waiting for Percy to continue.

"Are you free for another walk on the beach today, maybe about noon, at the same place?"

"Sure," I said, hoping my chest would be feeling a lot better by then.

"Okay," she said. "Well, I guess I'll see you there then."

"Okay." Not knowing what else to say at the moment, I said, "Bye."

"Bye." She hung up the phone.

I hung up the phone on my end, and my mother asked, "A girl? That's nice."

"Yeah," I said. "Hey, can I borrow the car to go down to the beach today about noon? I'd take my bike, but I'm not feeling that well, and I'd rather take the car."

"Sure, we don't need it then," she said, smiling broadly. She then frowned and said, "But what's wrong? You don't look well."

As I walked back into my room, I said, "Oh, it's just a chest thing. I'm sure I'll survive."

At noon I was standing on the beach next to a huge jetty jutting out beyond the substantial surf. Again I was staring over those bubbling waves at the beautiful Channel Islands in the distance. They were indistinct smudges of brown earth against the brilliant blues where water and air merged on the horizon. The fiery sun was shining hot, directly overhead. The vast Santa Barbara Channel kept the islands at bay, like the River Styx separating my life from the dead of the underworld. I was feeling the void of D.'s absence; even his ghost was now gone. I was hopeful that I had found a good friend in Percy to help fill that void in my heart. I waited for Percy to join me in my vigil.

At length I heard Percy walking toward me from behind, laboring through the hot, dry, resistant sand. I turned and beheld an agitated being. Her normally curled golden locks were stringy and askew, she had a small Band-Aid on one cheek below her left eye, and she held a very serious demeanor. I surmised that there was some sort of a problem she wished to discuss with me. As she approached, I said, "Hey. What did you want to tell me?"

Percy quickly dismissed my question. "Oh, that can wait. Something else has come up that is much more important!" When she finally arrived where I was standing, she continued past me and said, "Can we walk?"

"Sure," I said, and I trudged through the sand next to her. Serious in our walk up the coast, we toyed at the waves with our bare feet, playing with the waters of the Styx separating life and death.

As we proceeded up the coast, Percy looked long and hard out over the waves as if trying to catch a glimpse of D. in the underworld. Except for a groan now and then due to the pain in my chest, I was silent, waiting for Percy to tell me what was on her mind. Percy looked away from the waves on her left, over in my direction to her right, and asked, "Are you sure you're okay? You don't look so good, and you're groaning a lot."

I said, "Yeah, I think I'll be all right. But you look kind of beat up too."

She smiled for the first time that day and said, "Yeah, we both took a beating. But nothing that time won't heal. It's better being back in the solid world, where the brunt of our recent injuries don't physically manifest." She grew even more serious. "Something's come up after I called you this morning." I waited and walked beside my new best friend. Percy looked me straight in the eyes and said, "D. visited me this morning after our call."

"What? Are you sure it was *D.'s* ghost?" I asked, desperately seeking an alternative explanation for this apparent visitation.

"Oh, yeah, it was D. all right. I couldn't mistake him for another," she forcefully stated.

"How could that be?" I asked myself as much as I was asking Percy. We both thought about that question for some time, causing a pause in our conversation. "Okay," I said, "I guess that makes sense. D.'s ghost was—is—animated by those that keep D. in their hearts and minds. And by the way, that substantially includes you and me. And as long as we keep him in our minds, then the ghost is sure to reappear."

"Yeah," Percy said gloomily, "that's what I was thinking also."

"Did it seem any different from before? I mean, was it the *very same* D.'s ghost, or a kind of different D.'s ghost?"

Percy said, "That's what's interesting; he didn't have any real memory of us attacking the monster, or even that we wanted to kill it. I had to tell him the whole story of his original death all over again."

I began a sterile investigation into the metaphysics of the phenomena of the reappearance of D.'s ghost. "So it seems that the monster, in killing D.'s first ghost, cut off the causal connection between the original ghost and this new ghost that exists now. But the real causal force substantiating D.'s ghost's existence, all those truly existent sentient beings, is still out here in the real world, so of course D.'s ghost will reappear, just a little different from before." Percy was staring at me, wondering when I would grasp the terrible implications of my academic ramblings.

It finally struck me like a bolt of lightning. "Oh no!" I cried. "That means we didn't kill the monster after all!" I stopped dead in my tracks and looked at Percy in horror.

Percy almost inaudibly mumbled, "Yeah, that's what I was thinking too," and she turned around to continue her gaze over the waves.

I stared at the back of her ruffled head in disbelief. I thought, *So our efforts were for naught after all! The monster still lives!* I forced myself to attain a semblance of rationality. "Well, we don't know that the monster has been reconstituted by its disciples—the individual voices giving it substance. Not yet anyway. That would probably take some time. And as with D.'s original ghost, the causal efficacy emanating from the original monster has been severed permanently. But it's just a matter of time before all those evil existent sentient beings—or, to be more humane about it, all those sentient beings expressing some evil intentions—start up new unconscious extrasensory conversations. Those new conversations will eventually coalesce again up higher and higher levels until there is a new monster with the same evil nature and power as the original monster ... Great!"

Percy turned around and said, "Well, at least it's unlikely to remember that it was out to get you, if that is any consolation."

"Yeah," I agreed, "I wonder what sort of memory it will have, being based upon real flesh-and-blood sentient beings, all with their own memories to add to the mix?"

"I don't know," said Percy, "but D. this morning seemed to have lost a lot of his memory."

"You said D.'s ghost didn't remember that it desperately wanted to kill the monster? Okay, maybe we can lessen the damage by not telling the ghost about all of that." I was hoping for something positive in all of this.

"I did tell D. that," confessed Percy. "Remember? I just told you."

I groaned again. "Damn, then all of those that loved D. are in trouble with the monster again. It's like we didn't do anything at all! Except get hurt."

"But I told D. that we had killed the monster. Really, I told him that *he* killed the monster. So in his mind there isn't anything out there for him to go after any more. I didn't tell him the other stuff about the monster possibly being reanimated."

"Oh, thank God!" I said.

Percy turned to look out over the waves again, and looking back at me, she asked, "So what are we going to do? You said you had another plan?" By this time we had reached the point in our walk where we normally turned around to return down the coast.

We turned around, and I considered her question. "Okay," I philosophized, "so we're back stuck in the situation that we all find ourselves in, in the normal world. But now we're without a wacky ghost running amok and threatening the safety of all those who loved it in real life. Also, we know a little more about the hidden realm than a lot of people who are trying just to get by in their lives."

Percy's face showed that she did not like my reference to a "wacky ghost."

"No," I responded, "this is really important. Listen; I'm going to try to say something I've been thinking about but don't really know how best to say."

Percy said, "Okay." She then protested, "But don't call D. a 'wacky ghost,' okay? I love D."

"Okay," I agreed. "What I've been thinking about is that alternative plan I alluded to for killing the monster," I said.

"Good," said Percy. "What is it?"

"It's going to be really hard. Without a doubt, it will be the hardest thing you or I have ever done," I said softly.

"What is it?" she repeated.

I took a deep breath, and my chest ached. "Love."

Percy looked at me in surprise and smiled. A ray of sun caught a strand of her hair, and it shone golden again, brightly, just for an instant. "Oh, I see," she said, almost sounding somewhat sarcastic. She slightly increased her pace down the coast, trolling her toes in a small wave.

After a long while, with us trudging through the loose sand to go around the base of a jetty, Percy finally asked, "So how are we going to use love to kill the monster?"

I replied, "We're not going to kill it. We're just going to stop it from forming in the first place. The plan is kind of simplistic in concept, but it's infinitely hard in execution. It's based upon the fact that the monster—as with all evil monsters that live in the hidden realm and wreak havoc in our own world—exists in virtue of the existence of violent and aggressive thoughts emanating from existing sentient beings. So the plan is to get all those sentient beings to express only nonviolent and nonaggressive thoughts, always."

Percy looked at me as if I had just suggested we drink up the Santa Barbara Channel in one giant gulp or bring the dead back from the underworld.

"Yeah, like I said, it's easy to conceive but almost impossible to implement."

There was another long pause in our conversation as we walked down the beach, and I added, "But if you think about it, I think you'll see that there is no logical contradiction involved here in this plan, so it is *possible,* if not very *probable.* The plan is not impossible. But fighting the monsters in any other way *is impossible;* to fight the monster with violence only further feeds the beast, which is self-defeating. So the plan based upon love is the only possible way we have."

Percy thought about this and nodded solemnly. She then asked, "So how are you going to implement this plan?"

I replied, "With unconditional love expressed to all beings; anything less would be feeding the monsters. We've got to stop feeding the beast!"

Percy looked worried and said, "The monsters will not like that. They'll see what you are doing and try to stop you. They'll ... kill you. And it won't just be the monsters; there are plenty of hateful people here in the solid world that will perceive your love as a weakness and take advantage of you. How will you protect yourself?"

"I'll have to try to avoid violence directed against me, all the while promulgating unconditional love to all. I agree, I'll be a target, but not a sitting one." I sighed. "Like I said, it will be the hardest thing that has ever been done—much harder than building a great wall or sending people to the moon."

"Definitely," added Percy.

I repeated, "It's the only way. This plan for expressing love is *possible,* and any other plan will not achieve the desired result. None of the alternatives are even possible. We're constrained here by circumstance."

"I see," said Percy. "I wonder what D. will think of your plan. It certainly goes against all the two of you did in your childhood. You've got to admit you were very violent boys."

I thought about her question and then replied, "Well, it doesn't go against what we were trying to accomplish. It's just a different way of accomplishing our ultimate goal. I think D.'s ghost will understand that once you explain the plan to it. But don't get me wrong; I understand how hard it is going to be for me to change my behavior midstream, if you will. I'll need to take that proclivity to violence that was so much a part of D. and me and, with strict discipline, turn myself into a warrior of love. Like I've been saying, this plan is going to be incredibly hard to implement. I know I'll slip often. But I'll need to love myself too as I strive to love others and not dwell on my inadequacies. I just need to do the best I can. And hopefully others will join in and we can all begin to minimize the evil in the world. It's the only way."

Percy said, "You sound pretty serious about this."

I did not try to hide the fear of failure in my voice. "It's the only way. It is *the* way." Percy was now very quiet as we approached her small foreign car. I said, "Percy, maybe you can join me in this. It sure would be helpful to have a friend to share the burden. We could help each other along the way."

Percy stopped on our path and said, "The reason I called you this morning is that I needed to tell you something." I stopped with her on our path and waited. She looked at me and said, "My mom and I are moving away." I groaned again, this time in great disappointment. Percy explained, "My mom got a call from work and they need her to relocate again. This time we need to move somewhere back East. I wanted to stay here to finish my last year of high school next year, with you and all, but my mom said no. So just after this school year ends, we'll move away. I just thought I should tell you."

"Oh," I said, looking at my shoes and then away into the distance. "That's really too bad. I'm really going to miss you. We have great conversations. And ... well, you know."

"Yeah," she replied, "I'll really miss you too."

"Maybe we can get together again before you leave," I offered.

"Yeah," Percy responded noncommittedly. I felt lost, and I tried to hide my pain.

We arrived at Percy's car. She said, "Well, here we are, back at *Machine*."

I looked quizzically at Percy and asked, "You call your car '*Machine*?'"

"Yeah, my mom and I name our cars. She calls hers her chariot."

"So this is *Machine*," I said, patting its low top with my hand. "Hey," I added with forced merriment, "So you're my deus ex machina! You're my goddess in a machine!"

Percy became even more serious. Smiling, she gave my right hand a good squeeze with both of hers, looked me in the eyes, and asked, "Now that wouldn't be such a terrible thing, would it?"

I laughed and said, "No, not at all. I'll be the first one to admit that I need all the help I can get. You sure have helped me out of more than one jam."

She let go of my hand and said, "You're great. You'll be fine." At that point, Percy forced her large, strong body into that small foreign machine, gave me one last big smile, and drove away.

I was now alone, standing in the parking lot at the beach. I did not feel like driving home just yet, so I went back down to the beach and carefully walked and hopped boulders until I was standing at the very end of one of the long jetties. It was a bit rough going to get out that far—especially midway, where the breakers were crashing upon the rocks below and showering me with their salty spray. But beyond the breakers out at the end of the jetty, it was cool and peaceful. The long, low swells of the blue-green sea lulled me into an introspective mood.

I thought long and hard about what I had been discussing with Percy. Unconditional love is not impossible. In fact, it is the only possible solution to hate and evil. No, unconditional love is not impossible. It is just incredibly hard to constantly project! There is no guarantee that love will eventually win out over evil. Maybe the best we can hope for is an eternal balance between the two, with periodic ebbs and flows. I was reminded that I had once thought of myself as a phoenix rising from the ashes when the monster first informed me of its plan to kill me on sight. It now came to me that that is exactly what we all need to be—what we all really are by nature. We all continually arise from the ashes of the suffering wrought upon us by the forces of evil. From that mass rising, a huge communal phoenix is born. This universal phoenix of love sustained by the love of existent sentient beings will always be contending with the dragon of evil. It is up to us to maintain that cosmic balance; no one else can do it for us.

The vast ocean before me now was no longer a symbol of separation, the River Styx, but now became a huge, dynamic net of interconnected souls. Instead of separation, the ocean now became emblematic of relatedness. We all bobbed along in the waves of the universal soul, and we all had a significant part to play. The ocean was the invariant relatedness of us all; the shore was where there existed the individuated worlds within which we all lived and played out the scripts of our separate lives.

On the end of the jetty, I was thinking that to carry out this program of universal unconditional love, I would need to focus upon the solid realm, not the occult realm of unconscious, extrasensory conversations. *I will, I must, devote myself to the realm of the living. This is the only way to cut evil off at the knees. It is the only way to lessen, and perchance finally end, suffering. To violently go after the voices and conversations existing in the aether is totally ineffectual. Killing them is no solution. They will invariably sprout again from the evil thoughts expressed by living beings in the real world, like weeds perennially arising in a witch's garden. No, I will focus upon all real sentient beings, and help relieve them of their suffering. It is the only way. It is the way.* I made that vow to the vast infinite ocean of souls before me. I have not traveled in the aethereal realm all these many years—not to my knowledge, anyway.

Standing upon the panicle of that rocky precipice, looking out over that ocean of souls, I paradoxically felt alone in the world. All was up to me alone. And yet I knew that I was not really alone. I was connected to the entire universe even in my aloneness. My life's path was up to me, but in fact the delicate balance of the universe was up to all of us working together—no slackers allowed. The party-line theory of consciousness demanded this universal responsibility of us all. I laughed at the triteness of the puny term "party-line theory of consciousness." The term certainly did not convey the enormity of the effort required to keep the society of sentient beings in balance.

I laughed again, this time at the realization of my own smallness combined with the tremendous importance of each individual, me included. *Another paradox,* I thought to myself. *Another example of ... of ... well, the inadequacy of our understanding of it all.* I breathed in a great volume of humid, salty sea air. My chest no longer hurting with each breath, I laughed out loud, surprising the sleeping seagulls and sending them jumping up from the safety of that solid jetty. They flew out over the boiling waves, squawking at me for having rudely awoken them from their nonconscious slumber. I laughed again and returned ashore to begin my journey.

Epilogue

The next morning, as I walked down the hill from my parents' home to the high school, I thought about all that had transpired in the last couple of months. I thought about consciousness and its laws, the existence of evil and its veritably unstoppable will to power, and the fact that for suffering there is no separation between appearance and reality. I thought about my choice to combat evil by diving back into the world and trying to do good and trying not to cause any unnecessary suffering—to manifest unconditional love. This was a lot to carry on the shoulders of a seventeen-year-old boy.

These thoughts were especially poignant because during the last couple of months, when all of the above had been transpiring, I had also waged a successful campaign for student body president of my high school—a story in its own right, the telling of which is better left for some other time. As student body president of my school, I would be expected to be some sort of a leader, albeit a leader on a commonly assumed inconsequential level. "But is any leadership inconsequential if it can be harnessed to add even a miniscule impulse of good against evil?" I queried myself.

Still, I had doubts about being up to the task at hand. I asked myself, "How am I to return to the world, with all that recently transpired, and be a good leader?" I decided that I should not make known what I had recently experienced. If I were to do that, then my colleagues would likely be surprised at the least and would more than likely think I was mentally deranged. I would be shunned, and any hope of leading a substantial group of people to do no harm, to only think good thoughts, and thus to contribute our small share to the cutting off of evil at the knees would be lost. Being shunned by my peers, how could I successfully combat the pure will to power of evil—a will that seemed to corrupt and ferment most everything?

Consumed by these concerns as I descended the hill on my way to school, I recollected a story I had once been told long ago by an old Greek. Or at least it seemed vaguely as though I were recollecting the old Greek's story from long ago. That did not make much sense, however, since I was at the time only seventeen years old. With the thought lingering in the back of my mind that I had first heard this story long ago, the clarity of the story as I went through it in my mind made me think that I had been told the story only yesterday.

That old Greek had told me an interesting tale about prisoners being held in a cave. This cave had a very long and extremely narrow passage leading from the entrance down into a large cavern, where the prisoners were kept. From the time they were born, long before when their memories began, these prisoners had been chained to the cave floor so that all they could apprehend was the back of the cave. They could not see the other prisoners; nor could they even look down to see themselves. Behind these prisoners was the faint flickering flame of a fire. Between the faint fire and the prisoners ran a short wall along the width of the cavern. This wall allowed enough light from the dim fire to cast shadows of the prisoners upon the back of the cave. Between the fire and the short wall was a small cadre of people holding puppets up over the wall, casting more shadows upon the back of the cave. Some members of this group of puppeteers called themselves teachers. Some called themselves priests or ministers. Some called themselves politicians, and some even called themselves scientists. They held up the puppets, cast shadows upon the back of the cave, and made the appropriate sounds for the shadows they held. Those sounds in turn echoed off the back of the cave and gave the prisoners the impression that the sounds came from those shadows themselves.

The only experience for these prisoners was the shadows on the back of the cave. The prisoners came to identify themselves with their own shadows, and they identified the other prisoners as those prisoners' shadows. Otherwise, they intently watched the shadows cast upon the back of the cave by the puppeteers hidden behind the wall. Some of the prisoners became particularly adept at determining the regularity of the appearances of shadows based upon the appearances of other shadows. These adepts claimed to have found causal laws connecting those shadows directly between them. They were completely unaware of the fact that there was an utter lack of causal efficacy between the shadows themselves and that those causes lay elsewhere.

The old Greek told me that there was once a prisoner that grew uncomfortable with her predicament, thinking that there must be something more to life. After a long struggle, she was able to loosen her chains and take a look at herself and at some of the other prisoners. She was astounded to see that she was not a shadow at all and that neither were her colleagues. She desperately wanted to know from whence came the shadows. After long and painful exercises, she was finally able to free herself from the chains and stand up, at first teetering off balance from the pain all along her body. She turned around and saw the wall with the puppets being held above. She jumped over the short wall, surmised that she had found out what was really happening in the world, and joined the propagandists with their puppets.

At first she was content being just another puppeteer. Soon, however, she became dissatisfied with this endeavor also and decided to roam around the cavern in curiosity. Looking directly into the flickering fire hurt her eyes; she had never seen anything so bright. It blinded her to look at it. Eventually she got around the fire and began to explore the part of the cavern closer to the tunnel leading outside. After her eyes became used to the darkness of the cavern again, she thought she saw another faint light at the end of the tunnel. Not knowing how bright or how far away that light was, she decided to seek out this second source of illumination.

After extreme effort, she clawed her way up the tunnel, the light at the end of it becoming more and more intense with every foot gained. She finally found herself at the end of the tunnel, but she could not stand the intensity of the light. She held her hands in front of her face, trying to block the painful luminosity. Eventually it grew dark for some reason unknown to her, and she peeked out from behind her hands. It was blackness again, but with millions of tiny dots of light in the upper region of her field of vision. Her eyes soon became tolerant of this sparkling multitude, but periodically the intense brilliancy of light would again arrive and she would need to hide her eyes behind her hands.

Soon another source of light became ever more noticeable during the times when the intense light abated and when the millions of sparks were evident. Through a number of periods of alternation between millions of sparkles and painfully intense luminosity, this other source of light became more and more evident. Eventually she was able to directly look at this shining orb hovering over her. Soon it became so intense that it seemed to swallow up all those millions of separate shining sparks. Then, over a number of light and dark cycles, it slowly went away again and then came back again. After becoming completely adjusted to this luminous orb, she decided to try to see around her environment during the frequent periods of intense light. Initially she tried to become comfortable with the times when it first began and when it seemed to drop off again.

After much effort and pain, she could keep her eyes open right through the entire cycle of intense light. She was never able to look directly at the source of that intense brilliance, however. What she did see astounded her. She found that she was on the face of a cliff forming a beautiful valley. A gurgling stream softly ran down that valley, which was filled with brilliantly green trees, themselves filled with multicolored singing birds. Along the stream flew soft butterflies and metallic dragonflies. She was in a paradise, and she delighted in it. She thought that she would stay here forever. In fact, she did stay there for a very long time.

After many years of enjoying her paradise, she finally decided to listen to that nagging in the back of her mind about the plight of the others in the cave. She was especially concerned with the prisoners chained so as to see only shadows on the wall, who individually believed themselves to be one of the many shadows. She knew the truth of the matter, and she wanted to share that truth. She picked herself up from lying on her back in the cool grass, where she had been watching bright, fluffy white clouds pass above her, and struggled to climb the valley face so as to gain entrance to the cave, her former prison.

When she reentered the cave, she was plunged into darkness and could not see. She slowly moved down the tunnel using her hands to guide her along the sides of that rocky chute. Finally she saw a very faint flicker of light that she supposed was the fire in front of the wall where the puppeteers stood. She still could not see very well, and she accidently tripped over a small rock and kicked the fire, knocking the wooden fuel askew and nearly putting out the flame. The puppeteers were startled and shouted at her in agitation. She hurriedly began explaining all the wonderful things she had seen outside the cave. She described the stream, the birds, the butterflies, the dragonflies, the cool grass, the lofty clouds, the stars, the moon, and, finally, the brilliant sun itself. The puppeteers did not have a clue what she was talking about—they considered her speech to be rambling nonsense. They thought that she posed a serious danger because of her having nearly extinguished the fire and her flailing about as if she could not see the obvious reality around her. They therefore immediately killed her.

When I first heard this story long ago from that old Greek, a lot of it rang true—especially the ending, when the puppeteers summarily killed their savior out of evil's pure will. But I noted to the old Greek that certain aspects of the story did not seem realistic. How were the prisoners fed? How could they be kept alive in their captivity? Were not some of the puppeteers a bit more enlightened than just being merely cynical propagandists? In that paradise, where the former prisoner lived so long, how did she survive? Was she a vegetarian, or did she need to kill animals to eat? To eat, she would have needed to kill something, if not just plants. Surely that must have degraded her paradise. Did she have a house? Were there wild beasts out there trying to harm her? Was not there a strong possibility of harm to her person from some evil will—especially as she was out there all alone?

After conveying my doubts as to the realism of the story to the old, gray, fully-bearded Greek, he exhaled loudly and took a long, hard look straight into my eyes, finally smiling and saying with a shrug, "Well this is just a *story*. Goodness. It is an allegory, if you will."

"Jeez," I said, "if this is just a story, then I'd like to see an ending where she doesn't get killed but rather goes on to lead all the prisoners out of the cave. Even better would be one in which she helps the prisoners gain the knowhow needed to crawl out of the cave on their own, by their own efforts."

"Even better," agreed the ancient Greek, with a nod and a wink.

Motto

Don't feed the beast!

Reader's-Guide

1) Who is the narrator? Whom, or what, does the narrator symbolize?
2) What is the party-line theory of consciousness? What does the narrator mean when he asserts that the theory is "bottom-up" rather than "top-down?" What sorts of social and psychological phenomena can this theory explain?
3) According to the narrator, what role does science play in human knowledge? What is the birthday-cake fallacy, and how is that concept used to argue that we can never prove a scientific theory true? How, according to the narrator, does scientific physical truth relate to the purported laws of consciousness? Why does the author consider it important to discuss the tenuous nature of scientific knowledge at that particular point in the book?
4) What is suffering? Does the narrator change his views on the nature of suffering during the course of the story? If so, how?

5) Why is the violence in this story so graphic? Alternatively, are the discussions of human suffering in this story too academic and removed from real life? How can we apply something as abstract as logic to something so concrete as suffering?
6) Who was D.? How is D.'s ghost different from D.? Is D.'s ghost alive? Does it exist?
7) Who is Percy? What role does she play in the story? Is she a goddess? Is the narrator a god?
8) Compare and contrast Freud's notion of the id, ego, and superego with the interrelations between D.'s ghost, the narrator, and Percy.
9) How do the concepts of existence and nonexistence play out in this story?
10) Discuss the image of the Santa Barbara Channel as the River Styx. How does this image relate to other themes in the story?
11) How do the themes of life, death, and rebirth play out in this story?
12) What was the meaning of the narrator's dream? How did the narrator finally come to understand that meaning?
13) Was Resident Teacher helpful to the narrator? What did the narrator learn from Resident Teacher?
14) Why did Sage continue to ask if Percy or the narrator wanted more tea? Where is cube 1? What was the meaning of the stick hitting the narrator's head when talking with Sage? Is there a self?
15) How do paradox, contradiction, and relativity play out in this story?
16) Is everything consciousness, as the narrator frequently asserts? Why does he seem to take this position? Do his reasons for this thesis change during the course of the story?
17) How does the notion of free will contribute to the story? Do we have free will? How does the narrator finally demonstrate

to himself and others that he has free will? Is there a mechanism to free will? What sorts of responsibilities go along with freedom of the will?

18) According to the narrator, how can we all be living in separate worlds yet be connected with and relating to one another in a single universe? What is invariant between separate worlds? Can that invariance be discussed and described in words?
19) Why, according to the narrator, is fighting evil with violence an impossible task? Why does he think that the only way to lessen evil in the world is through unconditional love? Is unconditional love possible? Is it *possible* that unconditional love can eventually win out over evil? Is there any other way to remove evil?
20) In this story, what does the ocean, or water, symbolize? What is the significance of a jetty jutting out into the surf? What does it mean for the narrator to leave the tip of the jetty and to come ashore? Why is his journey just beginning at the very end of the story?
21) What is the monster? Why can the monster not be defeated with violence? Does the narrator, through his own unconscious thoughts, give substance to the monster?
22) Is this story a fictional narrative, or is it instead an allegory?

CPSIA information can be obtained
at www.ICGtesting.com
Printed in the USA
LVHW021309220622
721815LV00001B/33

9 781480 858299